Forget the rumors about mind scans; all you feel is warmth and a slight pressure. That's it. That's all I felt. Kind of like having someone placing their hands on your head and blowing in between their fingers.

Suddenly the four Chorian Elders went crazy: harmonized gabbling, bouncing up and down on the spot, ears flapping. Then all at once, they stopped screeching. I felt a burst of incredible pressure in my head, like a migraine gone nova. Everything went black for a second. Mavkel grabbed my arm.

"Partner, pair," it sang loudly.

Camden-Stone turned almost as white as the Chorians.

"There is some mistake," he said, but his voice was lost in the song of the four Chorian Elders. They had walked over to us, caroling their congratulations. The biggest pair, with enormous jowls that hung down to their chests, stopped beside Camden-Stone.

"This human is one of two. How did this happen?" one of them sang loudly. It leaned forward, its forehead almost touching Camden-Stone's.

Camden-Stone stepped back.

"I don't know what you mean," he said.

FIREBIRD
WHERE FANTASY TAKES FLIGHT™
WHERE SCIENCE FICTION SOARS™

SINGING THE DOGSTAR BLUES

ALISON GOODMAN

FIREBIRD

AN IMPRINT OF PENGUIN GROUP (USA) INC.

FIREBIRD

Published by the Penguin Group

Penguin Group (USA) Inc., 345 Hudson Street, New York, New York 10014, U.S.A.

Penguin Group (Canada), 90 Eglinton Avenue East, Suite 700, Toronto, Ontario, Canada M4P 2Y3

(a division of Pearson Penguin Canada Inc.)

Penguin Books Ltd, 80 Strand, London WC2R 0RL, England

Penguin Ireland, 25 St Stephen's Green, Dublin 2, Ireland (a division of Penguin Books Ltd)

Penguin Group (Australia), 250 Camberwell Road, Camberwell, Victoria 3124, Australia

(a division of Pearson Australia Group Pty Ltd)

Penguin Books India Pvt Ltd, 11 Community Centre, Panchsheel Park, New Delhi – 110 017, India

Penguin Group (NZ), 67 Apollo Drive, Rosedale, Auckland 0632, New Zealand

(a division of Pearson New Zealand Ltd.)

Penguin Books (South Africa) (Pty) Ltd, 24 Sturdee Avenue, Rosebank, Johannesburg 2196, South Africa

Registered Offices: Penguin Books Ltd, 80 Strand, London WC2R 0RL, England

First published in Australia by HarperCollins*Publishers* Pty Ltd., 1998
First published in the United States of America by Viking,
a division of Penguin Putnam Books for Young Readers, 2003
First published by Firebird, an imprint of Penguin Group (USA) Inc., 2004
This Firebird edition published, 2012

"The Real Thing" originally appeared in *Firebirds Rising: An Anthology of Original Science Fiction and Fantasy*,
edited by Sharyn November, published by Firebird, an imprint of Penguin Group (USA) Inc., 2006

1 3 5 7 9 10 8 6 4 2

THE LIBRARY OF CONGRESS HAS CATALOGED THE VIKING EDITION AS FOLLOWS:
Goodman, Alison.
Singing the Dogstar blues / by Alison Goodman.
p. cm.
Summary: In a future Australia, the smart-mouthed eighteen-year-old daughter of a famous newscaster
and a sperm donor teams up with a hermaphrodite from the planet Choria in a time traveling adventure
that may significantly change both of their lives.
ISBN 0-670-03610-2 (hardcover)
[1. Time travel – Fiction. 2. Science Fiction.] I. Title.
PZ7.G6353 Si 2003 [Fic]—dc21 2002012161

ISBN 978-0-14-241642-6

Set in Bulmer MT

Printed in the United States of America

*For my mother and father, Charmaine and Doug Goodman,
my dear friend Karen McKenzie, and of course Ron.*

My Mother and Other Aliens

I saw the assassin before she saw me. She was eating noodles at one of the hawker bars, watching the university gates. I knew she was a killer because old Lenny Porchino had pointed her out to me at the Buzz Bar two nights ago.

"Hey, take a look at that skinny kid with the frizzy hair," he'd said, nodding his head towards the doors behind me.

We were sitting in Lenny's private booth, hidden from general view. I shifted in my seat until I could see her. Skinny, frizzy, and mean.

"What about her?" I said, banging my harmonica against the flat of my hand. I had just finished jamming with the band and my harp was full of slag.

"That's Tori Suka. She's a culler for the hyphen families. If she's in town, someone's gonna die."

Tori Suka didn't fit my idea of someone who would work for the big-money families. Too rough. She was wearing the same kind of student gear as I was: black long-wear jeans, matching jacket. Standard stuff you can get from any machine.

One of Lenny's waiters came up to the table. He was all nerves.

"Mr. Porchino, there's a guy in the crapper done too much smack. Looks like he's croaking it."

Lenny shook his head.

"Don't know why they still go for that antique screte," he said. He looked over at me. "Joss, don't ever do any of that old-fashioned powder. Does you in and wrecks your looks." He turned to the waiter. "Get Cross and Lee to dump him outside St. Vinnies."

The waiter weaved through the crowd towards two bouncers lounging against the wall. Lenny watched until he saw Cross and Lee move towards the toilets.

"Suka's not the best gun around, but she gets the job done," he said. "I wonder who the mark is? And who's hiring?" He was pulling at the ends of his mustache. Lenny always made it his business to know who was putting out a contract.

I looked at the kid again. She was leaning against the bar, throwing nut meats into her mouth. She chewed with her mouth open. How did she become an assassin? Did Careers tell her she was suited to murder?

Lenny's son, Porchi, strutted over from the bar and slid next to me in the booth. He pressed his thigh against mine. I moved away from him. Porchi's been trying to snork me since we met after I pulled his dad out of the river a year ago. Old Lenny had "fallen in" the Yarra with a bit of help from some DeathHeads on a grand-final rampage. I happened to be cruising the area and grabbed Lenny out of the river before he was mulched by the cleaning system.

Later Porchi told me that half the DeathHeads were wiped out when their hangout was bio-bombed. Very ugly. Lenny believes in paying his debts: I saved his life, so now he looks out for me. I've even got a permanent bedroom upstairs at the Buzz Bar. I think Lenny's got some fantasy about me and Porchi breeding little Porchinos and living happily ever after. Like I said, Porchi would be happy to get stuck into the breeding part of that scheme.

Lenny is the closest thing I've had to family this past year. I haven't actually seen my mother for about eighteen months. She's always in production or in a meeting. I end up talking to Lewis, her secretary, via CommNet. Reverse charges, of course.

"I'm sorry, Joss, Ingrid is unavailable right now," he always says with his ferret smile.

"Well, tell her I called. She does remember who I am, doesn't she?"

"I'm sure she has a vague memory. I'll pass on the message."

Then he signs off before I bash my head through the screen.

Let's fact it, Ingrid Aaronson is not going to win the Mother of the Year award. Not that she needs it. She's won nearly every other award that a news presenter and VR star can win. She's even won the Thinking Man's Lust-Beast award, which is funny when you know she didn't even snork anyone to make me. I'm a comp-kid. Straight from the petri dish to you. Lust factor: nil. Ease factor: ten.

Sometimes I wonder if the petri dishes got mixed up and I should be living in the mall-highrises with Mamasan and Papasan. You see, my mother is all gold hair, big blue eyes, maximum curves, and honey skin (rejuvenated twice now, but who's counting?). I'm all black straight hair, brown cat's eyes, and pale, pale skin.

Once I asked Ingrid how many people were used to make me. A comp-kid like me can have up to ten gene donors. The bioengineers just split different genes and stick them together using viruses. It's like being glued together by the common cold. Ingrid swore she only used one male donor. Name unknown, of course. If that's the case, Ingrid's Nordic heritage has been bashed into submission by my father's genes. She's positive I also inherited my attitude problem from him. She says being chucked out of twelve schools must be genetic. Sometimes I imagine he knows I'm his daughter and is keeping tabs on me, waiting for the right moment to show himself. Yeah, sure.

I swung my pack onto my shoulder and walked past the noodle bar towards the university gates. The assassin eyeballed me as I passed her. She was smiling. I was tempted to stop and ask her about career opportunities, but Tonio Bel Hussar-Rigdon suddenly grabbed me on the shoulder. He was in dress uniform.

"You're late," he said. "Camden-Stone's so mad he's ready to expel you on the spot."

Professor Camden-Stone was always threatening to expel me. You'd have thought the Acting Director of the

Centre for Neo-Historical Studies would have better things to do than pick on a lowly student. Wrong again. Old Stony Face was building a career out of making my life miserable. Tonio thinks Camden-Stone has the hots for me. If he has, I'd hate him to really love me. He'd probably put a laser through my head. Even Lenny has dropped a word of warning about the dear professor. He told me Camden-Stone beat the screte out of a girl a couple of years ago and had to pay a lot of money to keep it quiet. You've got to wonder how a creep like Camden-Stone wound up in charge of the world's only time-travel training center.

Tonio was shifting from foot to foot, eager to get back to the ceremony. According to the campus bookies, he was going to be my time-jumping partner.

Every year, the top fifty first-year students at the university can apply to study at the Centre. If you're interested, you have to take extra classes with Camden-Stone and go through tons of tests. There's only twelve first-year places at the Centre, so it's ultra competitive. I just scraped in: number eleven. Tonio Bel Hussar-Rigdon was number eight.

Tonio wasn't bad for a hyphen kid, but he was so nervy it made me want to scream. At least he wasn't a wankman like all the other hyphens. Then again, it wouldn't have mattered if he was Mr. Nice Guy of the universe. The last thing I wanted was a partner. Especially a partner who lived, studied, and worked with me. Talk about cramp your style. There was no way I was going to survive six years living in the same quarters as Tonio. Or anyone, for that matter.

"Come on," Tonio urged. "You've got to get changed and down to the Donut. Partnering is about to start."

I looked through the gates at the Donut. The huge circular hall was buzzing with vid-crews. There was even a small group of protesters standing behind a banner. Something was up. The ceremony to partner time-jumping students didn't normally rate channel time or demonstrators.

"I thought partnering was supposed to be tomorrow," I said.

"No one could find you to tell you what's happened. How come you don't carry a screen?" He leaned closer, shifting into gossip mode. "Listen to this. They've moved the ceremony for diplomatic reasons. A flaphead is coming into our time-jump class."

Tonio stepped back, a smug grin all over his pointy little face. This was big news and he knew it. The university had finally accepted one of the Chorian aliens as a student. Not only had they accepted one, but they had shoved it in the middle of our time-jumping class.

"But, that makes thirteen in our group," I said. "It won't have a partner."

"Robbie's been dropped," Tonio said softly. "He was number twelve on the list. I don't think he's been sober since Stony told him."

Poor Robbie. He must be burning. I was lucky they weren't letting two Chorians into the course. I would have been skidding on my cheeks, too.

"Come on," Tonio said, pulling me towards the gates.

I let him pull me because I was in memory overdrive. Ever since I first saw the Chorians on the vid-news, I've been obsessed with them. I was ten and expected to see some kind of giant insect. Talk about chronic disappointment. Two arms, two legs, and a head with two eyes, just like us. Then again not many humans have two noses, two mouths, and two huge double-jointed ears that flap around.

The Chorians are really into this Noah deal: everything in twos. They even have two sexes in one, like slugs. When the anti-alien lobby got wind of that, they started calling the Chorians "sluggos." The government PR people knocked themselves out trying to stop that one. The campaign posters were a scream; a big slug with a red cross through it. Really subtle. I suppose it worked. Now everyone calls them flapheads.

When I first heard the Chorians were hermaphrodites, I thought they could snork themselves. You know, the ultimate wank. That sounded too good to be true, so I did some fancy detective work on the Net. I found out that self-snorking was out. Instead, two adults fertilize each other then each of them produces one child to form a birth pair. So every Chorian is a kind of twin. I've always thought it would be great to have a twin. Instant best friend.

A few years ago Ingrid made a documentary about the Chorians. She called it "Our New Friends from the Dog Star," which is a bad name for a bad documentary. The Chorians aren't even from Sirius A, the Dog Star. They're from a planet that has Sirius A as its sun and Sirius B as its white dwarf partner. Like everything else that has been written or made on the Chorians, Ingrid's doco was pretty short on information. At least it showed the original recording of the first contact. It's the funniest history vid I've ever seen.

Six or so years ago, the first delegation of Chorians appeared in Mall 26, just before it was joined to the Mall Network. The Chorians thought 26 was a center of government and the concert stage was parliament. A traditional Disney pantomime was playing, and it scared the hell out of them. Let's face it, an enormous mouse jumping around to tinny music isn't really the height of human culture. Of course, the panto audience went into panic mode and cleared out in about ten seconds. The only one left was poor old Mickey. So the Chorians were left standing alone in front of a stage with a big mouse cowering in the corner.

It took the government people exactly five and a half minutes to arrive, shunt Mickey off into the arms of a therapist, and set up their probe equipment. Meanwhile the Chorians were trying to say hi, mind to mind. They quickly worked out we're not telepathic, so they scanned the brain of one of the feds to learn our lingo. Now Chorians speak by harmonizing words using their two mouths. Imagine being confronted by a group of aliens who all dipped imaginary hats then sang, "Howdy pilgrims, sure is nice to meet you."

The fed was a John Wayne fan.

Later the PR people made "howdy ya'll" the most irritating phrase in the world. Whoever thought of setting it to lullaby music for the "Don't Be Afraid" campaign should've been shot.

About a year ago I bought an underground code from one of Porchi's contacts. It's supposed to only access RAVE-REVIVAL boards for free, but with a bit of jiggling, it also got into the government's news-boards. I found out why the Chorians were here. They've got some kind of time/space warp gizmo that lets them jump around the universe without a ship. Now they want to swap that technology for our time travel know-how. They need to learn how to manipulate time accurately. We want to learn how to get off Earth without expensive ships and space stations. So far none of these negotiations have appeared on the public vid-news channels. The PR people have been quiet, too. Although today, as Tonio pulled me past "official" vid-crews, it was obvious the government's policy of silence was about to change.

"This'll do," Tonio said, stopping in front of a reactor access hut. I opened the door. The faint thrumming of the reactor's cooling system buzzed through my feet. Tonio let go of my arm.

"I'd say you've got about thirty seconds to get changed and get back to the Donut. I'll see you there." He ran towards the crowd.

Tonio was right. I had to change into my dress uniform. Too bad it was still hanging in Lenny's office at the Buzz Bar. Turning out for a ceremony in jeans and a T-shirt, even if they were regulation, was not going to go down well. I was heading towards expulsion number thirteen, but this time I wasn't happy about it. And Ingrid would really crack the kuso. She'd spent a lot of money buying me a place in the university. She'd even bought mega shares in the Centre. The half-finished admin building is already being called the Aaronson Administration Complex.

I dumped my pack on the floor of the hut. All I could do was clean up a bit and hope Camden-Stone was in a good mood. I pulled on a new T-shirt and used the chrome handrail as an emergency mirror. What had I forgotten? My harp! I slipped it into my jeans pocket for luck and shoved my pack under some piping. Joss Aaronson was ready to meet her fate.

Escape Routes

By the time I got to the Donut, my class had already gone into the ceremonial hall. The main door was blocked by a group of fifth-year time-jumpers straining to see the stage. I'd met one of them at the Buzz Bar a few weeks ago when I was playing with the band. She was specializing in the history of rock and liked my harp playing. I tapped her on the shoulder.

"Hey, Lisa, how come you're not watching this on the screen? You could see better."

"What's it to you?" she said without looking. Then her eyes widened. "Joss, why aren't you up there with the others? Why aren't you in dress uniform?"

"The color doesn't suit me," I said.

"Old Stony is going to flay you alive." Lisa stood on her toes, scanning the stage. "That Hussar-Rigdon guy has left a space for you in the back line," she said. "Here, take my beret." She pulled the hat off her head, pressing it into my hands. "If you can get up there, maybe the screte won't hit the fan."

It was a nice thought, but I knew Camden-Stone

couldn't wait to boot me out of the program. He'd probably staged the whole change of day just to get me out. The man was creepy. He was always watching me, like some vulture eyeing up a bit of real-steak.

I twisted my hair into a loose bun, tucking it under the beret. Lisa turned to her partner, a tall guy with a huge jutty jaw. I'd seen him at the Buzz Bar, too.

"Derry, can you see if the back entrance is blocked?" Lisa asked. "Joss has got to get into formation."

Derry rolled his eyes at me, but looked around the stage.

"See that exit over there?" he said, pointing near the right side of the stage.

I saw the exit. I also saw Tori Suka sitting in the audience. What was she doing there? Was she going to kill someone during the ceremony? If I was lucky, she'd knock Camden-Stone off before he ripped me apart.

"That door takes you backstage," Derry said. "Look under the stage for a trapdoor with a big R-16 on it. You'll come out about where that red-headed kid is standing."

A ceremonial fanfare blasted out of the speakers. I grasped Lisa's shoulder in thanks and nodded to Derry. I hadn't expected them to help me so much.

The trapdoor was easy to find. So was a ladder. Everything was going my way except for one thing. The red-headed kid standing above R-16 was Chaney Horain-Donlevy, a kid from one of the most obnoxiously rich hyphen families in the city. He was more likely to push me off the ladder than help me.

I balanced on the top two rungs. First, a little test pull on the trapdoor. It moved. At least Chaney wasn't standing on it. I didn't fancy having him fall on top of me. It was time to take the plunge. I took a deep breath and pulled. The door opened with a clunk. Chaney stared down at me, his eyes bulging. I swung up onto the stage before he could collect his wits. Just in time. The door snicked back into place as his size-nine boot landed on my fingers. I almost bit through my lip trying not to yell. My hand was completely pinned. Chaney was grinning, but I wasn't beaten yet.

I looked for Tonio. He was being held back by Jorel, one of Chaney's disciples, but it didn't look like he was busting a gut to get free. The class was shuffling around, trying to see what was happening. Through the lineup of legs, I saw the bottom half of the Chorian guests and the university bigwigs walking towards our formation. Time to fight dirty. One karate chop in the back of Chaney's knees was enough. His legs buckled. I pulled my hand free and was on my feet before he hit the floor.

I slid into position just as Camden-Stone turned to face the class. We stared at each other. Three long seconds. His face was ceremony-bland, but his left hand was twitching. A vein pounded blue in his temple. When the ceremony ended, I wasn't going to wait around and get thrashed like that other girl. I finally looked away, but out of the corner of my eye I saw Camden-Stone smile. A vulture smile. I didn't hear the first half of the ceremony. I was too busy looking for an escape route.

I zoned back when Camden-Stone introduced the Chorian student.

"It is with great honor that the University of Australia accepts Mavkel into its prestigious Centre for Neo-Historical Studies. Mavkel will be studying Time Travel, which only accepts twelve first-year students who have displayed exceptional aptitude."

Everyone clapped.

"As we are a Centre devoted to the study of history in all of its times and guises, it is appropriate that such an historical event happen here."

More clapping. The Chorian student was standing a little apart from the rest of the Chorian contingent. Its ears were stretched back against its head. It looked like it was either sick or nerved out.

Camden-Stone continued, "The time has come for the very important task of partnering the students who have been chosen to study Time Travel. As you are no doubt aware, these human students are chosen not only for their talents, but also for their psychological, physical, and intellectual qualities and compatibility. These tests ensure that ideal partnering combinations are achieved. These partnerships usually result in an optimum working unit and a lifelong friendship."

Camden-Stone paused. His eyes flicked over to the group of Chorians. Even though he was smiling, you could almost see the distrust. The dear professor was an alienist.

"However," he continued, "since our new Chorian friend and workmate has not completed these tests, the Chorian government has requested that Mavkel choose its own partner by scanning the minds of our students."

A buzz of voices broke out in the audience and around me. Camden-Stone turned to face us.

A mind scan. Holy screte. That would rattle a few cages. There's a lot of tox floating around about Chorian mind scans. You know the stuff. Heads exploding, faces falling off, brains being wiped. Garbage like that.

"Naturally, if anyone is opposed to being scanned they may step down as a candidate for the honor of being Mavkel's partner. If you are opposed, please indicate your choice by moving to the left of the stage."

I knew for a fact that Tonio would be opposed. Chaney too. But not me. What a chance to meet an alien. Mind to mind. I never thought I'd see one up close, let alone get mind scanned. On the other hand, if I crossed over to the left side of the stage I could slip out while everyone was focused on the Chorian. Get out of Camden-Stone's sight for a while until he calmed down. What a choice.

The alien won by two short noses.

Chaney was the first to move across the stage. Jorel was next. That started the avalanche. Every hyphen kid in our class moved across. That left four of us: Peter, Sara, Jason, and yours truly.

The Chorian student stepped forward. It looked

nervous, gulping with its primary mouth, its secondary tightly closed. Even its skin was dull. Well, as dull as a sparkly white skin can be under bright spotlights. Camden-Stone ushered it forward.

"Do you all agree to be mind scanned by the Chorian named Mavkel?" he asked. He was leaning away from Mavkel ever so slightly. "Please state your answer for the record. Sara Ferrins?"

Sara looked like a rabbit under the wheels. She stared at the Chorian, then at Camden-Stone, and balked. Now there were three.

Peter was scanned first. It was pretty anticlimactic. Mavkel made a complicated gesture, then Peter's face kind of froze for a second. That was it. Mavkel bowed to him.

"My thanks. But you are not my partner." Its voice was a deep furry harmony that reached to the corners of the hall. Kind of like Billie Holiday with a cold.

Jason was up next. He was a total brownnoser and Camden-Stone loved him. But would Mavkel? Jason was scanned, but it was the same biz. Thanks, but no thanks.

It was my turn.

Forget the rumors about mind scans; all you feel is warmth and a slight pressure. That's it. That's all I felt. Kind of like having someone placing their hands on your head and blowing in between their fingers.

Suddenly the four Chorian Elders went crazy: harmonized gabbling, bouncing up and down on the spot, ears flapping. Then all at once, they stopped screeching. I felt a burst of incredible pressure in my head, like a migraine gone nova. Everything went black for a second. Mavkel grabbed my arm.

"Partner, pair," it sang loudly.

Camden-Stone turned almost as white as the Chorians.

"There is some mistake," he said, but his voice was lost in the song of the four Chorian Elders. They had walked over to us, caroling their congratulations. The biggest pair, with enormous jowls that hung down to their chests, stopped beside Camden-Stone.

"This human is one of two. How did this happen?" one of them sang loudly. It leaned forward, its forehead almost touching Camden-Stone's.

Camden-Stone stepped back.

"I don't know what you mean," he said.

He looked over at me, his eyes narrow. Obviously I had wrecked his plan. Someone else was supposed to be Mavkel's partner. Probably Jason.

"Aaronson isn't a good choice," Camden-Stone said. "Mavkel must try again."

"No," the Elder sang. "Mavkel has found its pair. The duality of life is restored." Its pair nodded.

Camden-Stone wasn't pale anymore. He was bright red. He knew I had him by the short and curlies. I was the chosen partner of the first Chorian student on Earth. He couldn't touch me.

I glanced at my new partner. It had flicked back its semi-opaque second eyelid and was squinting into the lights, staring at Camden-Stone.

The audience finally caught on that the Chorian had found its partner. Clapping started. Camden-Stone jerked to attention. He walked over to us, holding his arms up for silence.

"Honored guests, friends, students. History has been made in front of your eyes. The Chorian called Mavkel has chosen Joss Aaronson as its partner. Cadet Aaronson is the daughter of the highly respected journalist Ingrid Aaronson. Please join me in celebrating this new partnership."

The clapping became a thunder of approval. Mavkel leaned closer to me. I thought I heard it sing "be careful" softly in my ear, but when I turned my head it was speaking to the Elder by its side.

Camden-Stoned

The ceremony was almost over. We only had to parade down the central aisle, then we were free. The whole class was waiting backstage, sweating in heavy dress uniforms. A harried fifth year with an official clipboard was trying to get us in line, but it wasn't happening. Chaney was refusing to stand near Mavkel. The others were lined up behind him, pressed against the wall.

"After the ritual is over, I will be back in two of your twenty-four periods," Mavkel said to me, ignoring the whispering Chaney brigade. It absently stroked the vertical ridges along its noses.

"Where are you going?"

"My people want to finish my preparation." It paused, the first joint of its ears flattening outwards as it concentrated. "Your slangsounds would call it a major yawn."

"I can believe it," I said, smiling.

Mavkel leaned even closer, watching my mouth. Then it tried out a double-barreled smile. Not easy for someone with no lips. The result was hideous, but ten out of ten for effort.

"Joss-partner, be careful of your Elder Camden-Stone," it sang with that smile still plastered on its face.

"Yeah, I know. The guy's got it in for me. But don't worry, he can't touch me now that I'm your partner. Thanks for picking me."

"Of course I picked you." The quick lift of its ears was as expressive as raised eyebrows. "The Deetun in you called to me. The Elders felt it, too."

Huh? Had I missed something important in this conversation? Before I could ask, the fifth-year student pushed Chaney into line. The class was called back onstage.

When the procession finally ended, Mavkel and I didn't get another chance to talk. The vid-teams were all over us, trying to get an interview. Camden-Stone finally gave a statement. No interviews at this time. Then the security guards shut the gates on the media and an armed escort hurried Mavkel and the Chorian Elders away.

As I watched my new partner being hustled into a diplomatic hover, Camden-Stone caught hold of my arm. For an old guy, he packed a lot of strength.

"Don't rely on your luck too much, Aaronson," he said. "Be at my office at ten tomorrow."

A mob of excited parents was heading towards us. Camden-Stone let go of my arm and stepped back.

"Tomorrow at ten," he repeated, then turned to meet a short, shrill woman who was complaining about the hover facilities.

I quickly joined the crowd moving towards the free food and drink, but for some reason I had lost my appetite.

That night, Lewis contacted me at the Buzz Bar. I took the call in Lenny's office. Apparently my dear mother wanted an exclusive interview with me about the Chorian, but was too busy to ask me herself. I told Lewis I'd think about it. Then I disconnected the comm-line and headed for the bar.

I remember having eight shots of sake and beating Cross at pool, but after that all I get is static. Lenny said he put me to bed when I passed out under booth four. Luckily, I'd told him I had to be on campus by ten. He dragged me out of bed about nine and dumped me in the bather with a wake-up cycle. Pure torture, but at least I was compos mentis by the time it was finished. Even my headache had dropped two levels on the Richter scale. Lenny was in the Buzz Bar kitchen, frying up some of his special sandwiches.

"You staying on campus from now on?" Lenny asked, flipping over a hunk of real-bacon.

I nodded, catching a whiff of the meat. My stomach twisted in confusion: puke or eat?

"Semester starts tomorrow. I'm seeing Dr. Hartpury this morning to get my timetable and quarters." That is, if I survived my little chat with Camden-Stone.

Lenny handed me one of his hair-curling coffees. Bitter as hell, but the caffeine gets the synapses snapping.

"Come and see me soon. Maybe I'll have some hard info about Suka. She's a slow worker, that one. But be real careful. I got an idea who she's after." He wiped a spot off the white shiny counter. "You're not going to like it."

My esophagus went rock hard. I choked on the coffee.

"What? Is she after me?"

Lenny laughed.

"Only if you get in the way. I reckon she's after your new partner."

I suppose it made sense. All the political hoo-ha around the first Chorian student. The protesters. Suka in the ceremony audience. Just what I needed. A partner someone was trying to wipe out. The poor sod hadn't even moved into its quarters yet.

"Like I said, she probably won't try a hit for a while."

"That's a big comfort," I said, picking up my duffel. It was way too heavy to lug around campus. I'd have to fork out for a locker. "I gotta get going, but I'll drop in as soon as I can. When do you reckon you'll know if Mavkel's the hit for sure?"

Lenny shrugged.

"You know how it works. When the info comes, it comes. Meanwhile watch your partner's back."

And mine, too. I grabbed one of the bacon sandwiches on the counter, ignoring the roiling in my guts.

The small waiting room outside Camden-Stone's office was designed to intimidate. There was a row of framed degrees, a glass case packed with medals and awards, and a holo display that flipped through the university layout. The room even smelled intimidating—executive pine on the aroma-filter. To top it all off there was a human secretary,

Mr. Gareth Welton, hired to stare at you while you waited. I tried to make Gazza blink, but he had either glued his eyes open or had died in front of me.

The holo display was a more interesting distraction.

It was explaining the fusion reactor.

The University of Australia is circled by a huge fusion reactor built ten stories underground. I'd only been down there once, on the orientation tour. You can't see much, just a lot of piping full of water to insulate the heat. The reactor supplies most of the energy for Melbourne, but it also has a hell of a by-product: the Sunawa-Harrod Time-Continuum Warp Field.

The holo display flipped into a portrait of the guy who discovered the field: Daniel Sunawa-Harrod. He was also the official director of the Centre, but apparently he was heading for deadsville. That's why Camden-Stone had taken over.

The holo portrait was a still from a recorded lecture Sunawa-Harrod had given at the university. He was leaning forward as though making a point, and his eyes had lined up some poor jerk to be shot down. The holo was only a head/shoulder view, so I couldn't see his hands, but I bet he was drilling the jerk's argument to bits with his forefinger. You could tell Daniel Sunawa-Harrod had chutzpah.

I walked around the holo, watching the solid light slide around with me. Whoever had worked up the picture had done a terrible job. There was a gap in the guy's head. I looked closer. No, the gap was a scar. An implant scar. My own scalp crawled. So, Danny-boy had gone for the big IQ points and bought an organic implant. Never mind about the one in five chance of crushing your immune system. It seemed Daniel Sunawa-Harrod had played those odds and lost. I hoped someone was there to comb his hair and hold him up when the chutzpah wasn't enough.

Suddenly, the holo portrait disintegrated into a diagram of the time-continuum field. The commentary continued. Daniel Sunawa-Harrod had been experimenting with fusion technology when an accident produced a strange new field. It turned out to be the biggest scientific discovery since Absalom-Levy developed his universal laws. Daniel Sunawa-Harrod had discovered a way to warp the time-continuum. This discovery helped a team of scientists, led by Sunawa-Harrod, to develop time-jumping.

So there I was, about twenty years later, about to study time-jumping as a career and waiting to see Professor Camden-Stone, acting director of the Centre for Neo-Historical Studies. But what did he want? Hopefully just to scream and shout as usual. I had obviously got in the way of one of his little plans, but he couldn't do anything about it now. Mavkel and I were partners. If I was going to be logical about it, I knew he couldn't lay a hand on me. I was in the media spotlight. However, my survival instinct wasn't so convinced. It kept on whispering "what about that other girl?" A feather of sweat ran down my back. Was time-jumping worth this aggro? Then Gazza came to life and pointed towards the inner door.

"Professor Camden-Stone will see you now."

The door slid open.

Camden-Stone was working at his console and didn't look up when I walked into the room.

"You may sit down, Aaronson," he said, eyes not leaving the screen.

He was using psych-out tactic number one: make your victim wait. If it was supposed to make me sweat, it was working.

I sat in one of the large fake-leather chairs. The whole room was done out in Early University Professor: huge mahogany desk, real books lining the walls, even a holo fireplace with an antique analog clock on the mantelpiece. The whole place was one big lie. Everything was new, but had been treated to look shabby-old. The only things in the room that rang true were a gold antique ballpoint and a holo picture of Desmona Cartwright. The holo had a message written across the light unit. *To my dear Joseph, thank you for all your help, Desi.* What help had Camden-Stone given the most famous Shakespearian actress of the century? I'd met her once when my mother still thought it was cute to have a daughter. Desmona Cartwright was a dream. She didn't talk down to me, sneaked me extra biscuits, and let me play with her dog. How could she like Camden-Stone?

"She's lovely, isn't she?" Camden-Stone asked.

I jumped. Psych-out tactic number two: say something when your victim least expects it.

He turned the holo unit to face him. Camden-Stone was

a good-looking man, but there was something odd about his face. It hit me as he licked his lips. He had a woman's mouth. It was small with well-defined lips that made the rest of his face seem too heavy. He placed the holo unit back on the desk.

"One must admire her ambition and devotion to excellence."

"I met her once when my mother did an interview," I said.

Camden-Stone raised polite eyebrows. I gabbled on.

"She was doing *Hamlet* with Harley Leonard. The first season in London. You know, the one where Carol Poynard collapsed onstage and died."

"Yes, the critics weren't impressed," he said. "I believe the Sydney season was received more kindly. No ill-timed deaths to wreck the production."

I smiled politely, shifting forward in my seat. I didn't trust this one bit. Camden-Stone was being too damned nice. What did he want?

He picked up the gold pen and ran his fingers along its length, looking pensive.

"Joss, I want to ask you something."

Aha, here it comes.

"Do you really want to be partnered with that Chorian? I feel that you've been pressured into something for which you are not quite prepared."

His voice was deep with sincerity. He probably practiced the pitch every night before he went to bed.

"I don't think any of us are really prepared for the Chorians," I said, just as sincerely. "Anyway, Mavkel seems okay. I don't mind partnering it."

"Nevertheless, I wouldn't hold it against you if you decided to forfeit this partnership and join young Bel Hussar-Rigdon. That was our original plan."

"No, thanks. I'm happy with the assignment."

He leaned back in his chair and rolled the pen between his fingers. Things were not going the way he wanted.

Frankly, I was starting to think being partnered with the Chorian was going to be more trouble than it was worth. But I couldn't go along with one of Camden-Stone's plans. It was against my religion.

He stood up and walked around the desk. It was time for psych-out tactic number three: whenever possible physically intimidate your victim. Camden-Stone chose standing over me, his crotch in my face.

"Aaronson, you could just as easily be out of the twelve. Even out of the university. You must know you're in this course by default, so don't rock the boat."

Default? What the hell was he talking about?

"Oh, come on now," he said, watching my face. "How else would a misfit like you get into the Centre? Your mother paid for it, of course. Just like she's paid for every other school you've been to."

I knew my mother had bought me a place in the general university, but my place in the twelve, too? I thought I'd done that on my own. I'd worked hard enough for it. Damn her and her money. This once she could have let me do it by myself.

Camden-Stone leaned down, his face so close it blurred. I wanted to pull away. Create some space. Instead I sat there, staring past that sensuous little mouth.

"I'm sure you wouldn't want the Board to know of Mummy's little business arrangement, would you?" he asked.

I didn't move. His breath was peppermint fresh against my cheek. He moved forward slightly. The last attack.

"My dear girl, your mother may own an interest in this Centre, but it doesn't mean she can keep you here. You see, it won't be long before I have the controlling interest. Take my advice and change partners while you still have the chance."

He pulled back, looking down at me.

I was a throat ache away from bawling. It was time to get out of there. I'd rather take a laser in the head than cry in front of Camden-Stone. Why didn't I just swap partners? Make my life easier. Yeah, sell out and never be able to look myself in the eye again.

"You can do what you like, sir, but I'm not going to forfeit the partnership."

"Why are you being so stubborn?"

"Why don't you want me to partner the Chorian?"

We stared at each other. The old clock on the mantelpiece ticked on, timing the stalemate. Then Camden-Stone finally looked away.

The console blipped.

"Yes?" Camden-Stone snapped.

"Dr. Hartpury has arrived," Gazza's voice said.

"Have her wait, please." The screen blipped off.

"This is not finished yet, Aaronson. Think carefully about what I've said." He turned back to the console, the movement strangely awkward. "You're dismissed."

In the reception room, Gazza was sitting at his desk, staring out Dr. Hartpury. She was staring back, but smiled when she saw me come through the door.

"Hi, Joss. How have you been?"

"Fine," I said, my voice squeezing past the lump in my throat. Hartpury glanced at Camden-Stone's room, putting two and two together. She touched my arm.

"I believe you're scheduled to see me in half an hour. I'll be briefing you, so we can talk about it all then, okay?"

I nodded. The console sounded and Gazza stirred into life.

"Professor Camden-Stone will see you now, Dr. Hartpury."

Hartpury nodded to him, but kept on talking to me.

"Meet me at my office at eleven. We'll go right over to your quarters."

"Right," I said.

By this time Gazza was actually standing up, ushering Hartpury into Camden-Stone's room. Hartpury walked a few steps then stopped. Gaz hissed with impatience.

"Oh, and Joss, congratulations on being chosen to partner Mavkel. You must be very pleased," Hartpury said.

Yeah, over the moon. Gazza murmured something about the professor waiting. Hartpury winked at me, then the door slid shut behind her.

In a Mess

I needed a drink. The interview with Camden-Stone had sucked everything out of me. Even my teeth felt limp. I had about forty minutes before my session with Hartpury. It wasn't enough time to get back to the Buzz Bar. The mess hall would have to do.

I jogged to the mess, going back over the interview. Camden-Stone had a talent for flattening people. He'd get along well with my mother. She always made me feel like loser of the year. Had I even been close to the chosen twelve before she'd paid my way? Maybe I could get into last year's records and check out my standing. Maybe Hartpury would know. Maybe I should just contact Ingrid and tell her to stay the hell out of my life.

The mess hall was crowded with time-jump students on the mid-morning break. All of them were wearing the small gold circular arrow: the badge of the Centre for Neo-Historical Studies. I brushed my hand over mine. Whatever Camden-Stone said, I'd worked hard for it.

A short heavy-set fourth year walked by balancing four steaming containers in his arms. The spicy smell of coffee made me dry swallow. Why wasn't the bev-machine line moving faster? I checked out the groups of people huddled around the tables while I waited. One small group of sixth years looked me over. The word *alien* jumped out of their whispered conversation. Chaney and four of his friends were in the corner, playing a VR game. Tonio was sitting at a table next to them, slightly apart from some third years. He looked in my direction. I waved. His eyes slid over mine, avoiding contact. He was probably still burned up about the partnering.

I punched up a cold juice, pressed my finger across the payment pad, and collected the container. The juice cut through the furriness in my mouth as I walked over to him.

"Hey Tonio, how you doin'?" I asked, pulling a chair up to the table and sitting down.

He smoothed down the back of his hair and I noticed his forefinger was stained blue. The idiot was hitting the Bliss-sticks again. Everyone knew they chewed up your brain if you got hooked.

"I'm okay, I guess," he said. He looked over at Chaney, his leg jiggling against my chair.

"I hope you're not twisted about me partnering the Chorian. I know everyone thought we were going to pair up," I said.

He shrugged.

"I'm with Sara, now." He stood up. "Look, I've got to get going."

He looked about ready to jump out of his skin.

"Hey, Tonio, you still hanging around with that comp

screte?" Chaney's voice called out. He wasn't wasting any time getting me back for that karate chop yesterday.

Tonio and I swung around to face him.

Comp screte. It wasn't the first time Chaney had used my birth as an insult, but it still stung. I remembered what Master Roland, my Tai Chi teacher, had taught me. Take a deep breath and let the air clear out your anger. He was a comp, too, so he ought to know how to handle it. Once, when another class member called me a genetic monster, Master Roland had taken me aside.

"Don't make their fear your truth, Joss," he said. "They've been made by genetic potluck. We're made up from the best of six or more people. No wonder they're jealous and a little bit afraid."

For a while after that, I felt kind of special. Then it hit me: I wasn't even a proper comp. Ingrid says she used only one donor and kept the genetic manipulation to a minimum. So I'm not a comp, but I'm not a real-kid either. It was a no-win situation.

I ignored Chaney and breathed deeply, focusing on my breath as I exhaled. What a waste of time. I still wanted to throttle him. No wonder Master Roland never let me go on to the master level.

"Come over here with us, Tonio. You should mix with your own kind. What would your mother say if she knew you were sniffing around comp waste?" Chaney said.

The mess hall went quiet. Tonio's leg was doing double time. He glanced at me, then settled for staring at the floor, his face white. I tensed up, feeling a vertebra crunch in protest. I had two choices, a civ-libel charge or a fight.

I've never had much faith in the civ laws.

Chaney took off the VR visor, enjoying center stage.

"So, what's it going to be, Tone? Us or them? You've got to choose."

Tonio looked at me for help, but this time he was on his own. I was too close to losing it.

"I think," he said, and swallowed painfully. "I think we should all try and get along."

The Chaney camp screamed with laughter. Jorel started to imitate Tonio, swallowing between every word. "I," swallow, "think," swallow, "we," swallow, "should," swallow. He collapsed into giggles, Chaney raised his voice above the laughter.

"I. Think. We. Should. Ban comps from the Centre." He looked at me. "What do you think, Aaronson?"

I met his eyes. They were a strange light blue. So pale that there was almost no color.

"I think we should ban bigoted scum," I said, moving forward in the chair.

"Okay, that's enough," a dark-haired sixth year said, catching me by the shoulder. He turned to Chaney. "I want you and your lot out of here. Now."

Chaney shrugged.

"We've finished anyway." He drained his cup and strolled towards the door, his friends following in a close pack. As they filed out of the mess, a few people clapped.

Everyone started talking again. I breathed deeply. My last breath had been aeons ago. The sixth year dropped his hand from my shoulder.

"You shouldn't take the bait," he said, smiling to take the cut out of his words. "That guy just wants you to do something stupid so he can civ-suit you. Let this kind of tox ride, or it'll eat you up."

"Yeah? How would you know?"

"I'm a comp, too." He offered his hand. "Kyle Sandrall. And you are?"

"Joss Aaronson," I said, shaking his hand.

"You're the one who's partnering the Chorian, right?"

I nodded. He leaned forward, lowering his voice.

"I'm glad one of us got the job. That'll show them, hey? There's quite a few comps in the course and we're all behind you. Sometimes we get together, have a bit of blast. Why don't you come along?" He kept eye contact a few secs longer than normal. The invitation was for more than just a party.

"Sure," I said, knowing that I would never take him up on his offer. "And thanks for your help."

Kyle smiled and waved, moving towards his group of friends. I watched his smooth confident walk. He looked like he had the world all worked out. Nice bum, too.

"I'm sorry, Joss," Tonio said, touching my arm. I turned back to him. He was finally looking me in the eye. "I'm not very good at confrontation."

"Well, you tried," I said.

He bit his lip, staring at the scuffed tabletop.

I stood up. "I gotta get going."

There was still twenty minutes until my meeting with Hartpury, but I didn't want to hang around the mess. My stomach was burning for food, so I walked up to a vacant foodie. The 3D promised "delicious cuisine in less than a minute." I chose a tempeh jaffle and hit the button. Sauce? Yes. One of those tart plummy ones that burn your mouth with acid sweetness. Plum sauce always reminds me of Louise. She used to make prawn rolls with her special plum sauce every Friday night when I came home from boarding school.

The machine whirred as the jaffle slid onto the pick-up tray. I ran my finger across the payment pad. It beeped at me: try again. This time I pressed harder, moved slower. Maybe I was out of credit. No, Ingrid never missed a payment. The light switched to green and the thief cage slid back. I picked up the jaffle. The heat burned me through the cellulose packaging.

Louise was the closest I ever came to having a full-time father. She lived with us for about five years, until Ingrid switched back to men. I was seven when Louise moved into our big apartment in Mall 15. She was small and fine-boned, with a precision-cut bob that turned bruise-blue in the sun.

Back then, I looked a bit like Louise, so people often thought I was her kid. It used to give Ingrid the scretes. Louise was number three daughter of one of the big Japanese families, but she didn't pull any company line. In fact, she'd flipped the finger at her family and gone her own way, making fancy hats for hyphen society. Louise always told it how it was; she was straight and blunt. Too blunt, Ingrid often said after Louise had left us.

The plum sauce in the jaffle was a shocker. It was so sweet my jaw ached. Louise would have shaken her head slowly, the black bob swinging across her face in two sharp lines.

"You need tart plums that are still a bit green. Not ripe ones," she once told me. We had been at the old Queen Vic market buying fruit for the famous sauce. She picked up two plums and gave one to me.

"Here, press it like this," she said, pushing her thumb into the top of the plum. It gave way and the edge of her fingernail reddened as it cut into the flesh.

"This one's too ripe," she said. "Only choose the hard ones. They're tart and that's what holds back the sweet taste. It's the combination of the sweet and the tart that makes the whole." She tossed the plum she was holding back onto the pile. "You're selling the old screte again, Bernie," she said to the fruit man.

That famous plum sauce was just like Ingrid and Louise; the joining of opposites to make a whole.

My taste buds must have some kind of cell memory because every time I bit into that sickly jaffle, they longed for the taste of Louise's sauce. I hadn't had it for about six years. That's a long time to go without something you love. I dumped the jaffle in a nearby recyc and walked out of the mess. Time to get my duffel out of the hire locker and head up to see Hartpury. I'd be early, but there's always a first time for everything.

Hartpury's office was in D6, one of the original Melbourne University buildings. It was classified National Trust, so not too many changes had been made to it over the years. D6 was one of those twentieth-century boxes with lots of dark glass and gray concrete. The architect must have been having a personal crisis.

I stepped into the old-style elevator and pushed the sixth-floor button. The door ground across its tracks, jumped backwards, then finally closed. The stairs were probably a better bet, but I was trapped now. The floor numbers lit up across the panel as the elevator clunked past. I tried to look at the row of black buttons instead, but my eyes ended up watching the numbers. Riding one of these boxes takes a lot of trust. For all you know, you could be falling to your death or about to be launched through the roof. So you put all your belief in those little numbers marching across the top of the doors. Number six lit up and the doors slid back. Trust had been fulfilled. I was on Hartpury's floor.

As I walked along the corridor, I heard Hartpury talking to someone, her voice sharp. The old-fashioned hinged door of her office was partly open.

"I can't believe he dragged up that guidelines meeting from last year," she said.

"Joseph is a man who bides his time."

It was Dr. Lindon's voice. He was the other psychologist

for the Centre and Hartpury's boss. Ten to one they were talking about Camden-Stone. I stepped to the side of the door, hidden from view.

"He quoted me word for word," Hartpury said. "Well, I think it was word for word. Even I can't remember exactly what I said."

"You can bet it was word for word," Lindon said. "Joseph has perfect recall. I tested him myself."

Hartpury spoke again. Her voice was lower, pitched for dangerous talk. I leaned closer.

"You've known him a long time, haven't you, Bob?" She hesitated. "Have you noticed something a bit strange about his attitude towards the Centre?"

"Strange? What do you mean?" Lindon was hedging.

"He seems to be borderline obsessive. He takes any criticism of the Centre as a personal insult. He actually threatened me with an official reprimand over this guidelines thing."

There was a long pause. My back was beginning to ache from leaning forward. Lindon's mech-legs whirred as he moved across the room.

"If I were you, I'd leave this alone. Joseph doesn't appreciate people raking up his past for common gossip."

"What past? You can't leave me hanging like that," Hartpury said.

"Do you know the story behind the Centre?"

"I've read through the usual stuff. Mainly that history by what's-her-name."

"That's only official hype. It doesn't come close to telling the whole story. If you're really interested, do a cross-ref on Sunawa-Harrod and Joseph. Go back about twenty years. It'll all become clear then."

"What will become clear?"

"Why Joseph is so driven."

"Driven's an interesting way to put it."

"In a way I suppose you're right. He is obsessive," Lindon conceded. "But I also think the Centre is the only thing that's keeping him alive. I bet you didn't know that he's in constant pain, did you? You do that cross-ref, then I think you'll understand. Now, are you going to have a cup of tea or not?"

Lindon's tone said the subject was closed.

"Sorry, I can't. I'm settling Joss Aaronson into her new quarters and briefing her."

"Of course. Now, that will be an interesting little experiment. Personally I couldn't think of a worse combination. An alien and a delinquent."

"Joss is okay. She's just got a strong personality," Hartpury said.

Good ol' Hartpury. Defender of Joss Aaronson and small furry animals.

Lindon snorted. "It's a pity she won't be paired with Bel Hussar-Rigdon. He would have been a steadying influence."

"He would have driven her mad."

"Well, we've always disagreed on that one. It's a dead point now, anyway. Come on, cheer up. Don't let Joseph get to you. He's just letting you know who's boss. I'm sure he won't put a reprimand through."

The interesting goss was over. I knocked on the door just as Hartpury pulled it wide open. Well timed.

"Ah, Joss. I'll be right with you." She turned to Lindon. "Thanks for dropping by. I'll see you in the hook-up for the funding committee."

I stepped aside as Lindon neatly maneuvered through the door. He nodded to me.

"Aaronson. Congratulations on your new partnership."

"Thank you, sir."

"Good-bye, Janeen. And don't forget that cross-ref."

He waved, turning his upper body towards the elevators. The mech-legs swiveled a few seconds later. I didn't know about Hartpury, but I wasn't going to forget the cross-ref. Dirt on Camden-Stone was too good to pass up.

Hartpury watched Lindon walk stiffly down the corridor. She frowned, massaging the bridge of her nose in small hard circles that left the skin red.

"Are you ready to move into your quarters?" she asked.

"Can't wait."

"Okay. Let's get going."

Home Sweet Home

First year time-jumpers are usually quartered in the old Janet Clarke Hall. There're six units, one for each pair. The units are pretty basic: two bedrooms, a shared living room and a study area complete with consoles and VR hoods. Hartpury and I were headed in the opposite direction.

"Where are we going?" I asked. "J. C. Hall's over there."

I skipped two steps to keep up with her.

"Tell me, how do you really feel about all of this?" She swept her arm around, indicating the demonstrators just visible at the gates.

Hartpury was going into psych mode. I hated it when she tried to analyze me. I thought she had given up after I scored 100 percent on her ESP tests. She still doesn't know how I did it.

"I'm fine," I said. "How do you feel about it? Share your innermost feelings." I clutched my hands together over my heart.

I was halfway up the ramp before I realized Hartpury wasn't beside me anymore. I swung my duffel onto my other shoulder and backtracked. She had stopped walking.

"Be serious, Joss," she said, her hands on her hips.

"You've been dumped in the middle of a diplomatic nightmare. The next couple of months, maybe even years, are going to be tough. Look at those demonstrators."

We both turned towards the gates, where the demonstrators were hanging a banner. Only half of it was up, but it was obvious what it said: ALIENS GO HOME. Was Suka somewhere in that crowd, watching and planning her hit?

"That's not going to blow over tomorrow," Hartpury said. "There's even a backlash within the university. A lot of staff and students aren't happy with the decision to accept Mavkel."

"Yeah, including our illustrious leader," I said.

"Where did you get that idea? Professor Camden-Stone is working hard to make this whole thing a success. It's a pig of a job, too."

"He's trying to get me to quit the partnership."

"He's probably just worried for your safety. We all are." She bent forward, bringing her mouth close to my ear. "There've been threats against Mavkel, you know. We nearly didn't quarter you together. The professor didn't want to put you at risk. But we've decided you would lose too much bonding, so you're both being quartered in P3."

P3 was the state-of-the-art organic high-security building for visiting VIPs who were considered "at risk." Its design brief was "no one's getting into this sucker without clearance."

Hartpury leaned back, obviously pleased with the solution.

The pleasure was all hers. The last place I wanted to be quartered was P3.

"I don't want to live there. It'll be like living in a cage," I said. How was I going to operate? Every move I made would be recorded by the building. I'd heard it even had monitoring equipment down the toilet.

"It's the best way to keep you both safe. It's even been modified for Mavkel. Look, maybe all of this will just blow over in a few weeks. We could move you to J. C. then. But for now this is the committee's decision."

We started walking again. Hartpury was staring ahead. The stripe of red across the bridge of her nose made it look even bigger than normal. She had a huge nose, with nostrils the size of real-coins. Why didn't she have it fixed? It wouldn't cost too much, and everything else about her was okay. Maybe she was an anti-interventionist. No pills, no surgery, no rejuvs. Natural all the way. So far, I've only had one thing fixed. It was when I was born. I had some kind of skin tags on my eyes, almost like a second lid. Ingrid got her surgeon to remove them. She can't stand imperfections like that.

The ramp we were walking up intersected the university's central avenue. As we reached the top, P3 came into view. It was an armadillo of a building: armored and squat with an entrance annex that looked like a snout.

"Your new home," Hartpury said.

P3 was definitely going to be a problem. But, as Lenny often says, don't panic till you get all the facts. I'd have to check out this so-called high-security building and see if a small rat like me could get around the monitoring systems.

Lenny also says you should only ask a question if you already know the answer. That way you find out what the other person knows. He pinched the idea out of an old spy novel and swears it's how he keeps ahead of the game.

"When is Mavkel due back?" I asked.

"It should be back tomorrow night," Hartpury said.

So Hartpury was in the know and she was telling me the truth. So far.

She asked for the time from her armscreen.

"Damn, we're running late. That security guy is waiting to log your P3 clearance. We better hurry."

Major Donaldson-Hono was waiting for us in the security office next to P3's snout. He hustled us over to the console behind the counter, ignoring Hartpury's apologies.

You could tell Donaldson-Hono loved his job. He loved his little gold-plated insignia, adored his master coder, and got a hard-on when he thought of security breaches. He wasn't absolutely sold on the idea of giving me security clearance. It was written all over his fashionably altered face. He'd gone for that square action-hero look, but they'd botched the nose. Too flat. Maybe that was why Hartpury hadn't gone under the laser.

"Aaronson, I hope you realize a Code Green clearance is a big responsibility," Donaldson-Hono said.

"It's my constant thought."

Hartpury nudged me, frowning.

"P3 has a double-check security lock. First, a retina scan

then a code key, like this." Donaldson-Hono pulled back his sleeve to show a thin band of memory-metal, the stuff that shrinks to fit you.

"We've found that these used together are the best security. Especially when you have to be scanned to leave the building as well as enter it. P3 is as hard to get in and out of as the time-jumping labs." He slapped his hands together. "Righto, let's get down to business."

He handed me the eyepiece of a retina scanner.

"Place your eye on that and stay still. Don't blink."

I positioned the scanner against my eye. This whole security setup was a nightmare come true. Retina locks were practically impossible to bypass. My only hope was to hire a spyder to sneak into the security program and change my clearance. It would have to be an A-grade spyder. Someone who could breach defense programs and slide out without a trace. Lenny would know how to get in contact with the best.

My eye was watering by the time the computer accepted my scan. Donaldson-Hono pushed a wristband into a slot then punched up my details.

"I'm cross referencing this wristband to your retina scan and specifying your clearance. That is, entrance, exit, and full use of facilities in the Ledbetter suite."

The Ledbetter suite? Was it named after Damien Ledbetter, the artist? I liked his stuff. Ingrid bought one of his hard-copy originals when he had his first exhibition. She was in her "cultural enlightenment phase" and made me go through the virt-gallery with her. She even tried to get me into the spirit of things by buying the picture I liked, although she never hung it.

The wristband clicked out of the slot and Donaldson-Hono handed it to me. I slid it over my wrist and it shrank to a comfortable fit.

"Let me guess," I said, "this will only come off if I die."

"Don't be ridiculous. If you want to remove it all you have to do is report to the duty officer and run it over this scan." He pointed to a box on the desk. "Of course, it can also be removed if someone hacks off your hand."

Great.

Then a truly horrible thought hit me. "Does this thing have an inbuilt tracker?"

"No, do you want one?" He laughed at his own joke, then cleared his throat, glancing around to see if anyone had noticed. "Only VIPs have trackers. It's too expensive to fit them into all the mem-met bands. Well, that's you done."

He picked up a chunkier wristband, scanned it, then gave it to Hartpury.

"Doctor, here's your visitor's band."

Hartpury clicked it around her wrist. It was just a heavy bracelet with a regular snap lock. It didn't look like it needed to be scanned off like mine.

"If you want visitors, Aaronson, they'll have to be logged in at this office to get one of these bands," Donaldson-Hono said.

I nodded. He motioned for me to step up to the computer.

"We have to voice and vid record your understanding and agreement to P3 regulations. Are you ready?"

He positioned the screen to frame both of us, straightened his collar then started his spiel.

"Cadet Joss Aaronson is hereby cleared for entrance and use of the Ledbetter suite on the ground floor of building P3."

He turned to me.

"Cadet Aaronson, you do not have clearance to access any floor above the ground floor. Any attempt to access these floors will result in a security breach. Security measures designed to disable intruders may be used against you. Do you, Cadet Joss Aaronson, understand and agree to comply with these conditions and warnings?"

"I do."

I felt like I was getting married or something.

Donaldson-Hono suddenly relaxed his official pose and logged out of the computer.

"Have you ever heard of a neuro-needle?" he asked.

I shook my head. He smiled and picked up the scanner eyepiece, pushing it back into its protective covering.

"Level two is bristling with them. Take my advice, stay in your designated areas. It takes about six months to get over a needle. Complete paralysis."

"Thank you, Major," Hartpury said. "I'm sure the cadet is not intending to breach any security arrangements. I take it her clearance is on-line now?"

"Of course," Donaldson-Hono said.

Hartpury and I checked through the security entrance into the foyer of P3. The whole place was black marble: the walls, the floor, even the reception desk. The only door was the one we had just walked through. There were no corridors or lifts. Just four plain black marble walls and one door. Lenny would have freaked. He never goes anywhere without at least two exits available for a quick getaway.

We walked up to the desk. The security guy nodded to us.

"Good morning, Doctor."

"Hello, Sergeant. This is Cadet Aaronson. She's quartered here."

The sergeant looked me over. I looked back. Okay, if you like severe crew cuts and no lips. I smiled and leaned against the desk. Was this stuff real marble? I tapped it with a fingernail. It wasn't. Maybe they'd skimped on a few other areas too.

"Joss, this is Sergeant Vaughn. He's on day duty," Hartpury said.

"How's it hanging, Sarge?"

His eyes didn't even flicker, the sign of a great poker player. Maybe he'd join one of my games. Hartpury was frowning again. She edged me towards the back wall.

"Your quarters are up the corridor," she said.

All I saw was a black marble wall.

"What corridor?" I asked.

"Wait."

The wall shimmered, then broke up, dropping away to show a corridor. It was imaginatively decorated in black marble.

"Outrageous," I said. "How does it work?"

"The black marble is really a virtual wall that hides an energy grid," Hartpury said. "If you try and walk though it without clearance, it'll give you an electric shock. That band you're wearing turns off any energy grid that you're cleared to access."

"That's comforting."

"It's kind of like one of those mazes they used to use in psychology experiments," she said.

Yeah, and I'm the rat.

We walked down the corridor. A red line of light stretched along the floor next to each wall. I stopped to look.

"Don't go over the line," Hartpury warned.

I jumped back.

"That's the safety limit for the energy grid," she said. "Remember, those walls aren't real. There're corridors and suites behind them."

I stared at the wall. Was that the faint outline of a door or was I just imagining it? Lenny says you should never take anyone's word for anything. They could be bluffing. I reached across the line. An alarm beeped, but nothing else happened. Then my hand touched the wall.

I woke up flat on my back with my head in Hartpury's

lap. Vaughn was leaning over me saying it served me right.

"It's all right, Joss, you were only out for about a minute. Do you need a medic?" Hartpury asked.

I shook my head. All I felt was a slight zinging in my fingertips and toes.

"That was a stupid thing to do," she said. "You could have been seriously hurt."

"No, it can't do any serious damage. It's a low voltage," Vaughn said.

Hartpury glared at him. "Next time you might try believing me," she said, brushing my hair out of my eyes.

Vaughn offered me a hand up and hauled me to my feet. He must have had some kind of a master-band because all of the virtual walls in the corridor had dropped away. I could now see doors and other corridor openings, all safari-suit beige.

"Since you're okay, I'll go back to my post. Try and stay away from the walls," Vaughn said, his face carefully bland. The man was definitely on my poker list.

He walked towards the foyer, punching keys on his wrist pad. The black virtual walls re-formed.

I picked up my duffel and followed Hartpury in the opposite direction, keeping well away from the red lines. A second corridor opened up and we obediently turned into it like good little rats. A part of the left wall disappeared and the door to the Ledbetter suite became visible.

"Your wristband unlocks it," Hartpury said.

I waved my wrist across the lighted panel. The door slid back.

"Well?" Hartpury said.

"Aren't you going to carry me over the threshold or something?" I asked.

Hartpury snorted and pushed me through the dark doorway.

Organic Hardware

The Ledbetter suite stank of new plastic, that acidic smell that coats the back of your throat. It was mixed with a pinch of earthy cabling and a peculiar muskiness that I couldn't quite place. Then the lights came on. We were standing in a large hexagonal-shaped lounge room.

"Welcome Cadet Joss Aaronson. Welcome Dr. Janeen Hartpury," a smooth female computer voice said. "This unit is coded to the voices of Cadet Joss Aaronson and Cadet Mavkel. Environmental controls have been set at twenty-two degrees with a humidity level of fifty-three. Lighting is set to the equivalent of current levels of daylight." The voice rabbited on about lighting preferences and program changes.

"Is this going to happen every time someone walks in?" I asked Hartpury.

The computer answered.

"The welcome facility is automatic, but can be shut down at any time."

"Then shut it down."

"Completed."

Now I could place that musky smell. The Ledbetter suite

was set up with organic computers. The two access consoles were in opposite corners of the hexagon. A bio-tank was attached to each one, the organic gel heaving as it blended rainbow colors in a complex program. All that pulsating goo made me feel a bit queasy. Too bad you can't hide the stuff in some kind of casing, but without lots of light and air it dries up and dies.

The whole place was decorated in shades of Ledbetter's favorite color: blue. Even the food dispenser was blue. I could just make it out in the eating area that opened out from the back wall of the hexagon. On either side of this section there was a closed door. Probably the bedrooms. I bet they were blue, too. Whoever decorated this building had no imagination.

"The bedroom and console on the left have been modified for Mavkel," Hartpury said. "There's also a specialized food dispenser for it, too. Have a quick look round. Then I want to tell you about the research we've done." She was smiling as though she had personally built the place.

I wanted to check out Mavkel's room, but you can't snoop properly with someone watching. That would have to wait. Instead, I walked over to the console on the right side of the hexagon. My console. As I approached, the screen turned to face me. I feinted to the left. The screen swung with me. This machine was definitely state-of-the-art. As soon as Hartpury left, I'd have to check out its capabilities. The gel blurped at me. It sounded like a baby puking on someone's shoulder.

I dropped my duffel and took a look inside my bedroom. Finally, something that wasn't blue. The room was white, with a single bed, a side table, and one pale Ledbetter print. The room was big enough for a king-sized bed, but students only get issued singles. All in all it was a bit wishy-washy. The only bit of real color was in the ensuite. The whole bathroom had been molded out of yellow plastic. That kind of yellow you pee when you've been taking too much vitamin B. At least it had a full-sized bather. I hate cramming myself into a water-saver.

The food and living area at the back was straight out of one of Ingrid's home beautiful programs. I flicked over the choices on Mavkel's food dispenser. The names of the food had been translated into English, but I couldn't understand the descriptions. You've got to wonder, though, what Melch Daglon tastes like.

Hartpury sat down at the adjustable table, motioning me towards a chair.

"What do you think of the place?" she asked.

"It's okay. A bit too blue for my liking." I sat down opposite her. Actually, it was brilliant compared to normal student quarters. Being the partner of the alien had some problems but it also had some major perks. Like the fact that I was still at the Centre. Without my Chorian partner, I'm sure Camden-Stone would have eventually kicked me out.

"I think you could finally make a home here, Joss," she said. "This is your chance to really find out what you're about."

I shifted in my chair. Like I've said, I hate being analyzed. I feel like one of those butterflies with a pin through its guts.

"Lay off the psych stuff," I said.

"It's my job."

I didn't smile back. She held up her hands.

"Okay, let's just talk about Mavkel for now. We've been trying to get as much information as possible so you can get an idea of your partner."

Finally, someone was going to fill me in on Mavkel. Camden-Stone's little chat had made me realize how little I knew about the whole deal.

"Unfortunately we haven't been able to get much officially," Hartpury said. She paused, looking down at the table. My smell-a-rat detector shot up and bristled.

"Why haven't you got much?" I asked.

"The Foreign Affairs department isn't being very helpful."

"Why not?"

She shrugged, but she was holding back.

"Okay then. What do we know unofficially?" I asked.

Hartpury rubbed her hands together slowly, choosing her words.

"I got talking to a Chorian at an official reception. Its name was Refmol. It told me that Mavkel is more or less an outcast because its birth-pair was killed in an accident. Apparently if one birth-pair dies, the other is supposed to die, too."

"It's supposed to suicide?" I asked. A suicidal partner wasn't going to be very useful to me.

"No, I don't think so. I think it's more of a separation trauma. Refmol is some kind of Chorian medic. A Chanter. It was the one who saved Mavkel from dying and, from the sounds of it, started a huge controversy on Choria."

What would it be like to have someone in your mind all the time and then suddenly lose them? I thought a hole had been blasted right through my middle when Louise left, but I've never had someone close to me actually die. Sometimes I've wondered what it would be like if Ingrid died, but the idea is too hairy. My brain always hits the panic button and jumps onto a new subject.

"I don't think the Elders really know what to do with Mavkel," Hartpury continued. "A Chorian has to be paired to be able to communicate telepathically. Since Mavkel no longer has a pair, it's cut off from the rest of them. It has to rely on the spoken word—something the Chorians don't seem to be very keen about."

"We get along all right with it," I said.

"The Chorians think spoken language is very clumsy. Anyway Refmol let slip that they're not sure how the separation has affected Mavkel's mind. I think that's why the Chorian Elders think Mavkel is the best ambassador for this mission. It already understands in some ways what it is like to be a human: limited to its own mind and forced to 'communicate with sound.'" She singsonged the last bit, imitating the Chorians.

"They don't have a very high opinion of us, do they?" I said.

"Let's just say they have a very high opinion of our time technology."

"Is that all you've got on Mavkel?"

"That's about it. Most of the time we spoke Refmol was pumping me about you. Especially about your parents."

"Why?"

"I don't know. Their bloodlines are pretty important to them. Maybe Refmol wanted to check out your pedigree."

"What did you tell it?"

"Don't worry, I didn't say much," she said. "I know you're a bit sensitive on that subject. You know when all's said and done, I think I trust Refmol more than some of these Foreign Affairs creeps. At least Refmol is friendly. Look, it showed me one of their hand greetings." She took my hand in hers. "They seem to touch each other a lot more than we do."

She spread out her hand, pushing mine into a fist.

"You've got to remember that they have two thumbs," she said as she covered my fist with her hand, entwining our thumbs.

"What's this actually mean?"

"Refmol said it was a friendship clasp." She dropped my fist. "That's about all I can pass on to you. There's more information, but it's on a need-to-know basis."

"You're kidding. You mean that's all the information I'm getting?" I shook my head. "This really burns. I'm the one who's going to be living with Mavkel. I'm the one who needs the information."

Hartpury nodded.

"I know. I know. But the government has blocked our requests over and over again." She leaned forward. "I think they want you to report any information you find out about the Chorians."

"They want me to spy?"

This was getting severe. If they were into spying, this whole place was probably rigged for government eyes and ears. I'd have to find their little peepholes and plug them up.

"Well, they call it fact collection," Hartpury said, twisting her mouth into a half smile. "I think they don't know that much about the Chorians and it's driving them crazy."

She was probably right and wrong. It was more likely the government knew a lot, but didn't trust its information. Answer: corroborate from a different, neutral source.

"If you don't want to do it, you have my support," she said.

"I'll let you know," I said.

Spying for someone else wasn't really up my alley, but it wasn't a bad idea to play along with them. There was also a chance I could get a bit more information out of them. Right now, the Hartpury well of information had dried up. I needed to get onto the Net.

"If you don't mind, I think I'd like to unpack and get settled in," I said, putting on my tired-but-valiant face. If I was lucky, Hartpury would think I needed "some space." She took the bait.

"Of course, you'll have a bit to do. You've got the rest of

the day to settle in, like all the other students," she said. "Are you coming to the first-year cocktail party tonight?"

I shrugged. First I'd heard about it. Seems I wasn't on the top of the party list for my class.

"I hope you come. It'll do you good to mingle with some of the others," she said, standing up.

I grunted. Hartpury hesitated, as if to push the issue.

"I'll see you tomorrow, Doctor," I said firmly.

"Remember, I'm here to help you, Joss," she said. She walked out of the suite. The front door closed.

"Computer, lock entrance door. I don't want any visitors," I said.

"Entrance door is locked to all visitors."

I'd have to change that computer voice. It sounded too much like Louise.

Louise would definitely not have approved of me snooping. I can still see that little wrinkle she used to get between her eyebrows when I did something wrong. Ingrid, on the other hand, would think it showed initiative. That was one thing I had in common with my mother. The ability to rationalize any situation. It's not surprising I'm so good at it. Ingrid is a master. I still can't get over the way she rationalized why Louise left us. Ingrid said it was all the fault of the company directors. Apparently, they were insisting she have a male partner for a while because her hetero audience percentage had gone down. They said it would bring the conservative belt back on board. All I knew was that Ingrid and Louise were fighting. One night Louise yelled that she wasn't going to hide away while some testosterone pod jumped on for a publicity ride. She left soon after that. So did I. Boarding school number four.

Louise and my conscience would have to scowl in the background while I snooped. After all, a girl needs to be informed.

I had a tough choice on my hands. Play around on a state-of-the-art computer or sniff around Mavkel's room. The computer belched at me. It was a sign. First I'd download a bit of information, then explore the room.

The console of the organic computer was a new slimline large screen. I sat in front of it, pushing the VR hood to one side. I pressed my finger along the scan plate.

"Would you prefer virtual, voice, or keyboard recognition?" the computer asked.

Virtual was fun, but I always wasted too much time. I'd stick with voice. Then I had a nasty thought. Johnny Dirtbag, government agent, might be listening to all my conversations.

"Keyboard," I said.

The first thing I set up was a voice print data security lock so Johnny couldn't track my computer wanderings. It probably wouldn't keep him out if he really tried, but it might slow him down.

It was possible that this computer could check if there were any bugs in the suite. I typed in a request for a security schematic of the suite. Denied. Of course it wouldn't be that easy. It was a job for a spyder. I sent out the code that Lenny had made me memorize. Soon a spyder would contact me. Completely untraceable.

Next I requested two Net-wide searches: one on Joseph Camden-Stone/Daniel Sunawa-Harrod, the other on Chorians.

Finally I switched the computer to voice recognition.

The gel shivered into a rainbow as the organic started its scan of the world's computers. I could safely leave it to do its work while I tiptoed through Mavkel-land. I was almost out of my chair when the computer said, "Search completed. Three hundred and eight open entries. Fourteen retina-sealed entries. Do you want further details of entries?"

Snork me gently. This thing was fast! I looked around the console and pulled open a nearby drawer. There must be some Reader units around. I'd download this stuff and read it later. A stack of Readers clunked against the front of the second drawer as I pulled it open. Brand-new and not even formatted. The university wasn't counting credit when it came to their Chorian guests. I slipped a Reader out of its pack and pushed it into the download slot.

"Format Reader in Port A and download all of the open entries," I said.

"For your future information, this facility automatically recognizes data transfer units and does not require port addresses," the computer said.

Ouch. I'd just had my knuckles rapped by a computer.

"Similarly, this facility automatically formats data transfer units. A full instruction manual for this facility is available on request."

Double ouch.

"Transfer complete. Please remove data transfer unit from Port A," it said.

"I don't need addresses either," I muttered.

"Noted."

This computer was so formal, I was getting constipated just listening to it. Maybe it had a language modification program.

"Computer, do you have an informal voice and comment dictionary?"

"This facility can access up to level ten of the Johnson-Hargrave Informal Dictionary."

"Use that dictionary from now on. Also, if I get any commcalls, just take a message."

"Okay. Will do," the computer said.

Don't you just love level ten of the Johnson-Hargrave? Far more relaxed. I pulled the Reader out of Port A and put it in my duffel. Now for Mavkel's room.

Sprung Bad

Mavkel's bedroom was like a bad party; lights too low and no one around. It was hot, too.

"Can you increase the lighting?" I asked the computer.

"Not a chance. This is the level of light that's been program-locked for the room."

"What about the temperature?" I asked.

"Same deal," the computer said.

I stood still. All I could see were those colored cells that stream in front of your eyes until you adjust to the dark. If Johnny was watching, I hoped he was also having problems with the lighting levels.

I made out two groups of heavy-looking molded containers stacked against the back wall. A thermo-roll, the kind they use for hypothermic patients, was on the floor. By the time I got to the ensuite, I could see everything. I've always had great night vision. In the end I always got banned from the school games of Murder in the Dark.

The bathroom was outrageous. I couldn't even imagine how Mavkel used the strange-looking gizmo that stuck out of the wall. If it was a toilet, I wouldn't want to be peeing too often. That is, if Chorians peed. The bather was metal and all the taps were different. I turned one on. It rumbled for a second, then a blast of sand caught me on the arm just above my wristband, graveling about two layers of skin off. Thank God for soundproof rooms.

"Computer. Medical aid!" I yelled at the computer.

"Human or Chorian?"

"Human. Quick!"

I was probably giving Johnny a real laugh. It took two pain patches and some pseudo-skin before I was out of whine mode. Another pain patch finally had me zooming along, ready for more snooping. Something a bit safer. Something like the boxes.

Each box was molded to fit the one below, so that all together, they formed two purply columns spanned at the top by a longer carved box. I touched one and it ranked me out—just like living human skin. The whole construction stood a bit taller than me. All I had to do was pull the carved box down. I pushed at it to test the weight and found a hover switch. A minute later the box was on the ground.

There was no lock, only a catch made up of two inter-locking circles. I prodded and poked them until the top slid open. It folded in on itself until half of its mass just disap-peared. I felt around to see where it had been hidden, but it was just missing. I hunched my shoulders against that crawly feeling you get up your back and scalp when some-thing spooks you. It had finally hit home. I was dealing with something so different that none of the normal laws applied. Not even physics.

The first thing I pulled out of the box was an instrument. At least, it looked like an instrument. There were valves and holes and two mouthpieces. I blew into one. Nothing. It was obviously a duo kind of thing. The whole instrument was carved in something that was like rock except it was flexible. A line of symbols curved down the body and ended with the same interlocking circle design that was on the box. I placed the instrument carefully beside me on the carpet.

My next lucky dip produced a small matte-black cube. I tapped it. Shook it. Looked for a clasp. Then held it up to my eye.

"It is a thought cube," Mavkel's voice sang behind me.

I jumped around, my heart in overload. I was sprung bad.

"Holy screte. You scared the life out of me. How'd you get in?" I demanded. "Computer, I thought I locked the door."

"It's not my fault. You locked it to all visitors. Mavkel is a resident," the computer whined.

Sometimes that level ten dictionary could be a pain in the neck. "From now on, tell me if anyone even comes near that door."

"Sure thing," the computer said.

Mavkel held up its left hand. A mem-met band circled its wrist.

"This opened the door. Sorry to scare Joss-partner."

"Yeah, well, that's okay. You're early. Weren't you supposed to be coming tomorrow?"

Mavkel nodded. Its ears flattened on the top. For a second, it looked just like a guilty kid.

"Did not wait anymore."

"You mean, you gave all your minders the slip?"

Mavkel tilted its head to one side, obviously trying to understand.

"What I mean is, did you leave all of your Elders without them knowing about it?"

It nodded, double-smiling.

"Yes. It is easy to do what Mavkel wants to do when there is no . . ." It faltered, running out of vocab. Then it touched its head and moved forward, touching mine.

"You mean when there is no telepathy. That's what we call a link between minds," I said. Finally a use for all of those brain-numbing games of charades I'd been forced to play at my last school.

"Yes. Yes. No telepathy. Does Joss-partner like this no-telepathy?"

"I dunno. I've never felt telepathy."

"Maybe there will be telepathy soon," Mavkel said.

It knelt down beside me, a few centimeters too close for comfort. I leaned back on my hand. Mavkel was rearranging its heavy clothing and didn't seem to notice. I leaned back a bit farther, watching as it smoothed down about ten layers of regulation jumpers and woolen wraps.

"Joss-partner will not inform the Elders where Mavkel is?" it asked, its primary mouth pursed anxiously.

I had a feeling Joss-partner would not need to inform the

Elders. Johnny Dirtbag and Mavkel's wristband would take care of that.

"No. I won't tell."

"That is good. Mavkel will show Joss-partner the thought cube," it sang.

I gave it the cube. It was excited, resonating little harmonized scales as it placed the cube on the floor.

"The cube makes a memory come out of the minds," Mavkel sang, touching its head, "and run like . . . VR movie?" It looked at me to see if that was the right word. I nodded. "Mavkel show Joss-partner."

Mavkel leaned down until the cube was a few centimeters from its face. It flicked back its protective second eyelid, then stared into the top plane. The matte cube changed tones until it looked shiny wet. Then, a wisp of smoky color curled into an image a few centimeters above the top. It was a tiny Mavkel sitting in front of Refmol and a sour-looking government man. Refmol was bouncing up and down on the spot.

Then I think Mavkel laughed. It sounded like Indian music, rhythmic and discordant.

"Joss-partner can see Mavkel learning human sounds. There were many jumps of frustration. It is hard to learn your sounds."

The image rearranged itself. Mavkel pressed its primary mouth closed, its ears angled back and stiff. This next memory was obviously no laughing matter.

We were watching a rerun of the moment when Mavkel

chose me as its partner. It was weird seeing a tiny version of the ceremony from Mavkel's point of view.

First, I saw me being mind scanned. Suddenly the four Chorian Elders jumped up and down in shock. They seemed to move in closer together, as though conferring. Then they stopped, gestured with their hands, and concentrated.

"Your Elders scanned me again!" I said, recognizing the stance. Mavkel nodded, its eyes flicking to me. The image wavered.

I hadn't realized they'd scanned me again. They must have caused that sudden pain that had nearly knocked me out. Mavkel concentrated on the cube again.

I watched myself start to fall. Tiny Mavkel caught me. The Elders closed in, but Mavkel stretched out its other hand, commanding them to stop. Mavkel had stopped the pain. That bright white burn that had ripped through my head.

"Why did they scan me again? Couldn't they tell it was hurting me?" I said.

Mavkel pushed itself upright. Immediately the tiny scene disappeared, the cube fading to its original matte black. Mavkel twitched its ears around, almost as though it was looking over its shoulder.

"Joss-partner has resonance," Mavkel said softly. "The Elders searched. Too deep."

"What resonance? I don't understand."

Mavkel bounced gently against its heels, sounding a clash of frustrated chords. We stared at each other. Mavkel suddenly shielded its eyes with the milky second eyelids, a shutter being slammed down. It picked up the thought cube and placed it in front of me.

"The thought cube is for Joss-partner. Mavkel has learned of your custom for gift giving."

That drove the knife of guilt straight through my snooping little heart. I could almost hear Louise ordering me to apologize.

"Look, I'm sorry about going through your things," I said. "I just wanted to find out a bit more about you."

"Mavkel learned about sorry. Sorry is not right here." It motioned towards the two columns.

"These two are the pair. Before the fire the pair was Mavkel and Kelmav. Now it is Mavkel and Joss-partner." It pointed to the long box. "This is that which connects Mavkel and Joss-partner."

"I'm sorry I opened it up."

It bounced up and down gently.

"No. No requirement for sorry." It pushed the thought cube towards me.

"Try the thought cube," it sang. "Joss-partner must try the thought cube."

The computer interrupted.

"Joss, you've got a Comm-message from Diana Rosso-Pike. She's the head honcho at Foreign Affairs. Sounds like she's real excited, because she won't log off. There's also a group of people heading this way with a master-band."

So, the guano had finally hit the fan.

"Try the thought cube," Mavkel sang, pushing it up against my knees. "Joss-partner must try and make pictures."

"Didn't you hear the message? I bet your Elders are on their way."

"Elders coming?" Mavkel closed its long hand over the cube, placing it in one of its pockets. "Joss-partner try later." Its ears folded flat against its head.

What was the deal with that cube anyway? Mavkel was acting as if it was a gram of Bliss.

"It might interest you to know," the computer said, "that Professor Camden-Stone, Elders Gohjec and Jecgoh, Chanter Refmol, and Sergeant Vaughn will be coming through our front door in five seconds."

"Thanks," I said. "Come on, Mavkel. We'd better go and say hi."

"Refmol comes?" it asked.

"That's right," the computer answered.

Mavkel's ears stirred. Was it in relief? From what I could tell, Chorian ears gave away their feelings. I'd have to check that theory out. It could come in useful.

I grabbed Mavkel's arm and pulled it out of the room. We reached the middle of the hexagon lounge room just as the door slid open.

"Don't say anything. Just act cool," I whispered.

Mavkel started to shiver.

"Like this?" it asked.

"No, I mean act calm."

Mavkel stopped shivering.

"Act is your pretending. Yes?"

I nodded.

The posse charged into the room.

I couldn't understand what the Chorian Elders were screeching, but Camden-Stone came through loud and clear.

"Aaronson, what do you think you're doing?"

Good old Joe. Blame Aaronson and nine times out of ten you're right. But this was the tenth time, and I was going to enjoy it.

"What do you mean, sir?" I asked.

The Elders were ignoring Mavkel, but their ears were straight up in the air, stiff as plasboard. Refmol, the Chanter, seemed to be acting as some kind of intermediary.

"Mavkel left without authorization. Then we find out it's with you. What do you think I mean?" Camden-Stone demanded.

Refmol leaned closer to me. Its ears twitched as the Elders sang their disapproval in nasty discordant twangs.

"Mavkel has disobeyed the Elders. They may remove it from the school," it sang softly.

Why was Refmol telling me? I studied its face, but that was a waste of time. Carefully expressionless. The Chanter's ears were also at a neutral half-mast.

I had to admit, it would be bad news for me if Mavkel was removed from the Centre. This partnership was the only thing that could keep Camden-Stone off my back and me in the course. I also kind of liked the prestige of partnering the Chorian. I realized I was going to have to bite the bullet and let Camden-Stone win the round.

"I'm sorry, sir," I said loudly to Camden-Stone. "It's my fault Mavkel left without authorization." The Elders stopped screeching at Refmol and turned to face us. "I asked Mavkel to join me earlier than scheduled."

Refmol raised its ears. So I had done the right thing, although poor Mavkel looked completely confused. It opened its mouths to protest, but Refmol flipped its ears. Mavkel got the message.

Camden-Stone nodded with satisfaction.

"I thought as much," he said, bowing to the Elders. "It is the fault of Cadet Aaronson, not Mavkel. Now do you see why Aaronson is not a good choice as partner? I hope you will accept my sincere apologies. Aaronson will, of course, be disciplined."

I'd made Camden-Stone's day. Not only was he "right," he got to punish me. His favorite leisure activity.

Refmol stepped forward. "Refmol sees this new pair is eager to join." Refmol bowed to me. "Perhaps such eagerness should not be punished. This pairing is, after all, a bridge between our peoples and their knowledge."

The Elders sang their agreement. No wonder Mavkel liked this Refmol character. Smooth as silk. But Camden-Stone wasn't going to give in so easily.

"In our culture when one has done wrong, one must accept the consequences," he said, looking at me. "Isn't that right, Aaronson?"

Refmol spread out its hands. "As it is with our culture," it said. "However, this young pair was fulfilling the natural law. Two must join. No harm to any pair has occurred. Perhaps the young pair is correct. The time has come for them to join. The universe does not work to our time or our convenience."

I'd hate to debate this Refmol character. Camden-Stone knew he was on the losing team. He inclined his head.

"You have persuaded me, Refmol. Cadet Aaronson and Cadet Mavkel have now officially started their partnership. This episode shall be forgotten."

Refmol bowed again. Mavkel's ears had perked up a bit. We were in the clear.

"The official reception for Mavkel will be during the introductory lecture tomorrow morning." Camden-Stone told me. "You should both take the opportunity to get to know one another and settle in. I believe an official introduction to the rest of the class is important. You might do well to stay here until then."

Translation: don't leave this room until I've organized proper protection for Mavkel.

"Diana Rosso-Pike is still online," the computer said.

"I'll take that," Camden-Stone said.

While he calmed Rosso-Pike down, Mavkel sang its apology to the Elders. They ignored it. Refmol touched my arm.

"Refmol has felt the resonance," it sang. "The universe has prepared for the pairing of our peoples and Refmol is vowed to help."

I was getting sick of these cryptic messages. Just as I was about to ask "what resonance?" Refmol was called over by Gohjec. Very convenient. If you want to be mysterious, always have someone call you away at the critical moment. That way you never have to explain yourself.

The posse was leaving. Gohjec and Jecgoh turned away from a low bow from Mavkel. Refmol gave me a cryptic mysterious look. I nodded back. Hopefully, it was a mysterious nod. Finally they all left the suite. Mavkel and I were alone again.

"That was a close call," I said.

"Yes. My ears were heavy with their silence." It stroked my arm quickly. "Mavkel thanks Joss-partner."

"I think we should both be thanking Refmol," I said, moving away from its insistent hand. "I'm going to unpack. I'll see you later."

I picked up my duffel. Mavkel followed close on my heels.

"Joss-partner will try the thought cube now?" it asked, holding the cube out on its outstretched hand.

"No, not now. I want to unpack. You should too," I said, stepping into my room and reaching for the door sensor. "We can get together later."

Mavkel started to hum an eerie low monotone, its ears collapsing until they looked like limp pigtails. My hand found the sensor plate and the bedroom door shut between us. I leaned my forehead against the cool plasboard, slowly rolling my head until my ear was against the door. Mavkel was still humming on the other side. The lonely sound snapped at my nerves like an alarm that no one turns off.

I reached over to the sensor pad again, but dropped my hand. I needed to block Mavkel out, to block everything out. I dumped my duffel on the bed and wormed my hand through it. Of course my harp was at the very bottom. I can screen out the world when I'm playing the blues. I just slide behind the melody until the harp sings in my head. No more spooky humming. No more unanswered questions. No more Camden-Stone. The harp just fills in all my gaps.

I stretched out on the bed and stormed out some percussive tonguing, the fuzzy hard sound used in blues solos. I bent an A down to an A flat and let the note reverberate through my bones. It was the start of the blues duet I was writing. The whole idea was to make the two melody lines weave around each other like a Chorian harmony. I was even going to call it the "Chorian Blues" until that stupid group with the freckly singer stole the name for their pop song. How did it go?

Don't be an alien to me, baby,
Don't be an alien,
Don't be an alien to me, baby,
Cause aliens don't have lips.

What a load of tox, and it wasn't even blues. Anyway, I had come up with another name: "The Dogstar Blues." Not bad, if I say so myself.

The band at the Buzz Bar said they'd give "The Dogstar Blues" a go when it was finished. I'd even talked Jonas, the alto sax, into playing the second harp. The only problem was that I couldn't work out how to finish the damned thing.

I played the trill that I thought might work as the lead-in to the final section for the first harp. It sounded good, but I needed to hear the whole song to make sure it worked. So I started from the beginning, mentally humming the second harp part to check the movement. That's probably why I yelped when Mavkel ran into the room. It harmonized a sound that dug straight through my melodies, souring the chords. I felt like I'd been doused with cold water.

"Is Joss-partner ill?" Mavkel shrilled, its ears flat against its head. "Mavkel will call Refmol. Refmol will chant." It ran over and cupped its hands over my ears.

"I'm fine," I said. "For God's sake stop patting my ears." I pushed its hands away.

"Why does Joss-partner make healing sounds?" Mavkel had flicked back its second eyelids to peer closely at my left ear.

I moved my head away. "I'm just playing some blues."

"What are blues?" it sang. Its hands were still hovering near my ears. Mavkel didn't give up easily.

"It's a kind of music. Here listen."

I played the chorus of "The Dogstar Blues," ready to block Mavkel's hands with my elbows. It wasn't necessary. Mavkel was completely still as I played.

"Ahhh, this blues has many of the sounds Mavkel uses to heal minds," it sang as the last note faded.

"You use music to heal people?"

"Yes, Mavkel and Kelmav were Chanters. What do humans use music for?"

"We use it for lots of things. Mostly for fun and relaxation."

Mavkel sat back. I didn't need to understand ear-speak to see that it was appalled.

"Then how do humans heal?"

"We've got doctors who learn how to heal. They use drugs and surgery. Things like that."

"Doc-tors." Mavkel repeated the word a few times. "Doc-tors heal?"

I nodded.

"Then Mavkel and Kelmav were learning to be doctors."

"You were going to be a doctor?"

"Yes. Mavkel and Kelmav were learning the chants until the pair became a one."

I wanted to ask more, but Mavkel was backing out of the room.

"This is a time for apology, yes? Sorry for disturbing," it said. The door closed behind it.

How come no one had told me about the Chorians' using music as medicine? Or that Mavkel was one of their Chanter-doctors? I felt like I was picking my way through a VR maze without the help icon. I tapped out my harp and slipped it back into its case. Maybe there was more information on that Reader I'd downloaded. I pulled it out of my duffel bag. Time to start studying.

New Friends, Old Enemies

The next morning I was whacked. Serves me right for reading until four. But I did find some very interesting articles and interviews about Camden-Stone and Sunawa-Harrod.

The first thing I came across was a twenty-year-old Netnews article that reported a terrible explosion at the university. A young post-grad student, Joseph Camden-Stone, was critically injured during an experiment. His friend, Daniel Sunawa-Harrod, pulled him from the inferno and saved his life. Camden-Stone was reported to be in critical condition, with massive face and head injuries.

Maybe that explains Camden-Stone's strange mouth. Total reconstruction.

Then came thirty articles about how Daniel Sunawa-Harrod returned to the scene of the accident and discovered the time-continuum field. About fifty more articles reported his Nobel-Takahini Prize and his directorship of the new Centre for Neo-Historical Studies. I skipped most of them since I'd had the history of the Centre drummed into me during the intro courses.

Then I opened the most interesting file. It was a three part vid-interview with Sunawa-Harrod, dated fifteen years ago.

The interviewer was a woman named Joanna Tyrell-Coombes. She looked like the prototype for Ingrid: a glossy blonde with big curves and a bigger mouth. She seemed very high profile, but I'd never heard of her before. She was sitting across from Sunawa-Harrod in some director's idea of a "serious science" lounge suite.

Sunawa-Harrod looked a lot younger than his holo picture. He was kind of tired, but still exuded energy and confidence on the small Reader screen. Most of the interview was pretty boring, except for one strange moment when Sunawa-Harrod lied.

"Of course," Joanna Tyrell-Coombes said, "it was that awful accident involving Joseph Camden-Stone that resulted in you discovering the time-continuum field."

Sunawa-Harrod nodded. Wary. "Yes, one of my fusion reaction experiments went wrong."

Joanna leaned forward. Her smile was in place, but her eyes were ripping his throat out. I'd seen Ingrid in the same pose when she thought she had someone pinned down.

"Your experiment? My sources suggest that it was Dr. Camden-Stone's experiment that resulted in the explosion."

Sunawa-Harrod's eyes flickered for a second. He shifted his feet on the plush carpet. Ingrid used to say that if they fidget their feet, they're talking screte.

"No," Sunawa-Harrod said. "I was conducting the experiment. Poor Joseph was just assisting me."

Joanna suddenly glanced to someone offscreen. She frowned slightly then changed the subject.

In my mind there was no doubt: Sunawa-Harrod had lied. However, it seemed to be such a small thing to lie about that I nearly dismissed it. It was lucky I decided to check out part two of the interview, screened the following week.

Joanna Tyrell-Coombes was gone. Replaced by some dreary man who blatantly read the questions off a vid-cue. The third interview was the same. There was no mention of what had happened to Joanna.

So, at about half-past three in the morning, I trotted over to my console and looked it up in the archives. After that series Joanna Tyrell-Coombes's career went downhill fast. She never interviewed again and got stuck presenting some wildlife show. Hopefully a spyder would get back to me soon. Every bone in my body told me that something had been zelcroed tighter than a pair of cling jeans.

I was still on my first coffee when Mavkel's four body-guards arrived to take us to the lecture theater. I swear every one of them could have won Mr. and Ms. Hardbody. Not a bad way to travel. It took the pressure off me too, since five pairs of eyes on the lookout for an assassin is better than one. Although, according to Lenny, it was a bit early for Suka to strike yet.

The Centre for Neo-Historical Studies is the only school in the university that has no Net students. Everyone has to be on campus and most of the teaching is done by old-style lectures and classes. Camden-Stone says it builds better partnership and invokes camaraderie.

Mavkel was very quiet. Ears low, secondary eyelids closed. It was leaning towards me, but I kept on edging away until I bumped into one of the guards. He swung his gun around out of reflex.

"You're a bit jumpy," I said, holding up my hands.

He lowered his gun.

"I've been ordered to be jumpy," he said, smiling.

"Do you really think someone will try something?" I asked.

He shrugged, checking out a group of students who stared at Mavkel as we walked past.

"There're a lot of whackos out there. You never know if death threats are for real or just screte."

Mavkel jangled, his ears jumping all over the place. The guard's pill-tanned skin went red.

"I'm sure your friend will be all right," he said hurriedly.

He leaned over to Mavkel.

"Don't worry, mate, we'll look after you."

Mavkel bowed.

"This pair is honored," it said.

"Do they reckon I'm a target too?" I asked softly.

The guard hesitated, glancing at his sergeant who was walking in front of us.

"Come on, I've got a right to know," I said.

"No, they say you're not really a target. The emphasis is on the flap . . . I mean your friend. I suppose in the end you're pretty replaceable."

"Thanks for making me feel special," I said.

He laughed. "Better to be alive than special and dead."

I liked this guy's style.

"Hey, what's your name?" I asked, but we had just reached the lecture hall where the welcoming committee was waiting. Camden-Stone was up front, ostentatiously looking at his armscreen. I quickly checked out his face. Whoever had done the reconstruction job must have been good.

I felt Mavkel stiffen beside me as we approached the doorway. I didn't blame it. After going through twelve schools, I knew what it was like to walk into a new classroom. The first few minutes were always agony. Everyone's eyes on you, assessing, judging, testing. At one rich-kid school, I just gave them all the finger and walked out. It was the shortest enrollment that school had ever known.

The guards dropped back into a line as Camden-Stone stepped forward, Refmol beside him. For a second I thought Refmol winked at me, but maybe it was only adjusting its opaque eyelid against the light.

"Thank you, Sergeant Wolfendon. I'd like one of your team to keep watch inside and the rest on the perimeter positions," Camden-Stone said.

He pushed me towards the door.

"Aaronson, you and Mavkel take the two front seats that are vacant. We're running a bit late."

Mavkel dropped in close behind me, clipping my heels with its clawed feet. It was humming the same monotone from last night. A worried hum.

"Remember, just be cool," I whispered over my shoulder.

The humming stopped.

"Pretend again?" it whispered back, its breath hot on my ear.

I nodded.

"You pretend much, do you not?"

Mavkel didn't know the half of it. Right at that moment I was pretending not to see Chaney. He was looking at me, sniggering at something Jorel had said. Tonio was sitting in the row behind them and waved quickly. Sara smiled nervously beside him.

The lecturers sat in the front row in full academic dress, flat hats and all. Hartpury was sitting beside Lindon. She was chewing at her bottom lip. I'd be worried too if I was wearing that piece of black cardboard on my head.

Each of the classes sat together. The sixth years were at the back. I caught Kyle Sandrall's eye and he nodded. Lisa gave me a thumbs-up from the fifth-year section until Derry pushed her hand down, motioning towards Camden-Stone.

I led Mavkel to the vacant seats in the front row as Camden-Stone began to speak.

"Today is the official start of the academic year," he said. "As you are now aware, this year brings us many changes. Two special partnerships have been forged. Firstly, a partnership between Joss Aaronson and Mavkel, our first Chorian student."

He beckoned to us. Mavkel looked at me, reluctance in every line of his ears. We were obviously having the same reaction.

"What does Mavkel pretend here?" it asked softly.

"Just smile," I said.

As we stood and turned to face everyone, I wondered if the rest of humanity was ready for one of Mavkel's double smiles. To the school's credit, the clapping only faltered for a few seconds. Chaney was screwing his face up in disgust until Camden-Stone squashed him with a look. Mavkel and I sat down.

"I am sure you will all join me in extending a friendly and courteous welcome to Mavkel and endeavor to make it feel part of our family," Camden-Stone said, glancing at Chaney.

"We also have another partnership to celebrate. The partnership between Earth and Choria. This alliance will enable us to swap our technologies and our Centre is at the forefront of that information exchange. Beside me is Chanter Refmol, who is the official Chorian Ambassador. Chanter Refmol will be observing our operation and assisting Mavkel in its integration. Please make Chanter Refmol feel welcome."

So Refmol was sticking around for a while. That should make Mavkel happy. I stood up with the rest of the school as we clapped.

Refmol bowed and stepped up to the lectern, catching Camden-Stone by surprise. He moved aside awkwardly, motioning for everyone to sit down.

"Refmol thanks the Centre for the welcome. Choria is pleased to be allied with Earth and sees much alike. Before our contact to you, Choria had visited many other peoples.

We visited one peoples who did not have time like Choria or Earth. Another did not move in space as we do. But Choria and Earth have much in common. To find you who understand the universe in many ways as we do is the joining of a pair."

Refmol bowed as we clapped.

"Thank you, Chanter Refmol," Camden-Stone said. He cleared his throat, deepening his voice. "Unfortunately, I also have some distressing news. The founder of our Centre, Professor Daniel Sunawa-Harrod, is battling a serious illness. I have just found out he has taken a turn for the worse. I am sure you all join me in hoping for his speedy recovery."

"Not with that thing in his head," someone whispered behind me.

Dr. Lindon turned and scowled at the whisperer. I remembered the vid of Sunawa-Harrod and felt kind of sorry he was dying. After all, he'd made time-jumping possible. Camden-Stone seemed sincerely cut up about the news, too. Maybe Joanna Tyrell-Coombes had it all wrong and there was no conspiracy. Then again, she did lose her job.

"Now, it's time to start work," Camden-Stone said. "Would all first-year students please remain seated for their introductory lecture. All other students, please go to your first class."

The classes stood up, moving towards the door. I noticed Lisa pushing her way towards us, Derry following reluctantly.

"Hi Joss. I'd love to meet your partner," Lisa said. She

smiled at Mavkel, who bowed. Derry was standing back, nervously watching the guard at the doorway.

"Mavkel, I'd like you to meet Lisa . . ." Then I realized I didn't know her last name.

"Sholmondy-Rale," she said. She held out her hand. Mavkel took it in the peculiar grip Hartpury had shown me.

"Mavkel is honored to learn of your line," it sang.

"As I am to learn of yours," Lisa said. Mavkel's ears lifted at the courtesy. So, Lisa had studied up on the Chorians. A kindred spirit.

"Come on, Lis, we gotta go," Derry said urgently.

Lisa nodded, placing a soothing hand on Derry's arm. She was tiny compared to her partner, but she had ten times more presence. And it looked like ten times more guts.

"Okay. Just a sec." She turned to Mavkel. "I hope I'll have the pleasure of speaking with you soon. I'm very interested in your culture."

Mavkel bowed again.

"This pair looks forward to the meeting."

Derry pulled Lisa into the line to leave the room. She looked back over her shoulder until a tall sixth year blocked her view.

"Looks like you've got a new friend," I said.

Mavkel's ears did a quick affirmative flip.

We watched as the time-jumpers filed out of the room. The line was slow because Refmol was doing a bit of PR work at the door. I leaned over to Mavkel.

"How come Refmol's birth pair isn't around?" I asked.

"Molref stays on Choria," Mavkel said. "Refmol travels to other worlds with the Elders and Molref stays home to receive its thoughts. The pair is very strong."

"I thought they were doctors."

"Yes. Chanters are always strongest in the minds."

"So you guys can also telepath across space. That's incredible."

"Only some can. Only strong pairs. But even a strong pair loses contact. There is a problem with the time and the space."

"What happens then?"

"When a pair loses contact, they die."

"But you didn't."

"Mavkel is a freak," it said harshly. "Birth pairs should die together."

I sat back. Maybe Hartpury was right. Mavkel was tip-toeing at the edge of Deathwish Canyon. It brushed at its heavy jacket, its face turned away.

"The Elders are hoping that the time knowledge from Earth will solve the problem," it finally sang, flatly.

"I bet Refmol is hoping it will, too," I said.

Mavkel looked over at Refmol. The Chanter was talking earnestly with Camden-Stone and Hartpury.

"Mavkel hopes, too."

"Hey, Aaronson," Chaney said.

I turned around. Chaney had moved to the seat behind

me, his feet on the back of my chair. "Maybe you can settle an argument. Is it true a comp can't ever trace her bloodlines?"

What was he up to? Everyone knew that most comps can't really trace their family tree. It's one of the drawbacks of being tailor-made. You could have a hair-color gene from Mr. A, skin pigment from Dr. B and IQ strings from artists X, Y and Z. Splice it all together with a virus and what have you got? A major headache for a genealogist.

"Is it true you'll never know who your father is? Or should I say your main contributor?" Chaney asked again, but he was staring at Mavkel.

Chaney was leading up to something, but I couldn't work out his punchline.

"I'm sure I could find out, if I needed to. But I don't need to," I said.

Beside me, Mavkel stiffened, its ears up high, the ends quivering.

"Why do you want to know?" I asked.

"Just interested," he said, shrugging.

He'd backed down! Behind me, Camden-Stone called for order. Chaney pulled his feet off the back of the seat.

"You'd better turn around," he said to Mavkel, pointing at Camden-Stone.

Mavkel quickly faced the front of the room, pulling its top jacket tightly against its body.

"Why are you interested?" I insisted.

Chaney just smiled and ducked back to his seat next

to Jorel. I turned around. Mavkel was bouncing slightly. It grabbed my arm.

"Do not worry, Joss-partner," it said fiercely. "The Sulon will be recorded." It stroked my arm with two thumbs then flicked back its protective eyelids, squinting its unshielded eyes against the light. "Mavkel will help record the Sulon."

I had no idea what it was talking about.

"Aaronson, are you going to gossip with Mavkel all morning?" Camden-Stone asked.

"No sir," I said, sitting back in my chair. Mavkel's ears were still quivering.

As Camden-Stone told us about the time-jumping course, I forgot about the Sulon and Chaney's weird questions. It wasn't until much later that I realized how important those questions had been to Mavkel. But by that time, everything was well and truly set in motion.

All One

By Friday I still hadn't heard from a spyder. My code was probably too old, so I called Lenny and asked him to check it out. I'd also only managed to read another third of the entries on the Reader. It was hard fitting it in between classes and homework and with Mav hovering around like my shadow.

I swear I trod on Mav at least twice a day. It even followed me into the toilet until I explained that the cubicle was for private meditation.

In the end I did most of the reading in my "meditation box." But apart from the articles about Camden-Stone and Sunawa-Harrod, most of the entries were about stuff I already knew. In fact there wasn't much that was useful about the Chorians. I'd only found out two new interesting things.

New fact number one:

When attacked, a group of Chorians can join their minds together and blow out their enemy with a mega-powerful psychic mind-lash. They call it the Rastun.

I wondered what our defense forces thought of that.

New fact number two:

The Chorians have two brains: the Riko and Rikun. The Riko is kind of like a public brain that keeps tabs on what the rest of their society is yakking about. The Rikun is the brain that keeps up a Chorian's continual contact with its pair. This two brain setup means Chorians never have to sleep. They can shut off parts of one brain to "recharge" it while they use the other brain. Kind of like the way dolphins can rest one hemisphere of their brain while they use the other to party.

I actually didn't learn fact number two from my reading. Mav told me when I found it learning English at three o'clock in the morning. It was learning how to handle pronouns and sneezing its head off. Every time it sneezed, a little cloud of powder puffed up from its skin.

"Are you sick or something?" I asked, wrapping my bedcover around my shoulders.

"I don't have a sex pronoun," Mav said.

"And that's making you sneeze?" I joked.

Its discordant laugh turned into the sneeze of the century. White powder hung in the air.

"That is a language joke, is it not?" it sang, sniffing. "But it is the coldness that makes me sneeze." It pushed its two noses together to ward off another sneeze. "Tell me, you are a she. Is that right?"

"Yep. I'm female, so I'm a she."

"What am I?" it asked.

Good question.

"I suppose you're an it. You're not one or the other."

Mav shook its head.

"But an *it* is an object. Not a person."

"I suppose so, if you want to get technical."

"I am a person, so I must have a pronoun."

"Okay, then you're going to have to choose a sex."

Mav considered the problem.

"You are a female. A female pairs with a male. Is that correct?"

Did I really want to go into this? It could get very messy. I leaned back against one of the couches.

"Most humans pair with the opposite sex. Male with female. But some people pair with their own sex. And some go both ways," I said.

"So there are two sexes and two types of pairings. Same and opposite?"

"I suppose that's the basics."

Mav walked over to me, standing too close as usual. Way too close. I leaned away from it, sliding my bum along the back of the couch. I was going to have to say something about this personal space business before one of us got head-butted.

"We have many types of pairings, too," Mavkel said. "What is your pairing? Do you go opposite or same?"

"I'm more of an opposite kind of gal."

"Then to complete this human duality, I should be male. I will be a *he*."

"Okay Mav, you're a he from now on."

"What did you call me?"

"Mav. It's a nickname. I just thought that Mavkel was a bit formal."

"A nickname?"

"A name a friend calls another friend."

"But there is no Kel pool in this Mav name. It does not respect the Kel pool."

"If you don't want me to call you Mav, I won't," I said, shrugging.

Mavkel sang the name a couple of times. He nodded solemnly.

"It is proper. I am still of the Kel pool, but there is no Kelmav. Now I am just Mav. What should I call you, Joss-partner?"

"Just call me Joss. That'll do."

The only person who had ever given me a nickname was Ingrid. For about two years she had called me Jo-Jo. The first time I remember her using it was when I was six. Ingrid had booked us into the wildlife park for my birthday. As usual her whole entourage went with us. Twenty people all devoted to Ingrid and the money she made.

I was out of my six-year-old mind with excitement. Trees, animals, dirt, and a fascinating hole I'd found next to an old tree stump. Naturally I had to poke something down the hole. So I reached for a nearby stick. The stick rose up on six legs and ran up my arm. I screamed for so long I nearly passed out from lack of oxygen. Ingrid ran over.

"It's okay Jo-Jo," she said, swinging me up close against her body. "It's only an insect. A stick insect."

She bent down. I hung on tightly around her neck.

"Look," she said, gently picking up the insect. "It makes itself look like a stick so big things won't eat it."

That was probably the last birthday Ingrid ever spent with me. From seven to seventeen I spent my birthday at whatever boarding school I was stuck in at the time. Ingrid always sent me a present, but was "unable to leave the shoot." The class always sang "Happy Birthday," gulped down the soggy sponge cake, and left me alone. Not much seemed to have changed. My eighteenth birthday was in two days' time. No doubt Ingrid would be unable to leave her shoot, and Hartpury would make the time-jump class grind out "Happy Birthday"—soggy sponge cake optional. The only person who had ever done something special for my birthday was Louise. Each of the five years she lived with us, she came to my boarding school and gave me a special birthday hat. Once it was a pair of furry ears, another time an outrageously jeweled beret. I've kept them all.

"Joss, have you noticed that I am using personal pronouns?" Mav said.

"Yeah, that's great," I said, yawning. Time to go back to bed.

"I think the pronoun *I* is very interesting. It is the same symbol as your number one. See."

He carefully traced an *I* and a *1* on the back of the couch with his finger.

"The symbols are true," he said. "Only a one can be an *I*." He leaned closer until I could see the particles of white powder on his skin.

Let's face it, linguistic theories are a bit tedious at the best of times. At three in the morning they're unbearable. I tried to move towards my bedroom, but Mav was practically rubbing noses with me.

"Mav, move back. You're crowding me," I snapped.

Mav jumped backwards, his ears stretched back against his head. He jangled some kind of apology. Well, I finally had my space. I just didn't feel too good about it.

"Look, I'm sorry," I said. "I'm a bit tired. You've just got to remember that humans don't stand so close as you do. It gets on our nerves."

"You don't like being close?"

"Not all the time. Sometimes we like to be close, sometimes we like to be left alone," I said.

"Alone?"

"It means to be without anyone else around you."

Mavkel nodded.

"Show me its symbols." He patted the back of the couch.

I traced out the word, sounding the letters.

Mav made a triumphant sound.

"See, alone has one in it. If you separate the word it becomes all-one. It is very true. To be alone is to be all one."

It was a nice theory. I didn't have the heart to tell him he had put an extra *l* into the word. Mav stepped closer to me, then remembered and pulled up.

"I have felt very alone since Kelmav went," he said.

I nodded. Sensitivity warred with curiosity. Guess what won. "How did Kelmav die?" I asked.

Mav didn't answer for so long that I'd thought I'd really screwed up. I was about to apologize when he quickly touched my hand, his ears drooping, uncertain. I'm not too keen on touchy-touchy kind of stuff, but Mav was obviously hanging out for some contact. I took his hand. He quickly twined his two thumbs around my fingers.

"In the sun storm," he finally sang. There was a croon in his song, like an old ballad. "Kelmav died in the fires."

Mav held the last note for so long, it became a keen, his proper eyelids dropping over his eyes. Suddenly both sets of eyelids flicked back.

"I should not be doing this," he gasped, his thumbs digging into the back of my hand. "Music is for healing."

"If singing makes you feel better, isn't that healing?" I said.

I wriggled my hand, trying to relieve the pressure of Mavkel's grasp. He tightened his hold.

"I am alone," he cried, and the final syllable stretched into the tears of a blues chord.

Each note dug out my own loneliness, forcing it up into my throat until I ached from holding it back. Then Mav started to weave around the melody. He was swaying, his ears wrapped tightly across the back of his head, both eyelids closed. I recognized the song. Mav was singing my "Dogstar Blues," harmonized and heart killing.

There is a carving in Rome called the Mouth of Truth. You put your hand in the stone mouth. If you've lied, the mouth grabs your hand and bites it off. My hand was in the grip of truth, wrapped tightly by two thumbs, unable to move. Mav was showing me too much truth. But I couldn't move. All I could do was listen. My hand aching. My throat aching. Knowing that my own blues could never be the same.

Close Call

I woke up the next morning with a skull ache that would have had an elephant hitting the pain patches. Mav must have bounced some heavy subharmonics off me while he was singing. Hot strong black coffee was in order. But Mav was probably in the kitchen. What could I say to a guy who'd let his soul hang out in my face? "Nice day, isn't it" just wouldn't make the grade.

I pulled a regulation T-shirt over my head and found my jeans under the bed.

No, my best course of action would be to ignore the whole thing.

I jammed my feet into my boots.

But what if he brought it up?

I walked over to the door. It slid open and I peered around the corner. Well, he wasn't in the lounge room.

"How ya doing, Joss? You've got three Comm-messages waiting," the computer said.

I grunted, making my way towards the kitchen. No Mav there, either.

"Do you want me to play your messages?" the computer asked.

The kitchen looked the same as it had last night. Dishes stacked near the return hatch, Readers scattered over the table. Usually Mav cleaned it up every morning in some kind of crazed ritual. Maybe he wasn't up yet. Great explanation, except he didn't sleep. I leaned against my food dispenser and pushed the coffee button.

"Computer, where's Mav?" I asked.

"Mav left the suite at four A.M. Do you want me to play your messages?"

"All right, patch the first message through to the kitchen console," I said. The screen moved around to face me.

Where had Mav gone at four in the morning? Hopefully he was all right.

The food machine beeped and the cage slid back. I picked up the coffee container.

So far no one at uni had given Mav any aggro. Chaney and his gang had been very quiet. Too quiet. They hadn't even had a go at me for a couple of days, although I'd caught a few sideways looks and sniggers. Chaney was probably plotting another round of revenge for that karate chop at the partnering ceremony. Time to plan a counter strategy.

I peeled back the pull-ring on the cup. The heating mechanism kicked into action, pushing steam out of the drinking spout.

The console screen flickered then lit up with Lenny's face.

"Hey Joss. We've been having a bit of trouble getting hold of you. One of your friends is in town. Why don't you come around on Saturday night and catch up on all of the news. Bye."

His face faded into the CommNet logo. I took a sip of coffee. If I read Lenny right, he'd contacted a spyder for me and set up a virtual meeting at the Buzz Bar on Saturday night. Brilliant.

"Next message," I said.

The screen went black, then suddenly Ingrid was smiling at me.

"Hello Joss, darling," she said.

"Message freeze," I said. Ingrid stopped midword. She was looking great. Must have had her eyes done again.

"What time did this message come in?" I asked.

"At seven-sixteen," the computer said.

The console clock read twenty to eight. The first time in two years that Ingrid had contacted me personally and I'd slept through it. What a loser.

"Continue message."

"So, you're turning the big one eight tomorrow," Ingrid said. She raised her eyebrows, trying to look interested. "I'm sorry, but I won't be able to make it back for the party. I'll send a pressie by courier. Hope you have a wonderful day."

She looked away, listening to someone off-screen.

"Oh, yes. Darling, see if you can talk Professor Camden-Stone into letting me interview you and Mavkel. It would be such a coup. I'll speak to you soon."

She held her palm up to her mouth and blew me a kiss. It got lost somewhere along the data line.

The CommNet logo cut her off.

"Computer, keep that message."

I didn't have a current 3D of Ingrid. The picture of her blowing the kiss would be good to download onto my holo unit. I blew on the coffee. Still no Mav. If he didn't show soon, I'd check with the duty guard.

"Okay, that message is saved," the computer said. "Do you want the third message?"

"Go ahead."

For a moment I didn't recognize Louise. She'd grown her hair long, and the sharp planes of her face had rounded out.

"Joss, neichan, how are you doing? It's been so long." She bent down and picked up a baby.

"I want you to meet Mr. Perri Akinaro, my little boy." The baby made a grab at her hair. She pulled her head away then kissed the tiny hand.

"I know it's your birthday tomorrow. I was hoping you'd meet me for a coffee to celebrate. How about Mario's in Mall Fourteen? About eleven? Give me a call."

She recited her call code, waving the baby's hand good-bye. The screen cleared into the logo.

Louise had finally got in contact. A splash of hot coffee stung my fingers. I dumped the container on the bench. Handy hint for the day: don't start shaking with a cup of hot coffee in your hand.

I told the computer to rewind and freeze the last frame of the message. Louise looked ultra happy with her baby. Had

Ingrid ever looked that happy with me? They used to fight about babies. Louise had wanted one. Ingrid always said no way, one kid was enough. So Louise had to make do with me. Now she had her own kid, so why was she bothering to call me? After six years, too. Perhaps she'd been waiting until I was legally an adult. I wouldn't put it past Ingrid to have legally restrained Louise out of spite. Or there was the other option: Louise just hadn't wanted to see me until now. But I didn't like to think about that one.

I would call her and say no. I told the computer to link me into the CommNet. The call-code request flashed up almost immediately.

Maybe I should have a quick chat with her, just to let her know I was doing fine. Just to be polite. I repeated Louise's number and waited. A stranger appeared on the screen.

"Hello. Can I help you?" she asked.

She was stocky, with eyes that were big and widely spaced. High arched eyebrows made her look like she didn't believe a word anyone said. Was she Louise's new partner? If she was, then Ingrid beat her hands down in the looks department.

"Louise called me," I said. "Can I talk to her?"

"You must be Joss. Hi, I'm Barb." She smiled. "I'm afraid Lou's not here right now. Do you want to record a message?"

Damn, she wasn't home. A message was polite. Yes, I'd leave a message. I nodded.

She punched a key on the console in front of her.

"Okay, go ahead," she said.

The message logo came up, then counted down to the recording.

"Hi Louise," I stammered.

What was I going to say? I couldn't get anything out. My pause lengthened into a silence. I had to say something, quick.

"I'd love to meet you. Eleven at Mario's is great. See you then."

I signed off. So much for righteous indignation or grace under pressure.

The coffee was at gulp temperature, so I finished it while I punched up the breakfast menu. I was waiting for my bowl of cereal when Mav walked into the kitchen.

"Hello Joss. Are you well?" he asked. Not a hint of embarrassment about last night.

"Fine," I said casually. "Where've you been?"

"Rowley is teaching me slang."

Rowley was one of the night guards and a seriously hard case. She was probably teaching Mav the kind of slang that would get him killed in a bar.

Mav sneezed, wiping his noses with a handful of tissues.

He looked at himself in the chrome siding of his food dispenser.

"Look, I have wiped my noses so much they have no Toqua on them."

His usual covering of white powder stopped three quarters of the way down his noses, leaving stripes of sparkly white skin. He looked like he had dipped his noses in glitter.

"So what's this white powder for?"

"It is Toqua," he said.

"What's the Toqua for?" I asked, stumbling over the unfamiliar guttural sound.

"My home is much hotter than this world. Toqua stops our skin burning from us."

"It's a sunscreen?"

"Yes, but I am making too much. I think it is the common cold. It is not bothering you, I hope?"

He rubbed the side of one ear. I think he was embarrassed.

"No, it's okay."

"Can your doc-tor medicine take away these sneezes?" he asked.

I shook my head. "We've never found a cure for the common cold. You just have to wait it out."

"Refmol cannot chant the cold. Refmol is very annoyed."

The food dispenser beeped. I pulled out my cereal. This stuff was so heavy it would keep a whale going all day.

"We've got our first physical training class today," I said. "I've heard they're pretty tough. Better stock up on carbos."

"What are carbos? Do they taste good?"

I didn't fancy getting into a lecture on human nutrition.

"Just eat something that will give you lots of energy."

I shoved a spoonful of cereal into my mouth. It wasn't bad for something advertised as a high-energy gut-filler.

Mav flicked through his menu options, punched in a code, and waited.

Everything about Mav was a bit heavier than a human. Arms a bit chunkier, shoulders a bit wider, legs a bit shorter. The whole impression was strength. He'd be a good friend in a fight and would probably blitz the arm-wrestling competition. Was he good-looking in his culture? Maybe they didn't even consider looks. Remembering the Elders with their huge jowls, I'd say Mav was movie star material. Then again, they probably didn't have movies. I spooned up a huge mouthful as he collected his food from the delivery tray.

"Joss?" he sang hesitantly.

I grunted. My mouth was too full to get a word out.

"I am happy you heard the healing song. I am much less alone now."

I swallowed quickly.

"I'm glad you're feeling better," I mumbled.

Mav smiled, keeping his secondary mouth closed. He was learning. He picked up a handful of food in the scoop he had made out of his thumbs, pushed it into his secondary mouth, mulched it, then closed the primary mouth over it. Grisly. I smiled back, making a mental note to never again chew with my mouth open. We finished eating in silence.

Time-Jumped

Half an hour later, Sergeant Wolfendon and her merry men arrived to take us to PT class. I was under my bed looking for my other gym shoe. Mav was calling out helpful suggestions from the living area, but somehow I didn't think my shoe would have jumped into the air duct or crawled down the waste-disposal unit.

Wolfendon wasn't so sympathetic.

"Get a move on, Aaronson. No one's late on my watch."

Now there was a woman who badly needed the stick extracted from her bum. I picked up my other pair of jeans. Maybe the shoe was stuck in the leg somewhere. I had a habit of pulling everything off at once. Wolfendon's arm-screen beeped and she walked back into the living area, murmuring into the voice pad. I felt along the jeans leg and pulled out a pair of undies.

"Okay Aaronson, you can stop looking," Wolfendon said, standing in my doorway. "There's been a change in plans. Instead of PT this morning, your class is touring one of the labs."

I threw my jeans back on the floor. What a rush! We were finally going to see one of the Time-Jumpers. Maybe even touch it. I'd seen loads of holos, of course, but not the real thing. Only Centre personnel and students got to see the real thing. I picked up my badge and traced the gold circular arrow. Well, from now on, I *was* a Centre student and in six years I'd be a qualified time-jumper. Then the fun would really start. I could go to the jazz joints of the 1930s, see Toots Thielemans record with Quincy Jones, even sneak into the famous Rogue Henry/Dada Wells jam session.

That was my plan, anyway. I'd applied to specialize in music history—blues and jazz—but you don't get confirmation of your main research area until second year. According to my calculations, I had a good chance of getting the go-ahead. There were only six other music specialists in the Centre: four classical, one Eastern, and one rock. The place needed a blues/jazz expert.

Wolfendon and her men surrounded us in a protective diamond and we marched out of the suite. Mav was so excited that he was trying to bounce and walk at the same time. The guard beside him nearly got pushed through the virtual wall by a high-flying ear joint.

"Do we get to use the time mover today?" Mav asked as we scanned out of P3. He sneezed, barely catching the double load of snot in a wad of tissues.

"Time-Jumper," I corrected. "And no, we don't even get inside one until the end of second year."

He made an odd noise, a combination of a high A and a raspberry. My sentiments exactly.

The four labs were in the Daniel Sunawa-Harrod

Building, which was in the dead center of the university. The Time Building, as it was called, had no windows and only two entrances, front and back. The security measures were supposed to be somewhere between paranoid and homicidal. Dr. Harris, our class coordinator, was waiting beside the front entrance.

"Good morning, everyone. Sergeant, the rest of the class have already gone into the T2 lab as you asked," he said.

Wolfendon nodded.

"Okay. Allman and Greene," she said to two of our guards, "you scan into the building first and secure the area. Report in when it's clear."

Mav watched the guards scan through the security tube. He was jiggling up and down on the spot, his ears close to his head. I think he was a bit nervous about going through the full body scan, so I smiled at him reassuringly. Wolfendon's armscreen beeped. She acknowledged the message then turned to Mav.

"Right, you scan through first," she said.

Mav stepped forward, still rocking on his heels as the tube door closed. He didn't have to do the retina scan of course, not having a retina, but he was bouncing so hard that the body scan rejected him three times. In the end, I had to grab him by the shoulders, push his feet flat on the scan pad, and threaten dire consequences if he didn't stay still. He finally scanned through.

It was my turn. I stepped onto the scan pad and the tube

slid shut. A calm computer voice said, "Please do not move. Level three scan in progress."

I immediately wanted to scratch every part of my body. I tensed my muscles and shut my eyes as the scan light swept up and down.

"Please position the retina scanner over your right eye. Do not blink."

As usual, my eye started to water before the scan was accepted. I kept on thinking of that bit in *Bleeders* where the guy gets his eye sliced out by a booby-trapped scanner. Gross.

"Please place your wristband against Port A for access authorization download."

I pressed my wristband against the grid and waited.

"Cadet Joss Aaronson, you are now authorized for single entry/exit into the T2 Time Laboratory. Thank you." The inner door slid open.

Mav touched my shoulder as I stepped off the scan pad. I think he was reassuring himself, but it didn't do me any harm either. One of the guards, a young guy who already had gray in his hair, motioned me farther away from the scanner door. We all jumped when the tube door snapped shut. I had expected to step into an entrance foyer, but we were standing in a long central corridor with at least ten doors on either side. The guards had done a great job of securing the area: the corridor was completely deserted and eerily quiet. It seemed to affect us all, because we waited in silence as Wolfendon, Harris, and the other guard scanned through behind me. We walked up to the T2 lab door.

It was suspiciously easy to get into the actual lab. One swipe of your wristband across the scan pad and the door was open. There was, of course, the small matter of ten neuro needles set into the doorframe. No wishy-washy alarms for the Time Labs. It was a case of no authorization—no movement from the neck down.

As we walked through the doorway, the rest of the class turned and stared at us. They were grouped at the far end of an elegant console that stretched across most of the front wall. Chaney whispered a comment to Jorel, who burst out laughing. But I didn't have any time for those clowns. I was there to see one thing: the Jumper.

It was set back towards the far wall, surrounded by a ring of inactive force-field stakes. I'd kind of expected it to take up most of the lab, but it was only about the size of a sports-hover and shaped like an onion that someone had squashed. In comparison to the sleek surroundings of the lab, it looked a bit of a mess. Every part of it was angled or tubed except the smooth dome of the plasglass cabin. The official holos of the Jumpers made them look really smooth and elegant. But the squat compact crouch of the real thing was far more power-ful. T2 reminded me of a bulldog. Ugly as sin and all grunt.

A technician was kneeling near the Jumper, poking around inside a small hatch. Four fixer beams suddenly flick-ered on, securing T2 to the floor. The techo sat back on her heels, satisfied. Then someone tapped me on the shoulder.

"Hey, how are you guys going?"

I turned to see Lisa.

"Hi. What are you doing here?"

"Derry and I got suckered into helping out with your tour," she said, nodding towards her partner. Derry was standing next to the console, talking to Tonio and Sara. Tonio looked up at me and waved.

"Quick, look at this," Lisa said, grabbing my shoulders and turning me to face T2 again. "They're putting the fruz-field back on."

The hatch technician turned and gave a thumbs-up towards the console. There was a loud pop in the air and a faint purple haze crept upwards from the ring of stakes until it covered T2 in a dome that stretched from floor to ceiling.

"Fruz-field?" Mav asked.

"It's a security force field that totally immobilizes you if you touch it," Lisa said. "Literally freezes you to the spot until the security forces arrive."

"Does it hurt?" I asked.

Lisa smiled. "They reckon it doesn't, but I'm not too keen to put it to the test." She turned to Mav. "So what do you think of the Jumper, Mavkel? Isn't she a beauty?"

"Very much a beauty," Mav sang, but his ears dropped.

"What's wrong?" I asked.

"T2 has a pronoun," Mav sang. "T2 lives. We must make formal greeting. What are her bloodlines?"

Lisa looked at me, puzzled.

"Mav has discovered pronouns," I said, pressing my lips together so I wouldn't laugh. "It's okay, Mav. T2 isn't alive. It's just a custom to call any kind of ship a she."

"Why?"

I shrugged. He had me there. "It's just a tradition."

Mav nodded. "Yes, Mavkel understands tradition."

He turned to Lisa.

"According to the human tradition, I am a he because Joss is a she."

Lisa looked at me, her eyebrows raised.

"Let's just say Mav has chosen to be a he from now on," I said.

"Gotcha," Lisa said. She smiled at Mav.

Harris, who was talking to a tall round-shouldered man, clapped his hands for attention.

"Okay people, I'd like you all over here at the operations console. This is Mr. Roan. He's Head Engineer for T2 and will be taking you through the workings of the lab."

"Gotta go and do my duty," Lisa said. She hurried over towards Derry.

Wolfendon ordered her men to take up their positions around the room and waved Mav and me towards the console. Chaney and gang had lined up in front of Roan, taking all the good positions. I moved behind Jason, who wasn't as tall as the others, and checked out the rest of the room. Above the console was a glassed-in viewing level with a row of plush chairs. VIP territory. There were also four wall crawlers monitoring the lab and infra-red beam nodules evenly spaced at ankle level around the perimeter of the room. Heavy duty security.

"Lisa and Derry," Harris continued, indicating the pair standing beside him, "are fifth-year students who have kindly volunteered to answer your questions about time-jumping after the tour. Okay, the class is all yours, Mr. Roan."

Roan smiled shyly.

"As you may have gathered, this is the operations desk for T2. During a jump, it's always monitored by three support personnel and supervised by a senior time-jumper."

He moved behind the console and pointed to a bank of screens and readings. Peter, Chaney, and Jorel had pushed Jason along the console and moved directly in front of Mav and me, blocking our view. I stood on my toes, but still couldn't make out which display Roan was describing. Mav was even worse off. He tried to stand on his toes, but his claws stopped him mid-hoist.

"Hey," I whispered to Chaney, "move over. Mav and I can't see."

"Tough," Chaney said.

What a snorkwit. Roan moved on to the next section of the console. I wasn't going to see anything at this rate, so I tried to edge in between Peter and Chaney. Peter shoved me sideways, straight into a rib gouge from Chaney.

"Yeow," Chaney said loudly, covering my *hmmph* of pain. "You're pushing me into the console, Joss."

"Aaronson, stop messing around," Harris said. "This isn't a game."

Chaney was playing rough. I limped back, no ground made. Of course, I could just complain to Harris, but that was admitting defeat. And I couldn't let Chaney get away with that rib gouge. I figured that since Mav and I were stuck at the back of the class at the console, we'd automatically be at the front when we all moved towards T2. A satisfying switch that was full of payback promise. I looked over at Mav. If he was agreeable, I had some very interesting plans for his ears. He was bobbing about trying to see through the gap between Jason and Peter. He saw me looking at him and sidestepped across.

"I do not see," he sang softly. He squeezed his noses to stifle a sneeze.

I nodded, rubbing my rib cage. "Chaney's being a real pain, but I've got a plan. Will you help me?"

Mav's ears raised slightly.

"I will help you in all things. You are my pair." He flicked me his double smile.

"I was thinking that when we go over to T2, we could stop Chaney from seeing. Maybe with your ears. Can you make them go really wide or something?"

Mav started to spread his ears up and out. It was like seeing a beach umbrella opening.

"Put them down!" I whispered, glancing at Harris. Luckily he was busy snapping a stray thread off his jacket. "Just open them enough to stop Chaney seeing anything when we're looking at the Jumper."

"Why do we stop Chaney?"

"To pay him back," I said.

Mav tilted his head, puzzled.

"Revenge," I continued, "retaliation, settling the score."

"Ahh, it is a game," Mav sang, nodding.

Close enough. I started to edge backwards, pulling Mav with me by the edge of his woolen wrap. When the class moved to T2, I wanted us to be there first. Roan had moved on to security measures, pointing out the wall crawlers above the console.

"These four crawlers are continually feeding information to the shielded monitoring room. Most of the time it's just automated security stuff. However, during a jump, a backup crew keeps an eye on all of the systems. Just in case something happens to the personnel inside the lab."

A low murmur went around the group. We had all seen the vid-recordings of the early experimental jumps. You've got to wonder how long it took them to scrape six people off four walls and a ceiling.

"The viewing level is also shielded. We wouldn't want to accidentally disintegrate our VIPs, would we?" Roan said. Everyone laughed.

"Okay, now the bit you've all been waiting for," he said. "Let's take a look at T2."

That was our cue. I swung Mav around and we moved into place. Mav gave an experimental flip of his ears. I watched as Chaney tried to bulldoze his way into his usual front position. Exactly as expected. I was also counting on the group's eagerness to see T2, and they didn't let me down. Chaney got caught right in the middle of the surge and was herded straight towards us. Not enough time or room to divert. Mav calmly stepped in front of him just as he reached the Jumper. Chaney caught my look and smirked. He wasn't worried; after all, he was at least a head taller than Mav. For now.

"Calm down, people," Harris yelled. "This is delicate equipment!"

"Stay back behind the line," Roan said loudly, getting everyone's attention. "As you can see, T2 has a security force field over it. . . ."

I tuned out as Roan explained the fruz-field to the group. Mav was shifting from foot to foot, ready for action. I nudged him. He flicked his eyelids and very slowly started to unfurl his ears. Roan moved on to the plasglass cabin, pointing out how it was attached to the soft-metal body. So far, Chaney hadn't noticed anything. Mav was moving in geological time, the spreading of his ears almost imperceptible. Roan explained how the soft-metal stretched as the Jumper moved through time, and Mav's ears had somehow blocked the lower level of T2. By the time Roan got to the interior, Chaney was standing on his toes. I fought down a huge snort of laughter.

"If you look at this section of the Jumper, you can see the return countdown display and the oxygen level readout," Roan said.

We all leaned closer. Behind me, I heard Chaney grunt with annoyance. Mav had completely extended his ears and totally blocked Chaney's view of T2. Not only that, but he seemed to know which way Chaney was shifting and moved with him. It was classic.

"Put your ears down," Chaney hissed.

Mav's reply was to stretch them a bit higher.

"Put them down or I'll put them down for you!"

Mav didn't budge.

Suddenly Chaney pushed down on the top joint bones of Mav's ears. It didn't look like a hard push, but he must have hit something crucial, because Mav screamed. A shrill thin sound horribly unlike his normal harmonies. I twisted around, shoving Chaney into the people behind him. But I was off balance, and Chaney pushed back.

As I hit the fruz-field, I remember thinking that Lisa was wrong. It did hurt. The deep bone pain of extreme cold. And it was so quiet. Then the bone ache disappeared. In fact, all feeling disappeared, and I couldn't move. I was pretty sure I was still breathing and my heartbeat was probably around 200 bpm's, but voluntary movement had shut down. I couldn't even move my eyes. I think I preferred the pain.

Within my peripheral vision I saw Wolfendon and one of the guards running towards the Jumper. Then Mav reached into the force field. I wanted to yell out to him to stop, but I couldn't even moan. He grabbed a fruz-field stake, his two thumbs wrapping over one another as he strained to pull it out of the floor. A thick metal rivet hit me in the shoulder as the stake was ripped free of its moorings. Mav pulled it clear of the grid. I remember thinking, why isn't he fruzzed? Then

I dropped flat on the floor. I gasped for breath, instinctively curling into a ball, away from the sudden onslaught of feeling and sound. I felt Mav's rough-skinned hands on my head.

"Do you pain, Joss?" he shrilled, patting my ears. I looked up at him.

"Aaronson, are you all right?" It was Camden-Stone's voice. How did he get here? "Harris, get a medic. Everyone else move back and be quiet."

The class stepped back a few paces, the buzz of their excitement dropping a pitch. I moved my head experimentally. So far, so good. I grabbed hold of Mav and sat up. Not so good. The lab was washing up around me like a squally sea and my shoulder hurt like hell. I squinted, trying to stop the walls moving.

Camden-Stone stuck his face in front of mine. "Are you all right?"

I had barely nodded before he turned around to Chaney.

"What the hell were you doing hitting Mavkel and pushing Aaronson into the field? Can you imagine my embarrassment when I showed Chanter Refmol the monitoring room and we saw you attacking his charge?"

I looked around for Refmol. The Chanter was making its way towards Mav.

"Aaronson started it," Chaney said.

"That's not true, sir," Lisa said, stepping forward. "Chaney and his friends have been hassling Joss and Mavkel from the start of the tour."

Camden-Stone's hand was clenching and unclenching. Not a good sign for Chaney-boy.

"You are officially on reprimand, Horain-Donlevy," Camden-Stone said. "If you or any of your cronies go near Aaronson or Mavkel beyond your class requirements, you are out of this Centre. Do you understand?"

"Yes sir," Chaney said.

"You're confined to quarters for the rest of the day. Get out."

I'd never seen Chaney move so fast. Refmol was kneeling beside Mav, feeling his ears and humming.

"Are you okay?" I asked Mav. He was still gallantly propping me up.

"I am well."

Refmol nodded agreement.

"This force field does not affect our bodies as it does yours. And the violence to the ears is superficial. How do you feel, Joss Aaronson?"

The lab sea was settling down, only a ripple here and there. I rubbed the side of my head, thinning my eyes against the pain.

"Bit of a headache," I said.

Refmol reached across and circled my forehead with its thumbs, pressing against sore points. It crooned softly. The headache eased immediately.

"You are not permanently damaged," Refmol said.

A medic pushed his way through the excited class and

kneeled beside me. After a few questions and a bit of poking around he came to the same conclusion. He turned to Camden-Stone.

"I think she should come down to the medical center for observation," he said.

Camden-Stone nodded and beckoned to Wolfendon. Mav had been pulled to one side by Refmol and was in the middle of a heated debate, so I stood up with the help of the medic. Wolfendon offered me her shoulder to lean on.

"You know," the sergeant said, turning me towards the door, "I don't think your friend needs that much protecting."

I looked over at Mav. He was still holding the stake with its metal roots attached. He finished his conversation with Refmol in a burst of flat notes that didn't sound very polite, and walked towards us.

"I go to the medic place with you, not back to the Elders," he sang firmly. He took my other arm and patted my shoulder. "We not play this Chaney game again."

That sounded like a good idea. We had nearly made it to the door when Roan intercepted us, his mouth tighter than a cat's bum.

"I'd like my stake back, thank you," he said. Mav held it out, his ears drooping in apology. Roan snatched it out of his hand and strode off towards T2.

"He's a bit burned that Mav got through the fruz-field," Lisa said, walking up to us. "Are you both okay? I can't believe Chaney could be so stupid."

"We're fine," I said. "Thanks for sticking up for me in there."

She shrugged.

"It was the truth. Chaney started the whole thing."

"Well, it's no secret that Horain-Donlevy is a little thug," Wolfendon said.

She moved us forward. I smiled back at Lisa as we passed through the door. Definitely an ally.

"No secret?" Mav sang. "Does this mean it is knowledged by all?"

"Yep, everyone knows Chaney is a creep," I said, gingerly feeling my head. I pressed a sore point and clenched my teeth.

"Then a secret is not knowledged by all?" Mav sang, his ears stiff with concentration.

"If everyone knows a secret then it isn't a secret anymore, is it?" the sergeant said.

"Mav's people are telepaths," I said, frowning at Wolfendon. "I don't think they really understand secrets." I turned to Mav. "A secret is supposed to be kept to yourself. That's the whole thing about a secret. No one else is supposed to know it."

"Do you have a secret, Joss?" Mav asked.

"I've got tons of them."

"A secret is supposed to be kept to yourself," he repeated carefully. "Yes, I understand. It must be kept to the self." He nodded as though making a decision, then sneezed all over my arm.

Daniella

The medic cleared me of any aftereffects of the fruz-field, but advised me to take it easy and get a good night's sleep. Not likely. I had a late appointment at the Buzz Bar.

Mav wanted to come with me.

"No," I said.

"Why not?" he asked.

I motioned for him to lower his voice.

"Because you can't move without a guard up your bum. And I think your wristband has got a tracker in it," I whispered.

"The wristband is bugged, like these rooms?" he asked softly.

I nodded.

"That is good."

"What do you mean it's good? It's terrible."

"No, it is good. At home, everyone knows where you are. It is good. Comfortable."

Mav hadn't quite got the hang of being around minds that no one could read.

"Well it's not comfortable for me. I don't want anyone to know where I am or where I'm going. Especially tonight."

Call me paranoid, but I had a hunch that Mavkel wasn't the only one with a tracker in his wristband. It was possible that Donaldson-Hono had been lying through his teeth about my wristband. Even if he wasn't, I wasn't going to take any chances. That meant I had to ditch my wristband before I set foot out of the university.

"I'm sorry, Mav, you can't come. I want to get in and out of the Buzz Bar real quick. I can do that better by myself."

Mavkel sneezed, rubbing at his noses irritably.

"You want to be alone too much," he sang.

I thought about that as I left the suite. Mav was probably right. I did like to be alone a lot. On the other hand, sometimes I needed people around. Mav just hated to be alone. I think that's why he hums. To keep himself company. Either that or he does it to drive me crazy.

Barton was at the guard desk, still on duty from the afternoon shift. He grunted as I scanned my way out of the building.

I had a hazy kind of plan to get rid of my wristband. It was a bit disgusting, but it was the only thing I could come up with that might work. I peeled off the pseudo skin that I'd slapped around my sand-blasted wrist and arm a few days ago. Most of the abrasion was healed, but the bit near my wristband was still scabby. I picked at the crusty bits until they looked red and raw then headed towards the P3 security office. Operation Band-Off was go.

The duty officer was grossed out when I showed her my arm.

"How did that happen?" she asked, turning my arm over to get a better look.

"I think there's a rough bit on the inside that keeps on scratching me," I said.

She screwed up her nose. "You should have come earlier. That arm's a mess."

I nodded pathetically.

"Probably the best thing to do would be to plane it out and get rid of the sharp bit. Here, scan the band," she said, pointing to the unit Donaldson-Hono had shown me.

The wristband clicked open and fell onto the scanning pad without a hitch. The officer ran her finger around it.

"I can't feel anything."

"Maybe I'm just super sensitive," I said.

"Whatever," she shrugged. "I'll issue you with a visitor's band until yours comes back."

She logged my clearance onto the heavy bracelet.

"You should probably wear it on your other arm until that one heals."

"Thanks, I will," I said, ostentatiously clipping it around my right wrist.

Which brought me to step two of the plan.

"Hey, can I hire one of those security lockers?" I asked.

"Sure." She reeled off a list of prices.

I made my choice and she logged my fingerprint against the lock. While she was busy checking through a flower delivery, I slipped off the visitor's bracelet, wrapped it in my jacket and stuffed it in the locker. Call me paranoid, but also call me untraceable. I couldn't stop grinning. Don't you just love that feeling when a plan comes together? It's like holding a royal flush in a no-limit game of poker.

I was still pumped full of drene when I walked out the university gates. I gave the Venturi loop a miss, as I've never been very keen on the underground trans system. Being sucked through a vacuum tube in a metal box is not my idea of fun. It feels like you're being farted out by a giant worm. I prefer to take a route through the side streets.

The Buzz Bar was in Mall 16, so it was quicker to cut through Central towards the Mall 15 overpass. A group of No-Suns moved in front of me, slowing down my progress. These ones must have been pretty high in the sect because their head-to-toe robes were yellow and the face masks black. SPF 100. A few also carried large parasols, even though most of the levels are under cover anyway and the highrises put the top levels in permanent shadow. I saw an opening and ducked through the group, catching a glimpse of corpse-white skin along an eye slit.

With the No-Suns behind me, the run up to the overpass was fairly clear. Then, to my left, Berko Harris walked out of the Red Triangle, my favorite pool hall. Major spin out. As far as I knew, Berko still wanted to wrap a cue around my head for hustling him out of one hundred creds. I ducked into a side alley and squashed myself into a shallow doorway.

He must have seen me, because he headed towards the alley. Time to be scarce. I pushed the door behind me. It opened.

For a minute or so I just hid out in the scrappy entrance foyer. Then I heard Berko pound past, so I ducked inside the main room. Just to make sure.

It was time for a bit of deep breathing, Tai Chi style. A few breaths in I smelled something funny. Musty.

Where was I?

It was a huge empty warehouse, although a whole load of large bright squares were painted on the walls. There were more on the ceiling. And the floor. I leaned closer to the wall. It wasn't paint, it was cloth. Embroidered cloth.

For Luke. I'll see you soon, all my love, John.

It finally hit me. The walls, floor, and ceiling of the room were covered by a huge quilt made up of bits of old clothing, paper photos, paint, and embroidery.

In memory of Stephen Gossman, son and brother. RIP.
Daniella Tapp. Died age 20. My love always, Dad.

Daniella's square stood out because it was so plain. A large piece of white cotton, embroidered with uneven blue chainstitch. Even though it was so old, the plasglass cover had kept it clean. Daniella's father had tried to sew a large flower in the corner, but it looked more like a spider with an old style TV aerial.

"Hello. Would you like a tour?" a voice asked behind me.

It was an old man. Wrinkly old. Most people get rejuved

before they wrinkle up, but this guy was sagging and bagging all over the place.

"You gave me a bit of a fright," he continued. "Not many people come in here these days."

"I'm sorry. I came in by mistake. I should get going," I said, moving towards the door. Hopefully Berko was gone.

The old man sighed, his whole body getting into the act.

"Then I'll let you go on your way," he said. "Do come back if you remember."

For some reason, he reminded me of Mav. It must have been the droopy ears.

"What is this place?" I asked.

"The AIDS Museum and what's left of the Quilt Project," he said, as if he was announcing something important.

"The Quilt Project?"

"Have you any time to stay and look around? I could tell you about it."

He looked so hopeful that I nodded. The spyder at the Buzz Bar could wait a few more minutes.

"Oh, good. Come over here then."

He took my arm and led me over to the back wall. We stopped in front of a small screen.

"This quilt was started in 1987 as a memorial for viral AIDS victims. Each patch has been sewn or painted by a loved one. Of course, it should be about four times as big as it is, but most of it got destroyed by a fire. You can see how big it would have been on this picture."

He punched up a diagram onto the screen.

"The red bit is the section we have. The rest is gone."

"It must have been enormous," I said.

"Unfortunately, it was." He crossed himself in the old religious way. "The whole quilt was going to be put on the Net as part of Project Gutenberg, but before any of it was done, someone set fire to it."

"Deliberately?"

He nodded, rubbing his knuckles. "We think so. It was burned just after the same-sex marriage law went through. So most of this beautiful quilt is gone forever."

"Is it on the Net now?" I asked.

"This bit is. I'm a bit of a throwback, I know, but I think seeing it on the Net is nothing like seeing it for real," he said proudly.

He was right.

I'd never been in a real-museum before. Sure, I'd gone through the virtual Smithsonian and Louvre a couple of times, but they didn't have an atmosphere like this place. I looked down at one of the patches under the glass floor. As on so many of the other patches, someone had sewn in a large old-style photograph of the victim. This one was Roberto. He was laughing.

"That left-hand wall, floor, and all of the ceiling are the viral AIDS patches," the old man said, swinging his arm in a wide arc. "The rest is the implant AIDS patches."

He shook his head.

"People don't learn, do they? You can't play Russian

roulette with your body. They couldn't in those days and you can't today. You wouldn't stick one of those chips in your head, would you? Just for a few more brain cells?"

"No way," I said. Not when there was a chance that the thing would eat your immune system.

I walked over to Daniella's square in the implant AIDS section.

I couldn't get past Daniella. Dead at twenty. That was only two years older than me. Why did she go for an implant? Maybe she didn't know about the risks. Maybe she didn't care. Her father cared, though. For a second I envied Daniella that ugly spiky flower. At least she'd had a father who'd cared enough to sew her a patch, even though you could tell it was the first time he'd seen a needle. And it had worked, too, because here I was thinking about his daughter.

In a way, I suppose that's what a Time-Jumper is all about. We add patches of information onto history so that someone or something is remembered. But it's such a pot-luck business. There are so many missing patches. There's also a lot of wrong patches and not all of them are accidental. Take the Camden-Stone/Sunawa-Harrod thing. After what I'd read it seemed likely that most of that story was hidden. The question was, why? I had a feeling that the answers were at the Buzz Bar, courtesy of a spyder. Time to go and find out.

"People seem to have lost interest in sewing patches

these days," the old curator said. "There hasn't been an addition to the quilt for over fifty years."

"Maybe people have forgotten how to sew," I said, immediately regretting the joke.

"Maybe," he said, smiling. "Or maybe people have just forgotten."

I nodded, glancing at the door.

"You have to go now, I see," the curator said. "I hope you'll come back and visit us again."

Outside in the alley, the air tasted clean. That's one thing about virtual museums. You never get that old-things smell. Maybe that's why I gave up visiting them.

Itsy Bitsy Spyder

At the Buzz Bar, Lenny was sitting in his office watching one of the news broadcasts. The news item was about the president, one of Lenny's pet hates. He held up his hand as I walked in, motioning me to wait.

"How ya doing, Lenny?" I asked after he'd stopped listening.

"Fine, fine. You here to hire yourself a spyder, hey?"

He hauled himself off his chair.

"Here, sit down. One A-grade answered the call. Here's the new code. You'll have to sit tight but the spyder knows you'll be casting tonight. But remember, only use the keyboard. When you're finished, come for a drink."

He left the room abruptly. I heard him yell at one of the bouncers to get off the bar.

I keyed in the call code then sat back. Lenny had just bought this unit and it was already out of date. My P3 organic screted all over it. There was no doubt the organics were going to take over. That is as soon as everyone mortgaged their lives and bought one. Of course people might balk at having a computer made out of living gel. Everyone is still pretty spooked about the organic brain implants. Maybe the Takahini Corporation should rethink their strategy and market the organics as pets. Pat a heaving lump of gel today!

Something was happening on the screen. I hunched over, fingers ready on the keyboard. A sentence appeared.

This is Blackwidow. What do you need?

Just as I finished reading the line, it disintegrated backwards, character by character. Blackwidow was backbyting our conversation. They say you can never trace or recall anything that's been backbytten. They also say that if any spyder leaked the backbyte secret, they'd be dead in an hour.

I was lucky to get Blackwidow. She always delivered. I typed in my request. Find out about the security arrangements for building P3 on the university campus, emphasis on the Ledbetter suite. Break into any sealed files about Camden-Stone and Sunawa-Harrod, dating back twenty years. Finally, and I knew this was a long shot, any news on who had hired Tori Suka.

I tossed up whether I should also change my P3 clearance, but it would probably cost too much.

My message disintegrated. A dollar sign appeared.

Blackwidow was naming her price.

A line of numbers moved across the screen. Snork me gently! Any more zeros and I'd have enough for a game of Enow. It was lucky I hadn't asked her to change my clearance, too. As it was, I'd have to sell my soul. Luckily, I knew just the person who'd buy it. I typed in my acceptance of the price.

> Blackwidow will contact you. Payment will be through the big man. Half by 9 A.M. tomorrow. Other half on delivery. Agreed?

Agreed.

> Your key word is "conspiracy."

A small graphic of a spider ran across the screen and disappeared. The CommNet logo came up. Blackwidow must have been piggybacking on the CommNet line.

In a few days a courier would deliver a "novel" to me. When I loaded the disc onto my Reader, it would just look like a normal book. However when I activated the word "conspiracy" in the text, all of the novel's text would disintegrate and leave the embedded information that I had paid for. Ingenious.

But first I had to sell my soul. I switched to voice recognition and requested Ingrid's number. It was connected immediately.

"Hello, Joss," Lewis said. He had dyed his hair blond. Now he looked like an albino ferret.

"I don't suppose Ingrid is free?" I asked.

"I'm afraid not. She's with her masseur. Can I pass on a message? Or maybe I can help you? I do live for it, you know."

I didn't want Lewis to know I was asking for more

money. He thought I was a spoiled little kuso, already. On the other hand, I had to have it pronto. I'd hoped Ingrid would want to say hi, since tomorrow was my birthday. It looked like I'd have to sell my dignity as well as my soul.

"Perhaps you can help, Lewis. It's my birthday tomorrow. . . ."

"Happy birthday, Joss," he interrupted.

"Thank you. As I said, it's my birthday and I want to have a bit of a bash, but I need some money for it. Do you think Ingrid could forward a bit on?"

"As you know, Ingrid had given me authority to grant your financial requests, Joss. What is your proposal?"

Proposal? That was a sneaky one. I quickly invented the mega-party of the century.

"And how much will all of this cost?"

I gave him Blackwidow's price and a half again for miscellaneous expenses. You never know what might come up.

He raised his eyebrows. They were still black and he'd plucked them to the wrong side of thin.

"That's quite an amount," he said.

The creep was letting me sweat it. He looked off into the distance as if he was pondering the country's budget.

"Yes. All right. I'll put it into your account now."

"Thank you."

"And Joss," he said, smiling. "I hope you like Ingrid's present. When she asked me to get you something, I was a bit concerned. But as soon as I saw it, I knew you'd love it."

He signed off.

I jabbed the comm button off. At least Ingrid had remembered to tell him to get me something. I stood up, my chair rolling back so hard it hit the gun locker.

I found Lenny in his booth, shaking his head over some accounts.

"So, your business is done?" he asked, not looking up.

"Not quite. Half the payment has to be deposited now. Blackwidow wants to go through you. Should I put the money through the bar account?"

"No, put it through the restaurant. Safer."

"Okay. I'll give you a call when the stuff is delivered so you can put through the other half."

"Fine."

I went back to the office and transferred the money over to Lenny's restaurant account. Then I joined him back at the bar. He passed me a Reader when I sat opposite him.

"Tell me, can you see the problem?" he asked.

I scanned the spreadsheet.

"The Koli brothers are still paying last year's protection rate," I said, passing the Reader back.

"Ha, you're right." He made an adjustment to the sheet. "You want a drink?" he asked.

He held up his finger to Rocky, who was cleaning glasses behind the bar.

"How about a sake?" Lenny suggested. "I've got a good import."

"I'll just have a coffee."

"Two short blacks, Rocky. And don't be stingy with the

beans," Lenny said. Rocky nodded and headed towards the coffee machine. "He still doesn't know how to make a decent cup," Lenny confided. He reached into his jacket pocket.

"Here, something for tomorrow," he said gruffly, putting a long, slim package on the table. It was wrapped in recycled Christmas paper.

I picked it up. Weighty.

"You can open it now, if you want to," he said.

The paper was off in a second. Inside was a beautiful Hohner C chromatic harp. The best you could buy. I had promised myself one when I thought I was good enough to play it. I ran my finger along the smooth chrome top.

"Do you like it? Is it the right one?" Lenny asked anxiously.

"It's wonderful."

"Play something, then."

I played "The Dogstar Blues," experimenting with chord variations by pushing the slide. The tone was magnificent although it wasn't as loud as my Marine Band harp. The final note reverberated through my head like Mav's song.

Lenny clapped.

"It makes me sound better than I really am," I said.

"You're better than you think. Lots of people have been asking where you've gone. The band misses you, too."

"Come on, that's laying it on a bit thick. I've only been gone a week." I carefully wiped the harp down and laid it back in its case.

"Seems longer. How's it all going? How's that new partner of yours?"

"Okay. Have you heard anything about Suka?"

Lenny shook his head. Rocky arrived with the coffee. Thick and black. Lenny smiled approvingly and waved him away.

"Do you think the anti-alien lobby could have hired her? There's a lot of them hanging around outside the uni," I said.

"I haven't heard anything from that direction. Seems unlikely to me. They wouldn't have the bucks or the contacts. Don't you worry. I've got a few people sniffing around. They should dig something up soon."

"But what can I do to protect Mav?"

I sipped at the coffee. Whoa! Caffeine explosion.

"I heard the Centre has doubled its security," Lenny said.

I nodded. Lenny looked thoughtful.

"With Suka around that's probably slashin' in the wind," he said. "The ideal scenario is to get the alien out of the city, quietly so none of the ratters know. Otherwise as soon as you move, Suka's gonna hear about it. I can arrange it as soon as you want. When can you get away?"

"Not in the next six years. I'd have security and Camden-Stone down my throat before I could get him out of the grounds."

"Okay, then don't let your partner out of your sight. Let me handle this from my end. I'll contact you when I get something."

The kitchen door opened and Porchi walked into the bar. He had been beaten up. Looked like about twelve stitches down his face.

Lenny sniffed. "That son of mine is an idiot."

I'd known that all along, but I didn't say anything.

Lenny leaned back in his seat. "He goes and gets himself involved with that Pino. Very dangerous man, that one. Now I gotta bail him out." He turned on the light at the side of the booth. "Hey, Porchi. Come over here. See who has come to visit."

Porchi slunk over to us. I wondered who had done the beating: Pino or an annoyed Lenny? Porchi slid into the seat beside me.

"Hi Joss." He didn't even try to cop a grope.

"This stupid idiot is lucky to be alive. Aren't you?" Lenny demanded, poking Porchi in the shoulder.

Porchi nodded miserably.

"You're just lucky your father knows the likes of Pino." He leaned over to me. "I know how to look after you children. I told Cross and Lee to look out for this fool."

"They don't look like they did much of a job," I said.

"How does that joke go?" Lenny said. "You should see the other guy." He laughed, slapping the table with his hand.

Porchi winced. His head must have been killing him.

"Cross tells me you fought well, but don't ever forget about the arm sheath," Lenny said.

"I won't now," Porchi said glumly.

"Don't worry, Porch," I said. "The girls will love the scar."

"How about you?" he asked.

"Nah, scars turn me right off." I winked at Lenny.

"It is Joss's birthday tomorrow," Lenny announced. Porchi took the hint and wished me happy birthday, suggesting a rage on the town. Not likely in his condition.

"Thanks, but I've got to get back to the uni." I leaned over to Lenny and whispered "thank you for everything" in his ear. Then I kissed him quickly on the cheek. It was about the only time I'd ever done it, and it caught him by surprise. He grabbed my forearm for a moment. The closest he could come to a hug.

"What about me?" Porchi asked. He obviously wasn't as bad off as he looked.

I pushed him towards the edge of the seat.

"I wouldn't want to hurt you," I said.

Lenny was still laughing as I walked out of the door.

Happy Birthday to Me

Mav was working on his console when I got back to the suite. The lounge lights were dimmed to the same level as his bedroom. He'd also lined up three pads of tissues and wrapped himself in the thermo roll. Cold overkill. I threw the visitor's wristband I had collected from the locker on the side table and stretched out on one of the couches. Thank God tomorrow was a rest day.

Mav sneezed.

"Bless you," I said.

"Did you like the bar by yourself?" he asked.

"It was just business," I said.

"There was an announcement when you were not here. Your Elder called Sunawa-Harrod has passed away. What does that mean?"

"It means he died."

"Ahh. Refmol will be sad."

"Why?"

"Refmol was chanting Sunawa-Harrod. Refmol does not like to lose the life threads."

Mav walked over to me and gently touched my ear.

"The minds of Sunawa-Harrod will be greatly missed. May his line continue," he said formally.

It was a graceful way of putting it. I had never met Sunawa-Harrod, but I also hoped his line continued.

I leaned my head back against the arm of the couch. Another rotten headache was brewing. Maybe the doc was wrong and I did have some kind of fruz aftereffect. I closed my eyes and focused on my breathing. The pain got worse.

"Joss. Try the thought cube. You said you would try."

I opened my eyes. Mav was standing over me, holding out the cube. At least he was blocking out the rest of the dim light.

"Sorry Mav, I'm going to bed," I said, carefully swinging my feet onto the floor. "I've got a killer headache. I'll see you tomorrow."

"Tomorrow," Mav said, his ears dropping.

Even after two pain patches, I still couldn't get to sleep. A bath, some Ravel, and a classic comedy rerun didn't help either. I turned to the Reader.

I scrolled through until I found an article about Chorian mating habits. Just the thing for a sleepless night.

Apparently the most important thing to a Chorian pair is its bloodlines. They don't mate in the potluck way we usually do (not counting manufactured kids like me). Chorian breeding partners are chosen according to the talents needed in their society. I suppose that's one of the benefits of your whole race being able to tune into one another. If society needs a few more doctors, a number of bloodlines that have produced good doctors are invited to mate. I wondered if they sent out gilt-edged cards: Dear so-and-so, how'd you like to snork?

Probably less awkward than the way we do it.

However you can't just have a good genetic bloodline to breed on Choria. You also have to win some kind of mind challenge to prove your worth. When I think about some of the guys I've fancied, they wouldn't have had a chance in a mind challenge.

The scientist who wrote the article got pretty excited about the way the bloodlines challenge for the honor of breeding. She started going on about artistic spatial equations, which nearly cured my insomnia. But from the way she was describing it, the mating challenge is a favorite Chorian spectator sport. Having your whole society check out the way you snork seems a bit weird to me. But live and let live. Or in this case, live and let's watch.

After all the negotiations and challenges have gone down, the two winning Chorians impregnate each other so that a birth pair is born. The one who actually pops the baby out is called the Sulo. The impregnator is the Sulon. Each baby gets its Sulo name first, like Mav, and the Sulon name second, such as Kel. Mavkel is from the Mav line, Kel gene pool. Its birth pair is Kelmav who is from the Kel line and the Mav gene pool. Or at least it was.

The next morning, I woke up eighteen. Mav was knocking on my door.

"Are you awake, Joss?" he sang loudly. "I am giving you a breakfast treat."

"Computer, unlock the door," I said, rubbing my temple. The headache was still hanging around.

The door slid back.

Mav came in singing a harmonized version of "Happy Birthday." It actually sounded good. He was struggling to balance a tray of food and a package wrapped in white paper.

"Look. Your favorite meal. I searched much on birthdays and the Net said that favorite meals are made. And presents are bound in paper. This is right?" He dumped the tray on my legs, thrusting the package at me.

A plate full of trifle slid dangerously near my knee. I stopped it with one hand, catching the package with the other. It was wrapped in toilet paper.

"Yes, that's right," I said, moving my leg to prop up the tray.

"Now you open the present. There was no brightly colored festive paper with many-colored ribbons like it said. I could only find this dull one. No ribbons."

"The paper's fine."

"Open the present. It is the thought cube."

Maybe I was wrong, but I thought he'd already given me the cube. Obviously the Net hadn't covered the new occasion equals new present rule.

"You're not supposed to tell me what it is. It ruins the

surprise," I said. Might as well start teaching him for future birthdays.

"Ahh. That is why the paper, yes? To hide the present. Another of your human secrets."

"That's right."

I pulled the thick wad of toilet paper off the cube.

"You're right, it's the cube," I said. "Thank you very much. And for the special breakfast." I looked at the trifle leaning over on the plate—packed full of breakfast nutrition.

"Try the cube. Try it," Mav urged.

"How does it work again?"

"Focus on a memory and look into the cube. Like this."

He grabbed the cube, staring into it until the cube darkened. A tiny 3D of him trying to wrap my present wavered then solidified. The Net hadn't told him about sticky tape either. No wonder he had gone through three toilet pads. Then he broke concentration and handed me the cube. I turned it over feeling its slimy-smooth texture. It was quite heavy.

"Mav, how come you can make this work, but you can't use your mind to talk with your people?" I asked.

"The cube is simple," he sang, the harmony subdued. "We give them to the young pairs to practice their minds. I can do this. I can do simple scans. No more than that." He looked away. "For more I need a pair."

He straightened up.

"You try the cube."

"I doubt if I can get it to work," I said.

"Try."

I took a deep breath and concentrated on the cube, struggling to keep a single memory in my mind. I swear Mav was holding his breath, too. Nothing happened. Nothing, except the pain in my head throbbed fast for a second as I strained to form a picture.

Mav's ears were lower than I'd ever seen them before.

"Sorry, but it makes my head hurt," I said.

He didn't stir.

"Hey, when's your birthday?" My voice was fake jolly. Even I hated it.

He picked up the cube.

"We do not celebrate the day of births. We celebrate the joining day."

"What's that?" A change of subject would do us both some good.

"It is the day when a young pair joins their minds completely. It is the time of shared knowledge."

Great, this could only remind him of Kelmav. Next subject, please.

"This has been a great birthday treat, Mav. Thanks." I kicked the cover off my legs and wriggled off the bed. "I'm just going to get dressed. I'll be out in a minute." It was a cop out, but I didn't know what else to say.

Suddenly Mav lunged at me, wrapping me in a hug that verged on spine-snapping. Screte, he was strong.

"A hug and kiss is also traditional, yes? Happy birthday Joss-partner." He kissed me carefully, keeping his secondary mouth closed. It was like being kissed by a mild-mannered vacuum cleaner.

"Thanks, Mav," I said, patting him on the arm. At least his ears were a bit higher now.

I stayed in the bather a bit longer than usual, choosing a fragrance cycle rather than my usual dirt-off-get-out program. I decided to try a bit of makeup, too. Lipstick and maybe a bit of eye stuff. It didn't look too bad, although my hair could have done with a cut.

Mav was concerned when I came out of my room. "Why has your mouth changed?"

I looked in the wall mirror, just to make sure the lipstick hadn't worked its way up my nose or something.

"It's just makeup," I said. Maybe they didn't have makeup on Choria. "It's body decoration to make you look good. Make you attractive to other people."

"I have studied what humans think is look good. The information was not very exact, but you come into the parameters of acceptable without extra color."

I think that was meant to be a compliment.

"I have an incoming message for you, Joss," the computer said.

"Okay, I'll take it at the main screen."

"Well, well, well if it isn't the birthday girl," Vaughn said, leering. "Many happy returns. I've got a couple of packages for you here at the front desk that have just been cleared."

He was still leering when I got to the front desk.

"I hear you're eighteen today," he said. "You can get into the sex-scapes now, hey? I can tell you where the good programs are. Maybe we can link up."

What an innocent. Most people got into the Net sex-scapes before they were twelve, let alone eighteen. Vaughn probably thought I hadn't been kissed yet, either.

"Unlike some people, I've never needed to resort to VR sex," I said. "Can I have my packages, please?"

He handed me two packages: one small and square, the other flat and large. One was from Lewis.

"If you're not nicer to me, I'll tell you what's in your pressies," he said. "I saw them on the scan."

"It's too high a price," I said.

He flipped me the finger just as a man entered the building. The visitor frowned.

"What would the Major say?" I whispered.

Vaughn had already turned to the man, yes-sirring and no-sirring stiffly. The back of his neck and his crew-cut scalp were bright red.

I opened the packages back in the suite, Mav hanging all over me.

"You do not know what these are, yes?" he asked.

"They're a complete surprise," I said, struggling with the tight packaging on the smaller parcel.

Lewis had packed it in Outerlock, so I just about needed a blowtorch to get it off. Whatever was inside had to be fragile. Hopefully, it wasn't a vase.

It wasn't. It was the newest, slim-line, "do everything except breathe for you" armscreen. I'm sure it was very expensive, but it was exactly what I didn't want. Armscreens made you available to anyone, anytime. At least I would get a good price for it at Boney's pawnshop.

The card read:

Happy 18th Birthday, Joss, love Ingrid.

Short, to the point and written by Lewis.

"Who sends you this?" Mav asked.

"My mother's secretary," I said.

"You are friends to mother's secretary?"

"No."

Mav sat back, confused.

I ripped away the top layer of packaging off the flat parcel. It had an insurance sticker on it, but I didn't recognize the writing. After the third layer of spongy packing, I was beginning to get interested. Who had sent this?

Finally all of the packing was gone. Mav whistled with excitement. The final package was decked out in very bright paper with loads of slightly squashed ribbons all over it.

"Festive paper and ribbons," he said, fluffing up the blue and pink bows.

I pushed his hands away. This was getting more and more interesting. The paper and bows tore off easily. It was Ingrid's Ledbetter original.

I picked up the card. It read:

I thought you might like this now that you are living in the Ledbetter suite. You chose well. Love, Ingrid.

It was handwritten with two little crosses under her name. I scrabbled through the packing until I found the outer layer. She had even written out the insurance sticker. Lewis probably didn't even know about it. Ha.

"This is a good present? You smile a lot," Mav said.

"This is a great present," I said, slipping the card into my waist pouch. "It's from my mother."

"Joss, it's ten-fifteen," the computer said. I'd asked it to remind me so that I wasn't late for Louise.

"Okay," I said, ignoring the little lurch in my gut.

After a bit of a struggle, I managed to hang the painting up in my bedroom in place of the pale print. Mav stared at it for a while then agreed it looked good, although he couldn't see the use of it. Then we packed all of the Outerlock into the recyc bin and vacced it away. It was ten-thirty. If I didn't get going I would be late. Louise has always said being late for an appointment showed disrespect. She was always early. But not this time. This time she was six years late.

The Red Hat

I bit the bullet and took the Venturi to Mall 14. It was running on time so I got to Mario's five minutes early. Louise hadn't arrived.

Mario's is a monument to hard-core coffee drinkers. Even when coffee got blamed for Gosfords Syndrome, Mario's ignored the medical warnings. For a while it was one of the few places you could get blistering short blacks and real cappuccinos. Now that coffee drinking was back in favor, I was lucky to score the two seats at the front window bar.

I took Ingrid's card out of my pouch. Not only had she remembered I'd chosen the painting, but she'd also remembered I was living in the Ledbetter suite. Maybe I should start believing in Santa again. I smoothed out a slight crease in the left corner of the cardboard. It was already getting wrecked. I'd have to find somewhere safe for it. I slid the card back into my pouch, keeping it flat against the stiff front-piece of the bag.

Louise was now five minutes late. Maybe she wasn't coming at all. A guy in one of those awful cling business suits was eyeing up the spare stool. I took my jacket off and dumped it on the seat. He clicked his tongue, moving away.

Louise was out of breath when she walked in the door. She smiled at me as she slid a babypack off her shoulders. Her kid was asleep, his head flopped to one side. She maneuvered the baby, a huge bag, and a fluoro green hatbox neatly around the tables towards me. I stood up.

"Happy birthday, Joss. My God, you're so tall."

She paused, then kissed my cheek. Her skin smelled of powder with just a hint of baby puke. I kissed her, awkwardly sliding my arm around her for a quick hug. It was hard to act naturally, as though the six years hadn't gone by.

The waiter hovered over us, probably afraid Louise would knock cups off the tables with the pack.

"I don't think all of this stuff will fit under a stool," Louise said to him. "Is there a table free?"

Surprise, surprise, he found us a table in the back, away from anything breakable.

"Moving a baby is such a major production," she said as we sat down. She arranged the kid on the bench seat against the wall. The hatbox went under the table.

"I'll have a strong long black," she told the waiter. "You too?" she asked me. I nodded.

"You must be so proud of yourself, getting into the Centre," she said as he walked away.

I shrugged. For once I didn't want to talk about time-jumping. There were more important things to talk about, but all of them led straight to the big question: why hadn't I seen her in six years? So I said nothing.

"You're upset with me, aren't you?" she said.

All I had to do was ask, and Louise would tell me the truth. I picked up the chipped antique sugar dispenser, running my finger across the flip top. The waiter brought our coffees. Louise sipped hers slowly. She kept her eyes carefully on her cup. She'd always been able to outwait me. I curled my fingers around the edge of the table. Now or never.

"Why didn't you want to see me for so long? Did I do something wrong to make you leave?" I'd wanted to sound cool, as if the answer didn't really mean much. Instead, I sounded like a whimpering three-year-old.

Louise clacked her cup down on the saucer.

"Of course you didn't do anything wrong," she said.

"You're positive I didn't make you mad or something?" The three-year-old in me had to make sure. As sure as you can be when you can't read someone's mind.

"Absolutely. I left because your mum and I had a lot of problems. Not because of you." She touched my arm reassuringly. "I did try and see you after I left, but your mum asked me not to. But now you're officially an adult. You can see who you want to."

"I knew it!" I said, unclenching my fingers. "I knew you would have come if you could have."

Louise hesitated.

"We agreed it was best that I didn't. We didn't want you caught up in the middle of our fight. It was getting pretty messy. In the end I just had to get out."

I couldn't help smiling. Louise didn't hate me! Ingrid was the bad guy. Not me.

"I know," I said. "It was all Ingrid's fault. She wrecks everything."

"Come on, you know that's not true. I did some stupid things, too."

"But she was going to dump you for a man just to get her ratings. That's so low. I heard you fighting about it."

I was on a roll, President of the Down with Ingrid Club. The couple at the next table stopped midchat and stared at me. Louise glared at them until they looked away. She leaned closer, holding my hand so tightly that I winced.

"She wasn't really going to do that. That was just the flare-up point for a lot of other problems."

"Ingrid's the problem," I said, pulling my hand free to air-jab my point home. "She's so selfish, there's no room for anyone else."

"Isn't it time you saw your mother as a real person instead of a monster?" Louise said. "Even I don't think she's as bad as you do."

"Of course I see her as a person," I said.

Louise crossed her arms. "No, you don't. You're acting just like the spoiled kid you were six years ago. I'd have thought you'd have grown up by now."

Sometimes Louise told too much truth, too fast. There's something to be said for softening the blow. I looked at my reflection in the mirrored wall opposite. Lipstick, eyeliner, and six years had done nothing. I wiped the back of my hand across my red lips. In a way it was funny. I'd always thought I had grown up the day she left.

Louise was sitting very still, waiting for me to say something. Did strangled howls count? I gulped a mouthful of coffee. All right, I could be as grown up as the next person.

"If you know so much, you tell me why she stopped you from seeing me," I said. "But don't try and cop out. If you say it was all for my own good, I'll spray."

"You haven't been listening, have you?" she said. She placed her hands flat on the table. "Ingrid didn't want you dragged into the middle of our fight. You were so upset as it was. So I suppose you're going to have to spray, because Ingrid did want what was best for you."

I pretended to vomit into my hand, but I was really ducking away from a hot-knife memory of a twelve-year-old huddled against a heater, rocking herself too fast.

"Sticking me in all of those stupid schools wasn't the best thing for me. She just wanted to get me out of the way. I don't even know why she had me."

"She just wanted someone to love her, not her money or the way she looked," Louise said. "You know how she hates to be alone. It scares the hell out of her."

I used my trump.

"If she hates to be alone, then why didn't she ever want me around?"

Louise dragged her lower teeth across her top lip. Whatever she was going to say wasn't going to be good. I pressed myself back in the chair.

"She's afraid of you," she said.

I couldn't move. A rabbit in the headlights. Did Ingrid think I was a genetic monster, too?

"Maybe afraid is the wrong way of putting it," Louise said, studying my face. "I think Ingrid hates herself, and she's afraid you hate her, too. After all, the last time I saw you two together, you were treating her like dirt."

The cold wash of truths prickled up my spine and across my scalp. I scrubbed my hands through my hair, trying to push Louise's words away.

The baby started to whimper. Louise pulled him out of the pack, holding him close to her chest. I was glad of the interruption.

"I met Barbara when I called," I said into the silence. "She seems nice."

Louise watched me for a moment, slowly rocking the kid.

"Maybe I should learn to shut up," she said. "Are you okay?"

"Of course," I said, curling my fingers around my cup.

"I could be wrong about Ingrid," she said, but I could tell she didn't believe it.

"Barbara seems nice," I said again.

Louise nodded.

"She is. She's wonderful with Perri, too. Somehow she can get him to sleep when all he wants to do is cry."

The kid was wide awake now, trying to focus on me. His eyes were almond shaped and big, like mine.

"Is he a comp?" I asked.

"No. We thought about it, but we wanted the baby to know who he'd come from. So James, a friend of ours, volunteered to give us some sperm. He's absolutely gaga over Perri. Isn't he, sweetie?" she said to the baby, kissing the little curve of his nose.

"The father's around?"

"Of course. He's not living with us, but he comes and visits. It's part of our parenting arrangement."

The kid didn't know how lucky he was. Two loving mums and a donor who wanted to be in his life.

"He's got it all, hasn't he?" I said.

Louise stopped smoothing down Perri's wispy hair.

"Well, you know Ingrid did everything in her power to find your father for you. Personally, I didn't think she'd get as far as she did. It was too bad that code she bribed out of the nurse was no good."

I stared at Louise's mouth. A smeared red smile.

"What's wrong, Joss?"

"She never told me she looked for him."

Louise rubbed her forehead.

"She never told you?"

I thought about all the times I'd sat in class, dreaming up plans to find him. A private investigator. Lenny's underground network. A story by *60 Minutes*. Or my favorite one: my father finding me.

"Why didn't she tell me she looked?"

"I don't know. Why don't you ask her? Maybe it's time you cleared the air."

Louise waited for me to agree with her. Finally, she sighed, reached under the table, and pushed the hatbox towards me.

"Here's your birthday present. Guess what it is."

It was the game we used to play. Louise would give me the hatbox and I was supposed to guess my present was a VR game or a book or something. Anything but a hat. This time I didn't want to play.

I pulled the top off the box.

Inside was a small red hat. I picked it up, unraveled the cotton stuffing out of its crown, then balanced the hat on my fist. The rich velvet rippled in the light as the brim curved over my hand like an arched eyebrow.

"Try it on," Louise urged. She scrabbled around in her bag, holding the kid against her shoulder. "Here, I brought a mirror." She held it up in front of me.

"I'll look ridiculous," I said.

But I carefully placed the hat on my head, tilting it forwards the way Louise had taught me. The brim slanted over one eye, framing my cheekbone in red that sometimes flared with gold. I definitely didn't look like a twelve-year-old kid in this hat. In fact, I didn't look like me at all. I moved my head to the side, smiling at the woman in the mirror.

"What do you know," Louise said softly. "A dark-haired Ingrid."

"Don't be stupid," I said, pulling the hat off.

Louise caught my hand.

"Here, you know better than that," she said, pulling the hat out of my fingers. "Gently does it. And remember to stuff the crown so that it keeps its shape."

She pushed the wadding into the hat, her strong hands working it around the brim.

"It's a beautiful hat," I said.

"But you don't like it." Louise kept her eyes down.

"I do like it. I just can't see me wearing it. It's not really me, is it."

"It will be," Louise said, lifting her head. "That's why I made it for you."

She gently laid the hat in the box, pushing the top on with a tap of her fingernails.

"Have a good birthday, Joss," she said.

I nodded, not realizing that the day was about to go downhill in a big way.

Against the Wall

After I said good-bye to Louise, I walked for a while along the upper level. Sometimes window-shopping is better than a tranq. I remembered a saying that says you can never return home. I'd add a rider to that—if you do return home, give back your key and get the hell out of there.

At the mall junction, I decided to head back to the uni. That was when I noticed the creep following me. A big steroid guy in a red denim suit. I lost him on the split walkway. Probably a drugger who thought I was looking for some action.

When I scanned the visitor's band at the P3 security doors, it must have activated something in the security office. Donaldson-Hono and two of his private army shot out like scags on Guarana.

"Where the hell have you been?" Donaldson-Hono yelled.

"What's it to you?" I said.

The guards moved in beside me. I blocked one with the hatbox, but the other one slid in behind me. Donaldson-Hono was twitching. What had I done now?

"I've got half of my people out looking for you. Why can't you wear a screen like a normal person?"

"Who needs one when I've got a bugged wristband?" I said.

"What?" He looked genuinely puzzled. Okay, so maybe he hadn't been lying after all.

"Look, I've got a situation here," he said, rubbing his fist into his hand, "and I don't need a smart mouth. Your partner has gone off his head. Now the professor and all of those flapheads have gone to Sunawa-Harrod's funeral, so you're in the hot seat. I can't get the little sod out."

"What's wrong with him? What have you done to Mav?" I moved forward, but the two guards grabbed me by the arms.

"We haven't touched him," he said. He waved the guards back. "He's gone down into the fusion reactor and won't budge. He's making a hell of a noise, too. He says he won't talk to anyone but you or that Refmol. The tech guys are afraid if he goes any deeper he'll fry himself."

Screte! Had Mav completely flipped out? He'd seemed okay when I'd left. Well, sort of okay. He'd been upset about the cube, but he'd gotten over it.

"You'd better let me see him," I said. Not that I knew what to do.

Donaldson-Hono gave a quick nod.

"You're going to need a heat-protection suit. He's gone past the first level of insulation."

I crawled down the emergency ladder. The insulated overall and helmet I was wearing already smelled of sweat, but I couldn't work out if it was mine or the previous owner's. The gear made progress slow, too. According to Donaldson-Hono, Mav was somewhere near this ladder on sub-level three. As I passed the level two sign, I heard singing.

"Mav? Can you hear me?" I yelled.

Donaldson-Hono crackled through the helmet's comm-unit frequency.

"Aaronson, don't shout. You're distorting the sound. And move a bit faster. We can't hang around here all day."

What a drack. Too bad the suit wasn't linked to visuals. Then I could really show him what I thought of his precious sound link.

I stepped onto level three. The lighting was dim like Mav's room, the walls metal gray with color-coded pipes curling across the roof. It reminded me of those 3D anatomy diagrams. The low deep hum from the reactor was hitting me right in the skull bone.

"Mav?"

The singing was louder. He was using the fusion hum as a counter harmony.

"Can you see him yet?" Donaldson-Hono asked.

"No, but I can hear him," I said.

I walked along the corridor. Gauges, emergency equipment lockers, more pipes. It all looked the same. Maybe I should be leaving a trail of breadcrumbs.

Then I found him.

He was flat against the wall. Not human flat, but flat like a bear rug. He was humming at the same pitch as the fusion reactor.

"Mav? It's Joss. You okay?"

Dumb question. I touched him on the place that looked like his shoulder. He jumped, then curled off the wall.

"Joss-partner," he said wearily. His body began to morph back to its normal size, filling out in the proper places.

"Mav, what's going on? What's wrong?"

"I tried to record the Sulon," he said. "But I failed. I am sorry. It could not be found."

"Don't worry about it," I said. "It's not important."

"It is, it is," he wailed. "I could not record the Sulon and I could not reach you with the cube."

Time to get his mind off this Sulon stuff.

"Why did you come down here?" I asked. Limp, Aaronson, very limp.

He pressed up against the wall. Was he going to go flat again? I grabbed his arm.

"It's so warm, like home. And the hum. It fills my head. I don't feel the emptiness," he sang.

He squashed himself closer to the hot metal, humming loudly. His hand flattened. I closed my fingers around it. Something told me this flat business was not good.

"Tell me about your home, Mav."

"I should not be here. Kelmav is gone. Mavkel should be

gone, too. Why did Refmol and Molref save my life threads? It is too alone."

He sneezed then choked. His secondary eyelids flicked back off his eyes, taking me straight into Chorian hell. Half of Mav was missing. Kelmav. Now Mav was stranded in his own mind, just like all of us humans. He was right. Sometimes it was too alone. Maybe that's why some people want to believe in a god.

I didn't know how to help Mav. He really needed his pair, and I could never be Kelmav. So although I've never been very big on religion, I sent up a general SOS to any god out there, even the Net gods. Please, show me what to do. Then I shut my eyes and did the first thing that came into my head. I pulled Mav away from the wall, stroked his ears, and hummed a song that Ingrid used to sing to me: "Jingle Bell Rock."

"Aaronson, we've contacted Refmol and Professor Camden-Stone. They're on their way," Donaldson-Hono said, his voice low.

"Thank you," I whispered.

Mav shifted closer to me. I leaned against the metal wall, its heat seeping through my insulation suit. Mav's head was under my chin, his ears stretched back tight against his skull. "Jingle Bell Rock" turned into "Rudolph the Red-Nosed Reindeer." Mav seemed to like it. I stroked the ear that wasn't pressed hard against my chest, hoping I wouldn't run out of cheerful upbeat songs.

———

An hour later, Donaldson-Hono tapped me on the shoulder.

"Come on, Joss, it's time to go," he said, his voice scratchy through the helmet comm system. He held out his hand.

Refmol squatted down, taking Mav's weight as I stood up.

"Did Mavkel . . ." Refmol searched for a word, then held out his hand, pressing it flat against the wall.

I nodded.

"He went flat all over."

Refmol blinked back both sets of eyelids and looked me straight in the eye.

"Then, as you humans say, we are running out of time."

Sellouts and Sulons

Camden-Stone wanted me out of the way. He stepped in front of me, blocking my view of Mav.

"Go and wait in your suite. I'll speak to you later," he said.

"But I should be with Mav. I'm his partner."

I tried to push past him. No go, the man was solid muscle. He held me by the shoulder. Hard.

"Right now Mavkel needs his own kind to look after him. You'll just get in the way. I want you in your rooms. Now."

He motioned to a guard. My old friend Vaughn.

"Get Aaronson back to her quarters and keep her there!" Camden-Stone ordered. I'd never seen him so strung out.

Vaughn's hold on my arm was too tight to break. He pulled me towards the P3 security door.

"Do you get some kind of sick enjoyment pushing people around?" I asked him.

"Absolutely," he said.

I looked back at the crowd around Mav. I should be there with him. We were partners—we were in it together. He had to be all right.

The crowd broke apart, making way for a stretcher.

However, Camden-Stone wasn't watching the small procession that moved towards the medical building. He was watching me.

Vaughn pushed my wrist against the door scan and pushed my head around to face the retina scan. Then he checked himself through. The guard on front desk duties straightened up.

"Afternoon, Sergeant," he said.

"Afternoon," Vaughn grunted, steering me towards the back virtual wall.

"Excuse me, Sarge. This package has been delivered for Aaronson."

Vaughn sighed, pulling me around to face the front desk. The guard handed me a small box. If my guess was right, Blackwidow had delivered.

"Another birthday present?" Vaughn asked. "Aren't we the popular one?"

"Some people attract friends and some people don't," I said. The package fitted nicely into the inner pocket of my jacket, away from Vaughn's attention.

I didn't resist as he propelled me along the corridors to the Ledbetter suite. The quicker I got to a Reader Unit the better. Maybe I was finally going to get some answers. Even if I didn't, at least I had something to do until I got word about Mav. Otherwise I'd go warpo.

Vaughn stationed himself outside the front door of the suite.

I went straight to my desk, ripping the packaging off the

novel. Blackwidow had chosen to embed my information into the new best-selling thriller. Very appropriate. I slipped the disc into my Reader Unit.

A few hours later I had come up with three conclusions.

The Ledbetter suite was seriously wired for sound and sight.

Tori Suka didn't do any dealings on the Net.

Camden-Stone had sold out. In a big way.

I'd expected the first two conclusions.

Blackwidow had downloaded the current security schematics for P3. Every room was bugged except my bathroom. Even Mavkel's bathroom was bugged. Apparently the government knew enough about human bodily functions to let me sit in peace. The schematics also showed Refmol quartered in the next suite. Very interesting.

The fact that Suka didn't deal on the Net was as surprising as corruption in the government. If I was an assassin, I wouldn't advertise on a security nightmare like the Net either. But it had been worth getting Blackwidow to check it out just in case something useful about Suka had come up. Now it was up to Lenny to work out who she'd been hired to kill.

That left the story of Camden-Stone and Daniel Sunawa-Harrod. Blackwidow had done an amazing job breaking open the files. It seemed Sunawa-Harrod's fib to Joanna Tyrell-Coombes was just a nano-bit of a huge cover-up.

Joanna was on the right track—the experiment that

resulted in the time-continuum field wasn't Sunawa-Harrod's failed fusion experiment. It was Joseph Camden-Stone's successful time/space experiment. All the glory should have gone to Joe. The field should be called the Camden-Stone Time-Continuum Warp Field.

However, at the time, poor old Joe was comatose in the hospital. So in steps his best buddy, Daniel Sunawa-Harrod. He refines the field, rationalizes Joe's experiment as an accident and claims the discovery. On 10/10/50, the fiftieth anniversary of Australian Independence Day, Danny receives the Nobel-Takahini Prize for Science. The university rubs its hands together and helps him set up the Centre for Neo-Historical Studies. Danny is one of the major shareholders. He's set for life.

Two years later Joe gets out of the hospital with a new face and a major grudge. He's been intellectually ripped off. He threatens the university with exposure. Now the university has got a lot of mileage out of Sunawa-Harrod: it has the world's only time-travel center, a Nobel-Takahini Prize, and a lot of grants. They can't afford a scandal. They send their negotiator over to visit Joe. Gerry P. Brackman persuades Joe that the Nobel-Takahini committee would never overturn their decision, that the field would never be renamed, that Joe would only make a fool of himself. Gerry gives Joe an alternative. Silence. In return Joe will receive an associate professorship, shares in the new Centre, and a sizeable cash payment. Joe says yes.

When I pieced the story together, I almost felt sorry for

Camden-Stone. Almost. A little postscript to the whole affair brought everything back into perspective. Sunawa-Harrod had willed Camden-Stone his forty percent share in the Centre. Probably a guilt bequest. Now that Sunawa-Harrod had died, all Camden-Stone had to do was wait out a six-month caveat.

What was a caveat? I did a quick dictionary search. It's a warning, a proviso or law process to suspend court proceedings. So Sunawa-Harrod must have set up this caveat in case some lost relatives popped up to claim the shares. That means that if no one surfaces in the next six months, Camden-Stone will have controlling interest in a Centre that is making a historical swap of technology with aliens. Camden-Stone would finally get the fame and fortune he'd been coveting for over thirty years. The fame and fortune his best friend stole from him. No wonder the guy was a bit twisto.

"Professor Camden-Stone's at the front door," the computer said.

Speak of the devil.

It was time to hide the evidence. I pulled open my desk drawer. No one would find Blackwidow's Reader in the middle of a stack of empty Readers. Not that Camden-Stone would be looking for it.

"Let him in," I said.

Camden-Stone strode into the middle of the lounge room. He was holding his visitor's band, slapping it against his other palm. I stood up, stepping away from the desk.

"You're moving over to J. C. Hall," he said abruptly.

"Why? Is this something to do with Mav? Is he okay?"

"What did you call Mavkel?" Camden-Stone demanded, frowning.

"Mav," I said. "It's just a nickname."

"Mav?" he repeated, crossing his arms.

He turned his back to me, staring at the wall. At one point, I thought he whispered "Mavis?" Then he stared at the wall again. He really was twisto. The silence was just getting to that stifling stage when he shook his head and swung around to face me.

"I've decided your partnership is not working," he said. "You're moving to J. C. Mavkel is staying here."

"What do you mean it's not working? We're doing okay," I said.

Camden-Stone snorted.

"Some kind of okay. Mavkel's sick and you seem to be the cause of it."

"Me, the cause? Who told you that?"

"Refmol," he said smugly, knowing that I'd have to believe the Chanter's diagnosis. "You'll both be reassigned new partners as soon as possible."

I looked around the suite. It helps to move your eyes around if you think you're going to cry. Stops them from filling up. Camden-Stone was finally going to get me out of the partnership. And in six months he was going to get complete control of the Centre. Everything was coming up roses for Joey boy.

"I want you packed and out before they bring Mavkel back. Do you hear?" he said.

"Is Mav going to be all right?" I asked.

"I don't know," he said, shrugging. He didn't really give a damn about Mav. He only cared that his precious little technology swap might be in danger.

"I'm only going because I don't want to hurt Mav," I said.

"Very touching, but I don't care why you're going. Just that you're going. If I have my way, soon you won't even be at the Centre."

He moved towards the door. It slid open. Vaughn was standing at attention to one side.

"Vaughn, make sure Aaronson is out of here before they bring Mavkel back," Camden-Stone ordered.

"That would not facilitate Mavkel's recovery," Refmol sang smoothly, stepping past Vaughn.

Camden-Stone stopped still.

"I beg your pardon," he said.

Refmol walked slowly into the lounge room, followed by Hartpury and two Elders. Gohjec and Jecgoh? I couldn't tell.

"Refmol has chanted Mavkel and discussed the case with your Dr. Hartpury. We believe that Mavkel's partnership with Joss is vital to his recovery," Refmol sang.

I held my breath.

Hartpury nodded. "It seems that Mav is very attached to Joss," she explained. "Refmol believes he'll become even more agitated if they're separated." She turned to me.

"Mav's okay, Joss. He'll be back with you tomorrow," she said, smiling warmly.

I breathed out. I wasn't hurting Mav after all. I was helping him.

"But didn't you say Aaronson is the cause of his illness?" Camden-Stone demanded, pacing back into the middle of the room. He was slapping his palm again with the wristband. It was like watching an angry cat's tail.

"Mavkel is weak," Refmol sang. "The Elders say the Joss and Mavkel pair must not be separated."

The Elder pair bowed in unison.

Camden-Stone stared at me, but his eyes were unfocused. He was up to something. Something nasty by the look of the smile slowly curling his mouth.

"Of course," he said softly. He turned around to face the Elders. "Of course, the pair must not be separated."

For a man who had just been outmaneuvered, he was way too calm. Why the abrupt about-face? What was his game?

Hartpury smiled across at me. I unclenched my jaw and smiled back. She was still the defender of Joss Aaronson and small furry animals.

"Now I wish to speak to Joss as one," Refmol said. It bowed to the Elders and Hartpury, but only inclined its head to Camden-Stone. The battle lines had been drawn.

Camden-Stone knew when to retreat. He walked out of the suite quickly, leaving Hartpury to usher the Elders out with bows and murmured courtesies.

Refmol waited until the door slid shut.

"There is much to discuss," it said.

I pointed to my room. "Let's go in there."

Refmol's ears flicked with surprise, but it followed me through my bedroom into the bathroom. The door slid shut.

"Okay we can talk now," I said. "This is the only room in the place that's not bugged."

"Bugged?" Refmol asked, balancing itself on the edge of the bather tank. It smoothed the heavy metallic robe over its legs.

"Electronically monitored. You know, so other people can find out what we talk about."

Refmol shifted its weight. I got the feeling it wasn't really listening to my explanation.

It suddenly stood up again, its ears curled forward.

"We ask for your help, Joss Aaronson," it sang. The harmonies were so tight it came out more like a shriek.

"Help with what?"

"Mavkel must pair with you or his life threads will break."

Acid fear shot up my throat, lacing my mouth with bitterness.

"You mean Mav's going to die? But you said he was okay."

Refmol took both my hands and stroked them with its thumbs.

"Mavkel struggles with his doubleness in this single world. His threads grow weak without a pair. He strains to join with your one mind. Will you help him?"

"Of course. But how? I'm not telepathic."

"When Kelmav died, this pair caught Mavkel's life threads. We did not let Mavkel die," Refmol sang slowly. "The Elders wanted a pairless pair, to go to Earth and learn the one people's timecraft. Mavkel's pain was secondary."

Bitterness soured the chords. The Chanter clenched its primary mouth and continued.

"Without his pair, Mavkel has no bloodlines. He is not alive on Choria. So he tries to take on your bloodlines to be paired again. Such a thing has never been tried, but Mavkel is desperate. However, there is a problem. Your Sulon is missing." Refmol hesitated, searching for the words. "You would call it your father."

"Why is that a problem?"

"Mavkel cannot pair with you until you find the name of your Sulon and complete your bloodlines."

"I don't get it. How is my father's name going to pair us?"

"When the knowing is shared, the power is great. Is this not your truth, too?" Refmol cocked its head questioningly.

"I'm not sure I understand any of this," I said, shaking my head. "You're saying Mav won't survive unless I find my father?"

"Mavkel believes you will pair with him when you discover the name of your father. He thinks the point of knowledge will clear your mindways so that he can join you." Refmol paused. "Perhaps Mavkel is right. All young pairs must experience a point of knowledge before they fully join."

"You don't sound convinced."

"Can his double mind fit within your single?" Refmol's ears lifted in a shrug.

"Can it?"

"Maybe with you, yes."

"Why me?"

Refmol's primary mouth momentarily tightened.

"You have the same resonance as my people, Joss Aaronson."

"Resonance?"

"There is something in you that is of Choria. We have all felt it in your mind."

A strange fear uncurled in my stomach. A fear that pounded through my memory, putting together a jigsaw of strangeness: double lids, night vision, pale, pale skin.

"Are you saying I'm an alien?" My voice was a hiss.

Refmol drew back.

"No, you are human. But you echo our minds. It is why Mavkel tries to pair. He has given you a thought cube, yes?"

I nodded, sound unable to get past the knot in my throat.

"Mavkel tries to join your mind through it. Do you have pain here?" Refmol pointed to the side of its head.

I touched my temple where the dull pain throbbed. So it hadn't been a headache. Mav had been trying to get into my brain.

Refmol skimmed my head with his four thumbs. I pulled away, flattening myself against the wall.

"Mavkel does not mean to hurt you, but he tries dangerous ways to join your minds." Refmol stroked my ear. "Your resonance gives hope that the joining is possible."

I shoved Refmol's hand away.

"You must find your Sulon and pair with Mavkel." Refmol sang it as a chant. "This is the only way to save him. You must pair."

"Leave me alone," I shouted.

I hit out, my fist bounced off Refmol's chest. The rough metallic robe scraped my knuckles. The Chanter was so shocked I got in two more punches before it blocked me with its large hands. It backed out of the bathroom.

"You must pair," it urgently chanted. "You must pair."

"I'm not a pair," I yelled, as the door slid shut. "I'm not a pair!"

Mirrors

I stayed in the bathroom, huddled against the wall, for a long time. The side of my head and my arm were numbed by the cold tiles. I wanted to press my mind against them, too. Freeze the rush of questions.

There was always another way to stop the questions. I pushed myself off the floor. Lenny could get me out of the city in less than two hours. In four I could be underground in Sydney feeling fine on a Zoomer or two.

The bathroom door slid open. I ran into the bedroom, pulling my backpack from under the bed. A few T-shirts and my jacket would be enough. The rest I could buy on the road.

I scrabbled through the junk on my bedside table. The holo unit of Ingrid and the chromatic harp would be easy to carry. Then I saw the thought cube. I picked it up, turning it around in my hand.

Here's a bit of advice. Beware of aliens bearing gifts. Especially gifts that could fry your brain. I gripped the cube tightly, wanting to crush it. The sharp edges bit into my skin. I threw it at the wall.

It cracked against the plasboard, splitting in half. I

kneeled on the bed, expecting to see nano-chips or wires. Instead, two tiny identical black mirrors caught my reflection.

I leaned down to have a closer look. In one mirror my face was transparent. The broken cube had sucked away substance to leave only the outline of features. Long eyes that curved without pupils. Nostrils that dug pits into the ridged surface. A hint of mouth like a line drawing of a seagull.

The other mirror showed blocks of solidity that promised a face. The forehead was a rectangle. The nose a cylinder. A triangle chin.

I picked up the halves. The break was slanted, but no pieces were missing. I slid them together. The ridges and curves molded into each other, somehow repairing the break. The mirrors were gone, but I was left with the images of my half-finished faces.

I stared at the long crack still left in the dull surface. Focus on a memory. A picture of Mav in the reactor, curled in my arms, his head heavy against my shoulder. For a second the cube surface shined and the air above it wavered. Resonance. I closed my eyes.

Refmol had said I had to find my father. For Mav's sake. But I knew I had to find out who or what my father was for my own sake, too.

I carefully placed the cube back on the bedside table. Then I upended the backpack. Three T-shirts, my harp, and the holo unit fell out. I leaned back against the wall, too tired to put them away. My eyes were blinking fast, trying to stay open. A quick ten-minute rest would raz me up again. I curled around the backpack and my gear. Ten minutes only. I slept for three hours.

I woke up with one of those awful jolts that jump-starts your heart and plasters your lips to your teeth. I knew I had to talk to Ingrid and get my father's clinic code. And Louise was right. It was also time Ingrid and I cleared the air. I stumbled into the kitchen. Coffee first. Mug in hand I sat at my console staring at a late-night news channel: a triple murder, stock share fluctuations, Olympic demonstrators, and a cat who had gotten stuck in one of the Venturi valves. Business as usual.

"Computer, connect comm autocode one, please," I finally said.

"Okay, calling Ingrid now."

I wiped my palms along my jeans legs. The news channel flicked off and the CommNet logo appeared. It disintegrated into Lewis's smiling face. He'd had some beauty advice and dyed his eyebrows a lighter shade. He still looked like a ferret.

"Joss, whatever have I done to deserve two calls in two days? And so late at night," he said.

"Hello, Lewis. Sorry about the time. Can I please talk to Ingrid?"

Those awful eyebrows shot up.

"Well, that was very polite. Maybe . . ." he paused, his head to one side. "No, she's not available."

I didn't have time for his garbage.

"Tell Ingrid that if she doesn't speak to me, I won't help her get that interview with my partner," I said.

"Hold," he snapped.

The hold logo flipped up onto the screen. I only counted three seconds before Ingrid's too-young face appeared.

"Hello, darling. Are you having a lovely birthday? Did you get your pressies?"

She was in phony star mode. She used to put on that voice as a joke.

"I need to talk to you," I said.

She sighed, all drama queen.

"How much do you need, sweetheart? Surely that little advance Lewis gave you hasn't gone already?"

"No, it's not money. I just want to talk to you about something."

"Have you been thrown out of that Centre? They can't do that, you know. I have over ten percent of their shares."

"No. No, I'm fine. I want to talk to you about my father."

"Your father?" She frowned.

"I need his clinic code number. I know you've got it."

"How do you know about that?" Her voice turned from honey to plasglass.

"Louise told me."

Ingrid flushed. The color was uneven on her rejuved skin.

"You've seen Louise? How is she?"

"She's fine. She said you'd bribed some nurse to get the code from the clinic. I need it."

Ingrid suddenly swiveled her chair around to face Lewis, who was hovering in the background. She ordered him out of the room, then faced the screen again.

"I don't know what Louise has been telling you, but I don't bribe people. Anyway, that code is useless. The clinic files were all destroyed years ago. Now, if you've finished accusing me, I've got other crimes to get on with."

She reached for the comm off switch.

"Mum, don't go. I really do need your help," I said.

Her eyes widened. I hadn't called her Mum for a long time.

"What's this all about, Joss?"

"Can you secure this line?"

"If you think it's really necessary."

I nodded.

She flicked another switch in front of her. "Okay, we're clean now."

"Great. I'm going to change to keyboard for a while," I said.

"Why? I've secured the link."

"But I don't think this end is secure."

Ingrid raised her eyebrows. "Okay, I understand. Fire away."

I switched to the comm-text option and keyed in an edited version of the whole mess, skipping the bit about the resonance thing. Far too soon for that. When I finished, I switched back to voice. Ingrid sat for a while just swiveling the chair from side to side, biting her lower lip.

"This would make good newsvid," she said, then waved me back into my seat. "I'm not serious. And don't worry, I can be discreet. I'll get the clinic number for you although I don't think it will be much use."

She bent down, moving out of frame. When she straightened up, she was holding a box.

"This is where I keep all your kid stuff," she said, clicking open the lid.

She placed a heavy old-style holo unit on the desk and turned it on. A picture of me, circa three, lit up.

"Cute, hey?" She smiled, flicked it off and put it to one side. A very worn toy rabbit appeared, Bobby-Sox, I think, and a small plastic jar full of yellowed baby teeth.

"Aha." Ingrid slid an old piece of paper out of the box, waving it. "Here it is. For some reason the Newman Clinic thought hard files would be more secure than digital."

She lifted an eyebrow. Exaggerated comedy movement 334. I'd seen her practice it in the mirror when I was a kid.

She read through the file, nodding every now and again.

"What's the code?" I asked. I wanted to reach through the screen and grab it out of her hands. "No, don't tell me. Just send me a hard copy."

She fed it through the scanner. It took a few secs longer than I could stand. I ripped it out of the machine before it finished printing the last fancy border line.

"That's his code number written on the top," Ingrid said, pointing to it on her copy.

Number 8796632. Written in Ingrid's scrawl.

"I had a lot of trouble getting that number. As a client, I was only ever supposed to know his code name. Charles. I've always liked that name.

"Anyway, after a lot of legwork, I found out his number. My source told me it was linked to a hard file at the clinic which had his real name in it. But by the time I got the code, they'd destroyed the files. Standard procedure they said. I was this much too late." She measured the time between finger and thumb.

"Why didn't you tell me you tried?"

"I don't know. I suppose I didn't want to get your hopes up too much. You used to ask who your daddy was all the time. It nearly drove me crazy." She packed the jar of teeth back in the box. "Maybe I was just being chicken."

Her face was hidden by the fall of her hair. She picked up the holo unit, packing it away into the box, too.

"Louise said you comped me because you were afraid of being alone."

She jerked her head up.

"Louise hasn't changed a bit, hey?"

She laughed, roughly pulling the rabbit's ears through her fingers.

"Well, she doesn't know everything," she said. "You don't have a kid for a single reason. No one does anything for a single reason."

"But why did you comp me?"

"That's not an easy question, you know." She sighed. "I wanted you to have the best. I also wanted a kid to my own specifications. A bit stupid really, since all kids are up to chance. Even comps."

She dropped the rabbit into the box then snapped the top shut. Her hair obscured her face again as she fiddled with the lock.

"When you chose him, you checked out his genes and all that, didn't you?" I asked.

"Of course I did," she said. "I got the clinic to check out both our genes." She licked her lips. "Why? You're not sick or something are you?"

"No, I'm fine."

"I didn't think so. You come from good healthy stock."

She paused, her eyes flicking down the brief description of my father.

"You know, this sounds silly now, but one of the reasons I chose him was *Hamlet*. Look, he put it down as his favorite play. I thought you could trust a man who understands the 'To be or not to be' soliloquy."

"To be, or not to be—that is the question," I started. Ingrid joined in, her deep trained voice supporting mine.

"Whether 'tis nobler in the mind to suffer the slings and arrows of outrageous fortune or to take arms against a sea of troubles, and by opposing end them?"

She laughed. "I taught you well."

We looked at each other, eyes not quite meeting.

"I appreciate your help," I said awkwardly.

"I know," she said, wrapping her arms around her body. She suddenly looked a lot smaller.

"Take care of yourself," she said.

"I will." She'd taught me how to do that, too.

I cut the connection, slumping back in my chair.

The clinic file lay on the desk in front of me. The bare bones about my father. I picked it up.

DONOR CODE NAME: Charles. PROFESSION: scientist. EYE COLOR: brown. SKIN: medium. HAIR: black, straight. WEIGHT: 80 kg. HEIGHT: 178 cm. APPEARANCE: handsome, fit. PERSONALITY: vital, confident, warm. IQ: 280 on Saraen scale. HOBBIES: reading Shakespeare's plays (favorite—*Hamlet*), plays saxophone proficiently. BLOOD TYPE: A.

Hi Dad, whoever you are. Whatever you are. Ingrid couldn't find you. Mav couldn't find you. Maybe a spyder would track you down.

Are You Sure?

Lenny was pleased to see me.

"The birthday been good?" he asked, handing me a warm sake.

I so-soed with my hand.

"Ah, who needs birthdays anyway?" he said.

I threw back the sake. Yeow, it was the good import.

"You want another glass, or should I just give you the whole bottle?" Lenny asked drily.

I shook my head, waiting for the throat-burn to pass. One glass of brain damage was enough for me.

"Len, I need to get a spyder again," I said, when I got my voice back. "Actually, I want Blackwidow. Can you contact her?"

Lenny sucked his front teeth, holding his glass up to the light.

"It's not usual," he said, sipping the drink carefully. "They're not keen on being individually flagged. It makes it that much easier for the feds to track 'em. But I'll see what I can do." He looked at me slyly. "Maybe you won't need Blackwidow when you hear what I found out."

"You've got news about Suka?"

He touched the side of his nose.

"I told you the network would come through." He sipped again, watching over the rim.

"Well, come on."

"I couldn't get a name . . ." He paused, dragging it out. "But Suka is after an heir to some Centre shares. So it can't be your little alien friend."

My mind went into overdrive. Sunawa-Harrod had willed his forty percent share of the Centre to Camden-Stone. Suka was after an heir to Centre shares. Put two and two together and what do you get? A contract on Joseph Camden-Stone.

"Holy screte," I breathed.

"You got an idea?" Lenny asked.

"I gotta get going." I slid off the bar stool. At least one of the mysteries was solved.

"What about Blackwidow? You still want her?"

I pulled the copy I'd made of the clinic file out of my pocket.

"Here, if you get hold of her, ask her to find the name and any other info linked to that code number up at the top. Tell her the clinic was operating about nineteen years ago, at least."

Lenny took the paper. I ran towards the door.

"You going to pay her with kisses?" he called out.

"Can you cover me? I've got the money."

Lenny nodded, waving me away.

———

Although I didn't like Camden-Stone, I had to warn him about Suka. No one deserves to die because of some lousy shares. It was way too late to catch him at his office, but Donaldson-Hono might still be in the security hut.

The quickest way back to the uni was through Central and out through Mall 12. I was making good time until I dodged some people clustered around a fire juggler. Straight into a No-Sun woman. We both ended up flat on our backs. Her black-masked companion and I were helping her up from the pavement when I noticed a familiar face in the crowd. The steroid guy. Was it a coincidence? A paranoid freak like me doesn't know the meaning of the word. I took off again. Big guys like him usually can't run fast.

He kept up with me for a few kilometers until I dropped over the railing at Mall 10 onto the lower level. That fooled him. He went spinning along the top level towards the outer malls.

Donaldson-Hono was overseeing some security diagnostics in the security hut. He told me to wait by the lockers. The man was worried, a deep crease across his forehead. Finally he walked over to me, telling me to keep it short. I told him my conclusion.

"How do you know all this?" he asked, suspicion in every cell of his wiry little body.

"I heard it on the street," I said.

He snorted. "So one of your delinquent friends told you, huh?" He leaned across the counter. "Which one of them?"

"I have to protect my sources," I said. "If you don't believe me, don't check it out."

Donaldson-Hono licked his lips.

"Oh, I'll check it out all right."

That's all I needed to know.

Back at the suite, the computer told me I had two messages.

I flopped onto the couch.

"I'm too tired to move," I said.

"I can play them loud, or if you want to see them, project a 3D against the wall in front of you."

3D conference projection? This place had every gizmo you could ever want.

"Project."

I flinched when a huge Gazza appeared, a 3D mold on the wall. It was a good image too, although his skin looked a bit blue.

"This is a general memo to all Centre students," he said primly. "A memorial service for Professor Sunawa-Harrod will be held on Thursday at eleven A.M. All students are required to attend."

"On a happier note," he continued, summoning up a tight smile, "a cocktail party to celebrate Professor Camden-Stone's official appointment as director of the Centre will be held in the main hall on Friday between eight and nine P.M. This coincides with Professor Camden-Stone's fiftieth birthday. A donation for a gift has been added to all student's training fees. That is all."

Camden-Stone wasn't wasting any time. Memorial service one day, party the next. The last thing I wanted to do was contribute to a gift for him. I'd have to lodge a protest. If I was lucky, they'd ban me from the party.

"Next message," I said.

A 3D Lisa appeared.

"Hi Joss. I just heard about Mavkel. I hope he's okay. If you need any help or anything, just give me a call." She leaned forward, lowering her voice. "I think you already know Derry's not too keen on the Chorians, so just leave your name if he answers." She waved, pushing her long fringe out of her eyes with her other hand.

The projection disappeared.

Too bad she couldn't produce my father's name out of a hat. That was the kind of help Mav and I needed.

The next morning I was struggling through a chapter on time mechanics when Mav was escorted back to the suite. He looked really bad. Not a sparkle on his skin, and his ears were hanging like no-wind flags. His cold wasn't any better either. He sneezed three times as he walked in, each nose playing an off-key fanfare. Refmol was right; Mav was running out of time, and I was his last chance. But the whole idea of joining made me feel sick. There were so many unknowns. And deep down, I was also mad at Mav.

"Hello, Joss," he said, padding up in front of me.

I turned around and faced the other way. He sidestepped until he was in front of me again.

"Hello, Joss."

I grunted, keeping my eyes on my Reader.

He knelt, sticking his face in between me and the unit.

"I know not looking at me is rude," he said.

I dipped the Reader around his head, bringing it up to my face again.

"I know trying to get inside my head without asking is rude," I said.

He pulled away, sitting back on his rear claws.

"How did you know that?" he asked. "It was a secret."

"Refmol told me." I looked straight at him. "Where do you get off trying to get inside my brain without asking?"

"You said you would try the thought cube but you kept not trying."

"I tried."

"Not a true try. Five of your seconds is not a true try."

"You shouldn't have nagged me so much. *Joss, try thought cube, Joss try thought cube,*" I said in a screechy singsong voice.

Mav's ears were straight up and stiff. "You said you would try," he sang stubbornly.

"Then you just bulldozed right into my brain. You hurt me."

"I hurt you? I did not know you hurt."

"Some doctor you are."

"I did not mean to hurt you, I just try to join with you."

He touched my arm. A quick stroke. I shrugged his hand away.

"You didn't even ask me if I wanted to join. You didn't give me a choice."

"I see your truth now," he sang. "You do not want to pair."

"How am I supposed to know if I want to pair? I like being a single mind. It's what I'm used to." I turned to face him. "I've got my own plans! Things like jumping back to a Rogue Henry jam session by myself."

Mav watched me, his ears still.

"What's going to happen if we do join, Mav? Will I still want to see Rogue? Will I still be Joss?" I drew my knees up to my chest, circling my arms around them. "We don't even know if we can join."

"You are right," Mav sang. "We do not know." He pushed off the ground and sat next to me on the couch. His ears were flat again.

"Joss, I understand if you do not want to pair," he sang softly. "You should be one and I should be two."

I straightened up. "Don't you dare go all martyrish on me."

"I should have died with Kelmav."

"I don't want you to die, Mav." I squinted up at the ceiling. "It's just that . . . Refmol told me about this resonance thing. It scares the hell out of me. Do you understand that?"

"I understand," he sang. "I am scared of being a one."

He put his arm around my shoulder. The weight was comforting. We sat still, only Mav's sniffing breaking the silence.

"I've hired a spyder to look for my father," I finally said.

"You hired an insect with legs in many twos?"

I laughed. Too hard, but it was better than crying.

"No, a Net spyder. Someone who can find things other people can't. The spyder will find my Sulon."

"Thank you," Mav whispered.

Good Luck

We ended up being a couple of minutes late to our morning class, because Camden-Stone stopped me for a strange chat. He was giving instructions to Vaughn at the front desk as our mini army marched through. He called me over, telling Mav and the guards to wait at the door.

"Aaronson, I believe you discovered some information regarding my safety," he said, a strange smile twisting his little mouth.

"Yes, sir," I said.

"I just wanted to say thank you for your concern. It has confirmed a lot of my suspicions." The smile widened. "No doubt Mavkel is feeling more relaxed now."

He was watching my face intently.

"Yes he does, sir," I said.

"You can go to class now," he said. "Tell the sergeant to see me. I don't think your partner needs his chaperones anymore."

That was strange. Why was he taking off *all* the guards? There were still those twisto demonstrators out the front.

I walked up to the sergeant, feeling Camden-Stone's stare on my back. How did that poem go? Come into my parlor said the spider to the fly. Why did I feel like the fly?

Mav was studying the new violently colored virtual wall mural that had been installed. His ears were curled backwards, screaming distaste. For a being that had never heard of visual art, he was getting picky. I passed the message on to the sergeant then jogged up to the new art critic.

"Camden-Stone is stopping our guards," I said.

"Too bad," he sang. "I liked them. Sammy was going to teach me a game called poker."

After classes, Mav and I scanned our way back into P3. Vaughn called me over to the front desk.

"I'll meet you back in the rooms," I said to Mav. He nodded and walked into the virtual corridor. The wall closed behind him.

"Another package for you," Vaughn said. "You read a lot, huh?"

Blackwidow had delivered again.

I set a new land/speed record back to the suite.

"Mav, it's here," I yelled.

Mav poked his head around the doorway of our eating area. He was sucking one of his favorite food sticks. It looked like one of those old-fashioned cigars hanging out of his mouths.

"What is here?"

I mouthed "spyder." He ran over, his eyes wide and unshielded.

"Is the Sulon in there?" he jangled.

I held my finger to my lips. "I don't know," I whispered. "I just picked it up from the front desk. Come on." I pulled him into my bathroom.

"Shut the door," I said, kneeling on the tiles. Mav slapped his hand against the sensor pad.

The Reader was packed in Outerlock. My fingers were so sweaty I couldn't get a grip on it. "I can't get the damned thing open."

Mav snatched the package. He lifted a foot and ripped the pack open with his rear clawnail. A card fell out. I picked it up as Mav dealt with the rest of the packing.

"It says *'Good Luck.'*" I turned it over. Apart from those two words the front and back were blank.

Mav had finally got through to the Reader unit. He ran his hand along the side, flicking the switch.

"It is a story called *The Man Who Loved Children*. What do we do now?" he asked.

"The spyder's supposed to give you a key word, but I didn't talk to her. Lenny did."

Mav shook the unit.

"Quick. Go sound to Lenny," he said.

"Wait a minute." I turned the card over again. Spyders don't usually send cards. "Let me try a search on 'Good Luck.'"

Mav reluctantly let go of the unit. He leaned over my shoulder as I keyed in the search. We waited.

"It's working," I said.

Mav grabbed my shoulders, bouncing me up and down until my knees cracked.

The small screen rippled in purple. Then the color swirled, bunching up the words of the novel and draining them down the center of the screen as if it was a plug hole. One line appeared.

Donor No: 8796632

"That's him!" My finger smeared the screen. "That's my father."

Mav bent down closer. His ears were flapping so wide the right one kept hitting me in the side of the head. He ran one of his thumbs down the scroll sensor.

Donation 08/18/47 Usage:
Tangren-Poll, P: Gene: 564,332,887 Splice
    09/15/47
Dullam-Searle, C: Gene: 332,907 Splice 12/10/47
Aaronson, I: Full sperm donation. Fert 06/12/48

"What's fert?" Mav asked.

I counted out nine months on my fingers.

"I'd say it means fertilized. That's the date I was fertilized."

"But where's the Sulon name?"

"Wait, there's more stuff."

No digital record of name linked to No: 8796632.

Hard file stored at Newman Donation Clinic from
    06/05/43 to 06/05/54.
Incinerated 06/08/54.
End.

We stared at each other.

"One lousy name, and no one can find it." I hit the Reader screen. "Why the hell did they destroy the records?"

I wanted to go back to 06/08/54 and strangle the stupid idiot who had torched the med records. Just jump back and rip out his throat.

"There is no Sulon," Mav keened. The sound became a high-pitched screech. Unbearable in the small bathroom.

"Mav. Shut up." My bellow startled him out of his horror scream. "We can get the Sulon," I said, grabbing his forearms. "Don't you see. We can jump back. That's what we're here for. We can jump back in time!"

His ears shot straight up, stiff with joy.

"We can jump back in time!" he sang, bouncing up and down.

He pulled me to my feet, and we bounced and danced around the bathroom, laughing and yodeling. Suddenly, Mav caught me by the arm, stopping me mid-twirl.

"But we don't know how to do the jump," he wailed, his ears dropping flat.

Yes, there was that small problem. I stared at myself in the mirror, waiting for inspiration. It came.

"Lisa," I said.

"So will you do it?"

I had just spent an hour telling Lisa the whole story. We'd walked around the campus three times, but I figured we'd be safer on the move. Unless Lisa was bugged.

She sucked on the end of her braid.

"There's a lot of holes in your plan. A lot of big holes."

"That's why we need your help."

"For one thing, you don't even know how to operate a Jumper."

"I thought you said you could auto it."

"Of course I can, but what happens if something goes wrong? You wouldn't know an S.H. equation from a brick." She bit her lower lip. "Look, the Jumper only sits two, and the only way I can see this working is if I jump back with you instead of Mav. Otherwise, it's too risky."

"No, Mav has to be with me when I find out my father's name. It's called the point of knowledge or something. That's the only time he's able to get in my mind. It's his last chance."

"You really reckon learning your dad's name is going to make you two join minds? Sounds far-fetched to me." She shook her head.

"Yeah, I know it does. But we've got to try." I looked across the oval where a couple of guys were hand-passing a ball back and forth. "We've got to try," I repeated, hoping my own doubts would be pushed away if I said the words hard enough.

"All right, all right. No need to get frazzed." Lisa rubbed her forehead. "It's probably better if I back you up in the lab, anyway."

"So you'll do it?"

"We'd better start solving some problems, too. Like how are we going to bypass lab security? And have you thought of a way to explain an alien twenty years ago?"

"Are you saying you'll do it?"

She dropped the braid and shook my hand.

"Wouldn't miss it for a zillion creds."

Countdown

Two nights later, Lisa, Mav, and I met in my bathroom.

"Couldn't they forget to bug a room with a bit more ambience?" Lisa asked as she straddled the edge of the bather.

Mav was sitting on the toilet. He was shifting around uncomfortably until I pulled him to his feet and closed the toilet lid.

"Okay," Lisa said, calling us to order. "I did the usual research on landing time-location. About nineteen years ago, the Time Building wasn't finished yet, so you'll be landing in an open building site. That's why I think we should use T3; its lab is in the far corner, away from the other Centre buildings. It'll also be night, so that will give you some cover until you hide the Jumper."

"We're going to try and hide a Jumper?" It was going to take a lot of leaves and twigs to cover one of those snorkers.

"Camouflaging the machine is one of the first things you learn in second year," Lisa said, a bit pompously. "Don't worry, I'll show you how. I've got all the equipment in here."

She bent down and rummaged inside her backpack.

"I also think I've solved the problem of Mav," she said, her voice muffled.

"I am a problem?" Mav asked, bending down to look in the bag.

Lisa straightened up holding a pile of dark orange cloth and a white mask. Her face was flushed.

"I can't believe you got one of those," I said.

"What is it?" Mav picked the mask up and turned it over in his hands.

"It's a No-Sun robe and mask," Lisa explained to him. "They're a religious sect."

Mav stuck his fingers through the eye holes.

"No, look." Lisa took the mask back and held it up to her face. "You're going to have to disguise yourself because there weren't any Chorians around nineteen years ago. But the No-Suns have been around for at least thirty years."

"It's a great idea. How did you get your hands on it?" I asked.

Lisa took the mask off her face.

"Don't ask any questions and you won't hear any lies."

Fair enough. I was beginning to feel a lot better about the whole plan. If Lisa could swindle a No-Sun outfit and tell me to mind my own business, she could get me and Mav back in time.

Mav held the mask up to his face. He nudged me out of the way to look at himself in the mirror.

"The hood will hide your ears," Lisa said.

Mav insisted on a trial run of the whole outfit.

"This face thing hurts my noses," he complained, when I tightened the hood drawstring around his face.

I loosened it. Lisa and I looked at each other. She covered her mouth with her hand, not quite stopping a snort of laughter. That set me off. Mav looked at us through the eye slits, his ears flapping under the hood in disgust.

"It does the job, even if you do look a bit lumpy," Lisa said after she'd calmed down. "You'll also have to keep your hands hidden. Like a monk."

She pushed his hands up the opposite sleeves of his robe. Mav nodded. Then he pulled the mask off and started to fumble with the drawstring.

"There's really only one thing we haven't got covered. And it's a biggie," Lisa said, folding up the hood Mav had draped on the toilet lid.

"The security setup," I said.

She nodded. "We've got to override the security system. Any ideas?"

"All I can think of is busting it." I shrugged, spreading my hands.

"That will set off the alarms and I don't fancy getting a couple of neuro needles in the neck. Any other ideas?"

"How about . . ." I started, but shook my head. Seducing Donaldson-Hono for the override code wasn't a goer either.

"Refmol will help," Mav said. He swished the cloak Spanish dancer style around his body as he took it off.

"How could Refmol help us?" I asked.

"Refmol has dip-lo-matic im-mun-ity," Mav said, sounding it out carefully.

Lisa leaned forward. "This could be good. This could be very good. But why would Refmol help us?"

Mav looked at me and his ears gave a tiny twitch. We both knew why Refmol would help us.

"Mav's right. Refmol will do it," I said.

Lisa stood up.

"Are you sure?" she asked. "If Refmol says no, then we're lasered. Refmol might even rat on us."

"Refmol knows about secrets. Refmol will help," Mav sang firmly, bouncing on his heels.

"Then you ask Refmol for the override codes for the time labs and T3," Lisa said. Then she paused. "Actually, Refmol's going to have to scan it in, too, or else the whole diplomatic immunity stuff is gone. If Refmol says okay to all that, we're in business."

She held out her hand, flat in the air. The traditional seal for a street deal. I covered it with mine.

"Come on, Mav, give me your hand," I said.

I placed his hand over Lisa's and mine.

"Just like the Three Musketeers," Lisa said wryly. "All for one, and one for all."

"No that is wrong," Mav sang. "All for the pair and the pair for all."

Mav and Lisa left the suite together. Mav returned an hour later.

"Refmol agrees to mind-scan your security Elder. We will have the codes in twenty-four hours," he sang softly in my ear. Then he sneezed.

The following day, the memorial service for Sunawa-Harrod was running late. We'd been ordered at ease while a technical hitch was being fixed. I stood on my toes, scanning the milling crowd of time-jumpers and technicians, all in identical dress uniforms.

"I still can't see her," I said.

"Seek her pair. He will stand above all," Mav sang.

Good thinking. I scanned the courtyard for Derry. Nothing. Time to try a section by section search again. Finally, a group of fourth years broke their tight huddle around a bench. Derry and Lisa came briefly into view before the group reformed around them. No wonder I hadn't seen them before.

"Got her," I said.

We walked towards the bench. A lot of people were making a point of moving out of Mav's way. I caught a few ugly looks, and threw them right back. Mav's ears were at alert level. It still didn't make sense that Camden-Stone had stopped all our guards. Not when there were so many bad attitudes still around. At least Chaney was leaving us alone. He had obviously taken Camden-Stone's threat to heart and was keeping a very low profile.

"We'll wait here," I said to Mav. "You keep an eye on everyone."

I turned my back on the courtyard to face Lisa. She was playing it cool, but whenever she laughed her eyes searched the crowd. Someone in her group finished a joke, the upward beat of their voice reaching me. Lisa threw back her head to laugh and our eyes met. Her acknowledgment was barely more than a blink.

A general announcement shuddered through the courtyard, ordering us back into our class formations. The technical problem was fixed.

"She's seen us," I whispered.

Her group started to move towards the Donut doors. Lisa dropped to her knee to fiddle with her bootlace. She waved Derry to go on. When he turned to go, I grabbed Mav's arm and we walked slowly towards her.

"Refmol has the code," I said in a low voice.

She nodded, still hunched over her boot. "It's tomorrow night then. We'll meet outside the lab building. Eight-thirty sharp. Everyone else will be at Camden-Stone's reception."

She stood up, slapping the dust off her knees. Then she jogged up to Derry without looking back.

"Tomorrow night," Mav repeated, his ears dipping. "Now I fear two things. Being one and time-moving."

"I thought you Chorians liked things in pairs," I said.

Mav laughed. Seven on the hysterical scale.

Twenty-four hours is only 1,440 minutes or 86,400 seconds. It can also be a lifetime.

I was sitting on my bathroom floor surrounded by the time-jumping equipment Lisa had given me.

Four portable holo projection units with remote control.

Three stun stakes.

Countdown wristwatch.

Color frequency goggles.

About this time tomorrow night, I'd be using them to hide a time machine and break into a sperm clinic. I was either mad or desperate. Probably both.

I placed the four holo units to form a small square, putting the goggles in the middle. A flick of a remote switch. The goggles disappeared leaving a black smudge stretched between the four units. If you scale this idea up, you've got a fair idea of how we were going to hide the Jumper. A large black haze wouldn't be noticeable in the middle of the night. And even if someone did get nosy, there were always the stun stakes. Triangular formation force field. Stuns a trespasser for up to six hours. Not as sophisticated as the fruz-field that I got caught in, but good enough. For a non-interference academic pastime, time traveling was pretty violent. I turned the projection unit off and slid the holo units back into their softpack.

I added a tiny lock overrider to the pile of equipment. Lenny had given it to me last year for my birthday. It opened any security door except light-scanners, and they didn't have them nineteen years ago. I was also going to take my new harp. For luck. We were going to need all we could get.

That was the fourth check I'd done on the equipment. You can't be too careful or too paranoid. I'd also memorized Lisa's instructions. I was ready. At least for the physical stuff.

The last thing I packed into the carrybag was my father's file description. It was getting crumpled now like Ingrid's card. Tomorrow I'd find my father's name. I kept trying to tell myself it would just be a name on a piece of paper. Yeah, in the same way a death warrant is just a name on a piece of paper.

The Jump

Friday night. Eight twenty-five P.M.

Mav and I were waiting in the shadows outside the Time Building. Mav was draped in the No-Sun robes. He hadn't put on the mask yet. Didn't want to sneeze inside the face thing. I was bouncing on my toes. The carrybag slung over my shoulder thumped against my hip bone.

"Where are they?" I whispered. A weird feeling was frissing the back of my neck.

"They will come." Mav ran one of his thumbs around the drawstring hood.

"You're early," Lisa said, stepping out of a shadow. Mav jumped, his thumb claw pulling the hood over his eyes.

"I want to get this over and done with," I said. "Something doesn't feel right."

"What do you mean?"

I shifted the bag onto my other shoulder. "It just seems like the whole deal's a bit easy. I mean everyone's at the reception so we've got a clear run. And Refmol got the over-ride code overnight. Too easy."

"You just don't recognize luck when you see it," Lisa said. The light from the door's scan tube highlighted her frown. "It wasn't easy getting those robes. And it sure as hell wasn't easy checking all of the equipment out of the stores."

To my left a flash of metallic cloth flared against the shadows. Refmol. I ran my finger over the scabbed scrapes on my knuckles where I had hit the Chanter. It seemed eons ago. I hoped Refmol had forgiven me.

Its ears were doing some kind of aural scan as it walked up to us. It bowed to Mav and Lisa. I tensed. Had I lost Refmol's support? But then it turned to me.

"You bring much honor to your bloodlines, Joss Aaronson, whatever they may be," it sang.

Mav made an exultant sound and I felt his hard-skinned hand briefly touch my ear.

"Come, let us move smoothly," Refmol said.

It stepped onto the door scanner pad. The tube closed around it, abruptly extinguishing the light. Two beats later it opened again.

"Entrance not authorized," the security computer said.

Refmol braced itself. Keeping its secondary mouth closed, it carefully said, "Security override G Alpha Zed 213809." Its voice was a tight monotone. Imitation human.

"Security override recognized."

The inner door of the tube slid open. Next to me Lisa exhaled dramatically.

"Refmol must have practiced that a lot," she whispered as we walked into the building.

The long central corridor was dim, the only light coming from the security scan pads outside the four time lab doors. At the T3 door, Refmol repeated the override code.

"Security override recognized. Security levels A, B, and C are now non-operational."

We were in. Lights flickered on.

The room was a carbon copy of the T2 lab. Lisa pushed forward, heading for the large console. I walked over to the Jumper.

The fruz-field over T3 had been deactivated with the rest of the security. I reached over and skimmed my hand across T3's surface. Soft metal to allow for the time stretch. It was so beautiful. Like the skin of a dolphin.

"Refmol, you've got to override this lock so I can set up the jump."

Lisa's voice cracked my trance.

I turned back to T3 as Refmol hurried over to the console.

"Mav, come and feel this," I said. I placed his hand on the machine's body. "Soft metal," I said. "And this plasglass is the toughest stuff in the world, but it's still flexible. Even better than Rokwain. Nothing will get through it."

Mav tapped the cabin with a thumb claw.

Something moved in my peripheral vision. I jerked my head around, staring at the four deactivated wall crawlers above the console. Not a twitch between them. I could have sworn one of them had moved. Talk about jumpy.

"Joss, Mav. Come here." Lisa beckoned us over to the

main console. "Give me the date and time you're going back to. I've got to punch it into the T3 matrix." Her tone was professional, but her movements were nervy quick.

I felt inside the front pocket of the carrybag and found the copy of Blackwidow's clinic information. "That date," I said, pointing down to the day I'd been fertilized.

"You'll put down at 9 P.M. It will be dark by then." She punched a final key, then ran her fingers through her hair.

"Okay. The matrix is set." She looked up from the console. "You've got to remember that although we'll be using the S.H. field to go back and anchor you in the past, time itself is going to snap T3 back to where it belongs. So by my calculations you've only got six hours, eight minutes, and eleven seconds in the past. If you're not in T3 when the snap happens, you're stuck. Got it?"

"Six hours, eight minutes, and eleven seconds." I counted forward. "That means we'll have till 3:08 A.M."

"Don't cut it as fine as that. We usually give ourselves at least five minutes leeway. There's a clock in the Jumper here but I'll set your wrist countdown watch to give you an alarm." She pushed my jacket sleeve off the watch and locked in the alarm time.

She checked the console again, her fingers held against her mouth. Then she nodded.

"Be back by 3:00 A.M. That'll be plenty of time." She shook her fringe off her face and smiled tightly. "Let's get you two strapped in and jumping."

The cabin of T3 was as roomy as a pair of slink-jeans.

I wondered how Derry managed to fold himself up into a Jumper. Maybe that's why Lisa was so small. Counterbalance. As it was, Mav and I were pretty squashed, our legs jammed under a bank of displays. I only recognized the flashing jump date/time readout, the oxygen levels and the return countdown clock. Everything else was the stuff of technical nightmares.

"Do you understand all these readouts?" I asked Lisa.

"Yep, but it's taken four years of study," she said as she snapped my harness closed. "Don't worry about them. Just follow my instructions, don't touch anything and keep your eye on your wrist countdown."

"And everything will be all right. Right?"

"Right." We looked at each other, acknowledging how unright this whole thing could be. Lisa squeezed my shoulder and smiled.

"Are you ready?" she asked.

I gave her the thumbs up, then brushed my hand over the harp in my top pocket for luck.

"Mav?"

"Ready," he trilled, and held up his four thumbs.

"Then return in good time." She slammed the cabin hatch shut. Immediately the faint techno noises of the console room were cut off.

Mav looked over at me, his eyes unshielded and huge. "I feel fright," he said. I grabbed his hand tightly.

Lisa walked back to the main console where Refmol was waiting. Refmol asked her something and she nodded. Then the Chanter bowed to us. Very low and very elaborate. It looked like the Chorian equivalent of "those about to die, we salute"! My gut suddenly cramped and my mouth went dry. What was I doing here? I must be mad.

Lisa had warned us about the jump. She'd explained about The Nothing; the void that you slide through when you go back in time. She'd said a jump was never longer than ten seconds and to remember that when you want to scream and crack open the cabin door. Just keep your eyes closed and count out loud, she'd said. And hold onto each other.

Mav hooked his arm through mine. Lisa was counting down the seconds on her upheld fingers, mouthing the numbers. There was no whine of machinery or shuddering of power. Only heavy breathing. Mav's and mine. Lisa held five fingers up. Mav closed both sets of lids. Four fingers up. I tightened my grip on the safety strap. Three fingers up. Two fingers. Something wasn't right. There was the shadow of a person at the lab door. I yelled, pointed at it, but my hand was tangled in the strap. Who was it? Had security sprung us? Lisa held her forefinger up. Her mouth formed the word "One." Then the lab was gone. We were in The Nothing.

The soft-metal body of T3 rippled and spread out like a face hit by G-forces. The plasglass cabin elongated around us, washing outwards in waves. Mav's arm convulsed against mine. I looked across. Layers and layers of Mav spread across time. Genes, eggs, young Mavs, my Mav with closed eyes bulging, aging Mavs, dead Mavs curled and shrunken. Then I saw my own arm, embryo to skeleton, and I screamed. Kept on screaming until there was no more air. Blood surging in my ears, ready to explode. Heartbeat shaking my body.

Then I heard Mav sneeze.

The Nothing slid away. The layers of Mavs concertinaed into one Mav. I gulped for air, but it was too late. I passed out.

"Joss?"

My head was bumping against something hard.

"Joss, open your lids."

Mav's two noses came into focus. He was shaking me.

"Stop it. My head hurts."

He pulled back, stroking my forehead.

"You have been asleep a long time. We must move now, Joss. We are here. We have moved in time."

I tried to sit forward but bounced back in the seat. Harness. I squinted, fumbling with the buckle. Mav was already free. Through the plasglass window behind him, the sky was night-blue. A half-finished wall blocked any other view.

"Are you well now, Joss?" Mav asked, zooming in for a closer look.

I looked at the T3 countdown clock. I'd been out cold for over three hours. Screte, we only had about three hours left. What if it wasn't long enough?

"I'm fine. Let's get going."

The buckle released. I sat forward, dragging at the carry-bag under my legs. It wouldn't budge, so I cracked the cabin seal and pushed open the door. Air rushed in. My ears popped: a sharp pain that got rid of any grogginess. We pulled ourselves out of the cramped space, stepping onto gravel and sand. I reached back into the cabin and pulled out the bag. Mav was standing very still. Listening.

"The move was very strange," he sang.

"You're not kidding. I saw some mega weird stuff."

"I did not see mega weird stuff as you say. My lids were closed. But the sounds were not good." His ears flicked down.

"That's even weirder. I didn't hear a thing. I just saw . . ." then I remembered the shadow. "Hey, did you see someone at the lab door before we jumped?"

"No, my lids were closed. Who did you see?"

I put the bag on the ground. Mav squatted down, hands busy with the cling clasps.

"I dunno. It was just a shadow." I rubbed my arms. My whole body was suddenly cold. "Maybe it was the guards. I hope Lisa and Refmol are okay. They could be in real trouble. Maybe we should go back and help them?"

Mav looked up at me, one of the holo units in his hand.

"You forget what Lisa told us. When we return we will arrive at exactly the moment we left. No time will have gone so nothing will have happened."

I knelt beside him. He was right, but I was still worried.

Who was it at the door? The worst possible scenario was Camden-Stone. Please, don't let it be Camden-Stone.

The holo units and stun stakes didn't take long to set up. I checked my countdown watch against the clock in T3. They were still synchronized. I closed the cabin hatch and stepped back. Mav flicked the switch on the stun stakes then activated the holo units with the remote. A few seconds later, T3 was covered by a black splodge in the middle of the half-built room. About nineteen years on, Lisa and Refmol were standing in the same room, maybe even in the same place. I had a feeling they were in even more danger than we were.

Bless You

Mav and I had to cut across the campus to reach the Newman Clinic. We kept to the shadows, avoiding the occasional night student by ducking into alleys or behind buildings. Mav was having a hard time breathing under the mask. Every now and again he sniffed noisily, as if he was holding back a sneeze. He was getting slower and slower. Finally, as we passed a tiny park, he grabbed my arm.

"Stop here. I must get proper air," he panted.

He sat heavily on a bench, pulling the mask away from his face. I paced the edge of the park. It was just a few trees, the bench, and a fountain, one of those gray stone cupids peeing water. I couldn't work out what it was in our time. Then it finally clicked. This park was where P3 would be built in about eighteen years' time. It made my brain kink trying to keep the times in order. In this time Donaldson-Hono was still bullying other kids at high school, Camden-Stone still had his own face, and Vaughn wasn't even out of nappies. To top it all off, I was sitting in a petri dish half a klick away, meiosizing all over the place.

I squatted down in front of Mav. He was looking a bit better—a healthy dead white.

"You okay now?" I asked.

He nodded, trying to summon up a tiny double smile. I patted his knee.

"Come on then, let's get going." I pulled him to his feet. We had to keep moving. *I* had to keep moving or else the doubts would catch up.

The Newman Clinic was a small building hidden behind the university bio-genetic labs. A little card on the ground outside its double plasglass doors told me that the SafeAs Security Company was proud to protect these premises. They may have been proud, but they weren't very good. The door lock was only a basic code scanner. My tiny lock overrider opened it in less than five seconds. Mav snorted his approval beside me. I slipped on the color frequency goggles. SafeAs were definitely amateurs. Only three light beams crossing the foyer at thigh level. All we had to do was crawl across the floor to the fancy transparent reception desk.

"I take this face thing off now," Mav said, pulling the fastening band free. "No one will see me."

He opened and shut his mouths in a series of jaw-crunching stretches.

"Are my noses flat?" he asked. He felt along his four nose ridges.

"You're beautiful. Come on, get inside."

I shut the door behind us and placed the overrider on the internal lock pad. The lock clicked back into place. That would take care of any delay alarms SafeAs might have installed in a fit of efficiency. I pushed Mav down onto the ground, kneeling beside him.

"There's three trip beams across the foyer," I said.

"I know," he interrupted. "I can see them."

"You can see infra-red without goggles?"

"Of course. Can't you?"

"No." I snapped the goggles back over my eyes and dropped onto the floor, my head cranked back to keep an eye on the beams. I beat Mav to the desk by a short half head. I may be infra-blind, but I'm fast.

According to the polished brass sign on the desk, reception was the domain of Nurse Gregory Salway. He was a very tidy person. By the looks of it he used a ruler to line up his notebooks. The good side to all this screaming neatness was the carefully labeled codekeys hanging from a line of hooks. Toilets. Kitchens. Storeroom. Laboratory.

File room.

My gut clenched, right down to the exit sign in my undies.

Mav was watching the front door. His ears were stretched out to their fullest under the hood.

"Someone comes," he whispered.

Screte, SafeAs were more conscientious than I'd thought.

I crouched down behind the desk. Mav bobbed down beside me. The theory was good, but the desk was see-through. I stood up again. There was nowhere to hide in the reception area, not even a friendly potted plant. Mav pulled himself back onto his feet.

"What are you doing?" he asked.

"We've got to hide."

He reached over and quickly snagged a key off its hook.

"Good idea," I said, scooping up all the other keys. "Get going."

Mav dropped to the ground and wriggled into the foyer. I was so close behind I had to dodge his rear claws. A hover door slammed shut outside. We had a choice of two corridors. Mav chose right. I followed.

He stood up as soon as we were out of the foyer.

"No light lines here," he whispered.

I ran to the first door on my left, waving my hand frantically in front of the sensor. Locked. I pressed all the code-keys against the scan pad. Nothing.

Mav ran up ahead to the door at the end of the corridor. I tried my keys on the next door. Nilch.

"Joss," Mav hissed, "I've opened a lab."

I was beside him in a nano-sec. We both jumped as a loud click echoed from the foyer. The guard was inside. I could see a circle of torchlight scan the reception desk, flaring on Greg's brass sign.

A woman's voice said, "I'm in now, Jeff. Turn the infrareds off at your end, will ya?"

Mav grabbed my sleeve and pulled me into the lab. The door shut behind us. We were in complete darkness.

"Which one of these buttons is the lock?" Mav's voice was so low it was a vibration.

By the time I'd turned around to face the door, I could see clearly. I pressed down the lock then turned back to find a hiding place.

The laboratory was a standard setup. Four benches in a row with stools, VR hoods, and screens. At the end of each bench, a long-limbed machine hung from the ceiling like a limp orangutan. Three of the walls were lined with storage units. The fourth wall had a transparent security door embedded in it with a sign across the top that read:

INCUBATOR A
AUTHORIZED PERSONNEL ONLY
ENVIRONMENTAL CODE 6

A muffled slam sounded down the corridor. Mav hissed under his breath. The damn security guard was checking every room. Just when you needed a bit of negligence, along comes Ms. Conscientious.

"We gotta get out of sight," I whispered.

Mav opened a storage unit. Trays of petri dishes were stacked a few centimeters apart. I touched him on the shoulder. Pointed to the incubator room. He nodded, holding up a warning finger.

"There is a light line across the doorframe."

The door was reinforced Rokwain with a punch-code lock. I smiled. It was the same as buying a Rottweiler then pulling out all its teeth. I fitted the overrider onto the pad. I could hear the security guard cough. She must have been in the next room. Mav gripped my shoulder.

We both sighed when the lock finally clicked open. Mav went in first, tracing the line of the infra-red with his fingers.

We were in a tiny booth made up of the clear Rokwain door and the inner door. If the guard came in, we were still snorked. We had to get into the next room. I pushed the overrider against the inner swipe pad. It beeped: too hard. I eased off. As the door jumped open, a large hologrammatic sign flashed at eye level:

WARNING
INCUBATOR ROOM MUST BE MAINTAINED AT:
37 CELSIUS
03 LIGHT
3:1 OXYGEN

We stepped through the sign, its reds and yellows sparking off Mav's skin. The door closed behind us.

Dim light came from two swing-arm lights positioned above a long machine against the back wall. It looked like a foodie except the display window showed petri dishes instead of Chicken Kievs. The air was so warm it felt fluffy going through my nose and into my lungs. Mav sighed with pleasure.

"This is better weather," he sang softly.

He shook his head, flinging it back to breathe deeply. His eyes bulged. He squeezed his noses together, but it was too late.

The sneeze was like a full brass fanfare. We both froze, listening, but my heartbeat was pounding my ears deaf.

"I think we're all right," I finally said. "This room's probably soundproof."

"Sorry," Mav gasped.

"Try and control yourself, would you?"

I pressed myself against the door, inching my face across to the tiny observation window in the middle. The guard was silhouetted against the lab doorway. She scanned the room with her flashlight. The bright circle zigzagged across the storage units then swung towards me. I pulled back, signing for Mav to keep still. Our window flickered with light. The edge of the incubator glinted. I counted to ten. My breath dewed the door, wetting my cheek as I edged back to the window. The lab was empty. The door was closed

"She's gone," I said. "We're okay, she's gone."

I looked back. Mav was bent over the incubator.

"Joss, come see what I see," he said urgently.

"Did you hear me? She's gone."

"Yes, yes, but see what is here."

He tapped his finger on the incubator window. I leaned over his shoulder. All I saw was a line of petri dishes with labels.

"So?"

"No. Look at that one."

I pushed his finger off the plasglass so that I could read the label.

AARONSON/8796632

Holy screte.

Mav opened the hatch door and snaked his arm across the tray. He pulled out my dish, held between his two thumbs.

I grabbed his arm. "What are you doing?"

"This is very exciting," he said, easing the close-fitting top off the dish. "We are honored to see the beginning."

"Put it back. You'll drop it or something."

I tried to grab the dish, but he snatched it away and held it level to his noses, studying the glob of clear jelly in it.

"I saw movement," he said.

I bent closer. All I could see was a bit of goo. Mav half snorted. I looked up. His head was back, the muscles in his jaw straining to stop the inevitable. I reached for the dish, but the sneeze beat me to it.

"You stupid snorkwit! Look what you've done."

A glomp of snot had hit the jelly.

Mav was staring at the dish. He whirled around to the workbench, pulling down the nano-scope.

"We must look. Quick, put it in the view thing." He thrust the petri dish into my hands. "Put it in the view thing."

I fumbled, then slid it into the viewing slot. Mav held the goggles up to his eyes.

"I can't believe you snotted in my dish," I wailed.

Mav held up his hand.

"No. Be still." His voice was professional. "Yes. Yes. It is happening."

"What? What's happening?"

Mav passed the goggles to me. I held them up to my eyes.

"Do you see?" he sang happily.

Biology 101 came back to me in a rush. I was looking at a group of cells in the middle of a meiosis split. At the corner was a dark smudge of something else. A stranger working its way through the membrane.

"What's the dark thing?" I asked.

"It is your resonance," Mav sang. "You are of the Mav line. You are of me!"

The Point of Knowledge

The dark smudge broke through the cell wall, glooping in like oil dropped in water. I lowered the goggles. Mav was beaming the widest double smile I'd ever seen.

"You are of me," he repeated, his ears vibrating with excitement.

"You're saying I'm made out of your snot," I said.

Then a hyena cackle rolled up from my gut. Mav stepped back as wave after wave of sobbing laughs doubled me over. I hung on to the edge of the bench.

"Joss, what is wrong. Are you not well?"

"I'm made out of your snot," I gasped, each breath caught in the one before.

"What is this thing snot?"

I wiped my eyes and hiccupped.

"It's the stuff that comes out of your noses."

"Ah, I see. But you are not made of this snot, you are made of your gene material." He picked up the second pair of goggles and motioned me towards my pair. "Look, you can see the pairing of your Sulon/Sulo cells. My snot joins it like a grain of sand joins the desert."

A vision of sticky green dunes and camels with their feet

stuck jumped into my mind. I clamped my jaw and concentrated on the science.

"So your snot must have some DNA in it, right?"

"Of course. But only an insy-winsy bit as your slang-sounds say."

The insy-winsy nearly broke me up again. I took a deep breath.

"Doesn't that make you sort of my Sulon?"

Mav stopped smiling. He leaned forward so fast that I thought he was going to headbutt me. I pulled back. His face came back into focus, eyes wide, ears high.

"Please join with me," he whispered. I nodded.

He cupped his hand around the back of my head, the thumbs cradling my neck. Gently, he placed his forehead onto mine.

I closed my eyes. A sharp pain speared through my right temple. A burst of red behind my eyes. I frowned against it. Mav sighed, his breath hot on my chin and neck. I felt his fingers lightly brush my forehead. A soft touch of regret.

"No. There must not be enough of me in you. The Sulon must still be found."

"In the file room," I said. I touched my temple. The pain had gone.

"Yes. We will join in the file room." His unshielded eyes searched mine.

I know I should have kept eye contact. Showed him my belief that we would succeed in joining. But I turned away, sliding the petri dish out of the viewing slot.

"Joss?" he sang.

I stared at the gluey mound in the glass dish. That jelly was going to grow into me. It would be born, get chucked out of twelve schools, learn to make plum sauce, play the blues. Then, when it was eighteen and standing in a hot incubator room, it would be torn by doubt and the terrible choice between saving its friend and risking its whole identity.

"The Mav line is honored by your blood," Mav sang softly.

The temperature gauge on the incubator read 37.6 degrees, but I felt very cold.

The file-room door didn't have any trip beams across it. I fanned the tangle of codekeys out on my palm, squinting at the tiny labels. Mav looked over my shoulder, his body pressed against my back. Too close. His high-pitched hum vibrated through my body. I leaned away, turning over the last key label. *File room.* Mav exhaled a long hissing breath. I pressed the key onto the scan pad, my whole weight against it.

The door opened. An overhead light clicked on automatically. I blinked, covering my eyes with my hands. The small windowless room smelled of moth wings and chocolate. I separated my fingers, tensing against the slices of light.

A metal carousel full of files took up most of the room. Clamped to the carousel's fixed central strut was a robot with ten long search-arms. A selector console stood against the wall next to the recyc shute. Someone had left a Tutti Bar wrapper on the floor. Milk hazelnut. My favorite.

Mav pushed past me. He peered at the file compartments in the carousel, poking a finger into one of the thin openings.

"I cannot see the numbers," he sang. He jammed in two fingers, pulling at a file. "It does not move. How do we see the numbers?"

"We use that," I said, pointing to the selector.

The console was basic: key in the number and press go. I pressed the power button. The programming diagnostic flicked across the tiny screen. It beeped, prompting the first file request. I licked my lips and carefully keyed in 8796632.

Nothing happened. I looked around at the robot. Dead. What was wrong? Mav grabbed the central strut and shook it, rumbling his frustration. The console beeped again, flashing a message.

Press enter for file request.

Good one, Joss. I hit the enter key.

"It's okay. It'll work now," I said. "Stand back."

The carousel moved slowly around. The robot's search-arms swung across the compartments, scanning the numbers. It looked like a spider hit by a bug-o-sonic wave.

Then it all stopped. One of the top arms slid into a file slit, pulling out a green plasform folder. The robot flipped upside down until the top arm was level with Mav's chest. He pulled the file from the outstretched claw.

I tried to ask if it was the right file, but my throat had closed up. I swallowed and tried again.

"Yes, it is the file of your Sulon," Mav said, nodding.

"You read it, Mav." I tightened my grip on the edge of the console and closed my eyes, waiting to hear the name of my father.

"No," Mav said. He walked over to me, the folder flat on his palms. "You must be the first to know the name of your Sulon. Then we can join at the point of knowledge."

He pushed the hinged folder against my chest until I took it. I brushed my fingertips across the number etched onto the top of it. Dad. I could still back out. Then I knew that this jump back in time was not only for Mav, it was for me, too. Whatever happened I had to open that file. I had to know my father.

"Okay. Ready?" I asked.

Mav moved in front of me, his face close to mine, his hands on my shoulders. He nodded. One of us was shaking.

I flicked the snib off the edge of the folder. The hinge was stiff as I opened the green cover. There was only one typed page. My eyes flicked over the words and numbers, scanning for a name.

They found one.

DANIEL SUNAWA-HARROD.

I looked up at Mav. He grabbed the back of my head and pulled my face towards his. I yelped as bone hit bone. My hands were jammed against my chest under the folder. Mav pulled me even closer, his top nose ridges digging into my forehead. I tried to pull away. I needed space. The folder fell to the ground. My father's name pounded through my mind in a duet that pushed and tore and burned. "I can't do it,"

I yelled. The words *stay with me* sang in my ears, but they weren't made of sound. They were pale green, soothing. Suddenly a fireball of pain roared over them. Mav screamed and let go of me. He hit the ground. I fell onto my hands and knees beside him.

I couldn't move for a long while. Couldn't think. Mav was making a soft mewling noise, but all I could do was stare at the gray carpet. Any movement was agony. Even blinking.

"Joss?" Mav finally croaked. He rolled onto his side to face me.

"It didn't work, did it?" I said.

"No, it did not work." He struggled to sit up using the wall as a prop.

I eased backwards until I was kneeling on my heels. Pain dug in behind my eyes.

"It was my fault," I said. "I should have tried harder."

"If you had tried any harder, your brain would have burst." Mav threw his hands up in the shape of a small explosion.

"There's got to be something else we can do."

"No, there is nothing. I will join Kelmav. It should have happened long ago," he sang calmly. Under the hood, his ears dropped.

"No! We can try and join again. Let's just rest a bit then we'll have another go."

Mav reached over and took my hand.

"I did not have the strength to break through, Joss. That was the last try."

"Don't say that." I gripped his hand tighter. "We'll try again. Come on. Do it." I pulled him towards me.

"No," Mav sang flatly, shaking my hand away.

"What do you mean, no? Are you just going to sit there and die?" I struggled up onto my feet.

"Not right here. Later."

"Great. Well don't forget to tell me when you decide on a time. Just so I know not to schedule anything important."

I turned around sharply, smashing my thigh into the edge of the console.

"Screte!" I kicked the console stand, slamming my hand against the edge of the panel. It rocked. I hit it again. My breath shuddered into a sob so deep it hurt.

"Joss!" Mav stood up. He grabbed my fists, pushing them down.

"Let me go," I said, trying to pull out of his deadlock hold.

"You will hurt yourself."

"Who cares?"

"I do. You are my friend."

I stopped straining against his hands.

"But I let you down."

"We tried. It did not work. That is the way it will be sung."

"So, all of this was for nothing."

"It has not been for nothing," Mav said. "You have found your Sulon and I have found a ..." He tilted his head, then smiled. "I do not know what blood you are to me, Joss. But I honor it."

He released my wrists, gripping my hands in the Chorian friendship clasp.

"I'm honored to be of your line, too," I said, and I really meant it. I squeezed his hands, then let go, wiping my eyes on my sleeve.

"Now you know all of your bloodlines," Mav sang.

I looked at the green folder on the floor. Daniel Sunawa-Harrod was my father. I could hardly believe it. The guy who'd cheated Camden-Stone, developed time-travel, and set up the Centre was my father! Would he want to see me? I thought of his holo portrait. I even looked a bit like him. Then I remembered the scar on his head and the memorial service.

"He's dead," I said. "I'm too late. He's dead."

I slumped against the console, my face turned away. I frowned at the gold musical notes on the Tutti Bar wrapper, willing the tears away.

Mav's robes rustled behind me.

"Is Kings College near this place?" he asked

"It's on the other side of the campus," I said, turning around. He was holding the folder open, one of his thumbs marking a place on the page.

"Then we go there now."

"Why?"

"Because Daniel Sunawa-Harrod is not dead in this time."

Party Animals

Flat three at Kings College was thumping with the original jazz-rock version of "Pump Mama." A woman's voice cut through the guitar solo, whooping an Indian war cry.

"Are you sure he lives in flat three?" I asked Mav.

"That's what the file read," Mav said, nodding. He suddenly sneezed, and the No-Sun mask slipped sideways. He pushed it back in place, then slid his hands back up his sleeves.

"Okay, here goes," I said. I stepped onto the scan pad.

The door slid open. A tall woman with spiky black hair squinted down at us.

"You can't come in without a present," she said. "You got a present for Susie?"

"No. We just want to see Daniel Sunawa-Harrod."

But she had already hit the shut button. The door slid closed.

"What do we do now?" Mav asked.

The door slid open again. It took me two blinks to recognize the young Joseph Camden-Stone standing in front of me.

"Sorry about that," he said. "Maggie's a bit far gone."

His face was gentler than the Camden-Stone I knew. His mouth was more generous, the corners permanently turned upwards like a dolphin. The surgeons who would later reconstruct his face would get everything right except that mouth.

"Sorry, do I know you?" he asked. His eyes widened as he noticed Mav in the No-Sun robes.

"Actually, we've come to see Professor Sunawa-Harrod," I stammered.

"Professor? Don't you mean Doctor?"

"Yes, that's right."

"Are you a student of his?"

"No. I'm . . . I'm a relative."

"Oh, okay. Well, he's in here somewhere." He motioned us into the hallway. A new song started to boom. "I'm afraid you've caught us in the middle of a party," he yelled, making his way up the corridor.

We followed him, a pathway clearing as people caught sight of Mav's mask. We entered the crowded kitchen area. A large banner was strung across the wall. It read HAPPY 30TH, SUSIE. The thrum of a dozen conversations suddenly stopped. Mav shifted uncomfortably beside me.

"Hey, has anyone seen Danny?" Camden-Stone asked.

"I think he's in his bedroom," a tanned woman said. She stared at Mav.

Camden-Stone tugged my sleeve.

"Come on, this way."

We walked back into the corridor, a hiss of whispers behind us.

"Your friend's making quite a stir. We don't see many No-Suns around here," Camden-Stone said to me. "I'm Joe, by the way." He held out his hand.

"Joss," I said, shaking it. "And this is Mav."

Mav bowed slightly.

"Mav? That's an unusual name. Is it short for something?" Camden-Stone asked.

Mav rolled his eyes at me.

"Mavis," I ad-libbed. Mav gulped.

"Mavis?" Camden-Stone pressed his lips together, trying not to laugh. "It's a pleasure to meet you, Mavis." He bowed politely.

"Mav's taken a vow of silence," I said hurriedly.

We stopped outside a closed door. Camden-Stone knocked, but there was no response. He shrugged.

"Let me go in first," he said. "Make sure he's alone."

He opened the door, just wide enough to let himself through, then shut it quickly behind him.

I took a deep breath. I was only two meters away from my father. Would he believe I was his daughter? Probably not. I wouldn't believe it. I'd have to break it to him gently. Explain the whole deal.

Camden-Stone opened the door and poked his head out.

"He's a bit the worse for wear. Maybe you should come back tomorrow," he said.

"No! I can't. I've got to see him tonight." I pushed past Camden-Stone, nearly tripping over his feet. Mav was close behind me.

"Why don't you come in?" Camden-Stone said wryly.

The room was nearly all bed. Unmade bed. Daniel Sunawa-Harrod was lying facedown, his arms hugging a pillow. Camden-Stone pushed a pair of crumpled jeans to one side and sat on the bed next to him.

"I don't think you'll get much sense out of him. He hit the Bliss-sticks pretty hard tonight," he said. He shook Sunawa-Harrod's shoulder. "Danny, wake up. You've got visitors."

Sunawa-Harrod groaned. Camden-Stone gently pulled him over until he was lying on his back.

Sunawa-Harrod wiped his mouth with the back of his hand and frowned against the light from the bedside lamp.

"What do you want?" he asked, opening his eyes.

"Dan, this is Joss and Mav. They've come to see you."

"Who?"

He struggled to sit up then settled for propping himself on an elbow.

"I don't know you, do I?" he said to me. He looked at Mav. "I sure don't know you."

"I'm your daughter," I blurted out. Screte! So much for breaking it to him gently. I dug my fingernails into my palm. Take it slow, Joss.

"My daughter," he repeated blankly. Then he snorted, shaking his head.

"Is this your idea of revenge?" he asked Camden-Stone.

He looked at me. "Did he tell you the whole story? It's not my fault Jenny preferred me."

"No, this isn't my idea," Camden-Stone protested. "I'm still working on the Jenny payback."

I stared at Sunawa-Harrod, trying to make him see the truth in my eyes.

He had to believe me. I wanted a father. I wanted him to say *daughter*. "It's not a joke," I said slowly. "I've jumped back from the future. I came back in the machine that you developed. I'm your daughter."

Sunawa-Harrod looked over at Camden-Stone, his eyebrows raised. "Cute, but completely twisted."

"Too many Bliss-sticks?" Camden-Stone suggested.

They both laughed. A private joke.

Camden-Stone leaned closer to Sunawa-Harrod. "So, you got any other long-lost daughters you've never told me about?" he whispered dramatically.

I stared at Camden-Stone, the words "long-lost daughter" thumping through my head. I was Daniel Sunawa-Harrod's long-lost daughter. I was his heir. Then the truth hit my gut like ice: the caveat. I was the one Tori Suka had been hired to kill!

"What's wrong? You've gone dead white," Camden-Stone said.

"I'm fine," I managed to gasp out. Mav moved closer to me, trilling his concern. The two men stared at him. I half sat, half fell onto the bed. Camden-Stone leaned over and steadied me.

"I think you really are buzzed out on Bliss. Maybe I should get a doctor?" He was really concerned.

"No. I'm fine. I'm fine," I said, grabbing the sleeve of his shirt. "I've just got to prove that I'm telling the truth. Ask me anything you want."

There was an awkward pause. Camden-Stone gently pulled his shirt out of my hand. He looked at Sunawa-Harrod and shrugged. Sunawa-Harrod cleared his throat.

"Okay. So what was the date when you jumped back? What was the year?" It was obvious he was humoring me.

"March the twelfth, sixty-seven," I said.

"Hey, that's my birthday," Camden-Stone said. "It's June forty-eight now, so if you jumped back in sixty-seven . . ." He looked up, calculating. "My God, I'll be fifty. Do you know me? Am I still suave and sophisticated?"

He smoothed back his hair, pretending to primp in front of the mirror on the wall. I caught his eye in the reflection. What would happen if I told him his whole history? Would it make any difference? Would the knowledge make him or my father change the way they would act? I'd like to think it would have. But then if they do things differently, maybe Mav or me or the Centre wouldn't happen.

"No, I don't know you," I said.

Mav sniffed noisily and tapped his wrist under his sleeve. I looked at the countdown watch. Less than thirty minutes until T3 snapped forward to our own time.

"Well, tell us something that's going to happen," Sunawa-Harrod said.

"That's not going to prove anything," Camden-Stone argued. "She should write down something that happens in the future and seal it and then we'll open it just after it happens."

"Where on earth did you get that idea?" Sunawa-Harrod asked, laughing.

"I saw it in one of those old 2D movies," Camden-Stone said sheepishly.

"Well, it's stupid. I don't even know why we're even talking about it. She's as mad as a virt-junkie."

Mav nudged me, tapping his wrist again. He was right, we had to get back to the Jumper.

"It's not stupid," I said. "Have you got a blank Reader?"

"I've got something even better," Camden-Stone said. "Wait a sec." He hurried out of the room.

Sunawa-Harrod shifted his weight irritably. He reached over to the bedside table and tapped a Bliss-stick out of a half-empty packet.

"I'm telling the truth," I said.

He lit the stick. The tip of his forefinger was stained Bliss blue.

"Sure. I impregnated some woman when I was about ten. Happens all the time." He drew back hard and smiled as the narc hit his system. I sat forward.

"You could come and see the Jumper. Then you'll know it's true."

Mav's ears flicked under the hood. Sunawa-Harrod blew the used smoke upwards.

"Nothing is moving me out of this bed," he said. "Especially not someone else's Bliss dreams."

He leaned back against the wall, watching me. The only sound in the room was the soft hiss as he drew back on the stick. I stared at the floor, trying to find the magic words that would make him believe me. But who was I kidding? Nothing I was going to say was going to change the mind of this stranger sitting in front of me. I would have to make do with the sealed prediction. At least one day he would open it and know the truth.

Mav was motioning urgently towards the door, but I needed to stay a little longer. I looked around the room. An alto saxophone was propped against the wall by the bed.

"Do you play that?" I asked, pointing to the sax.

Sunawa-Harrod nodded.

"I play blues harmonica," I said, pulling my harp out of my top pocket. "Chromatic."

"Let me have a look."

I passed him the harp. He balanced it in his hand.

"Nice and light. It would have been a real drag to time travel with a cello, huh?"

He laughed at his own joke and passed the harp back.

"You any good?" he asked.

"I play with a band," I said. "I write stuff, too."

He carefully snuffed out the end of the half-smoked stick then leaned over and picked up his sax.

"Great. Play something you've written. I'll join in." He drew his mouth along the reed to wet it.

"Sure, why not?" I said, trying to be ultra cool. "I've just finished working out a duet. Here, I'll play your part first."

I took a deep breath and put the harp to my mouth, but the breath got caught in my thumping chest and I half choked, half gasped. So much for cool.

"You okay?" Sunawa-Harrod asked.

Mav crooned anxiously behind me.

"I'm fine."

I took another breath and looked my father in the eye. This time "The Dogstar Blues" came out strong and clear. Sunawa-Harrod listened with his head to one side, beating the time against the mattress with his foot.

"Okay, I got it," he said. "Mind if we jazz it up a bit?"

He didn't wait for an answer, but moved in with a quick, clever variation of his part. He played fast with a lot of notes and an emphasis on technique. A Charlie Parker fan.

An old bass player once told me that the blues and jazz were all about expressing your own voice, letting your rhythms show through the music. If he was right, then Daniel Sunawa-Harrod was expressing a deep-seated need to be number one.

I tried to bring us back to the melody line, but he cut across me, shrieking into another intricate solo. He obviously didn't know the meaning of "duet." I was being blown out of my own song. Then suddenly he slowed down the pace, each note becoming a statement. The change threw me right off and I stopped playing. He glanced at me, almost as if in apology, then closed his eyes. The music climbed into a high wail. He was playing for himself, unaware he was betraying a loneliness that echoed Mav's death keen for Kelmav. I glanced at Mav. He was swaying and I thought I heard him humming a soft harmony.

Camden-Stone came back into the room, shutting the door behind him. Sunawa-Harrod stopped playing.

It was suddenly silent.

"Don't mind me," Camden-Stone said.

"We were just having a bit of a jam," Sunawa-Harrod said. He cleared his throat. "So what have you got there?"

Camden-Stone was holding an elaborate folder with a gold design etched on the front. He opened it and took out a gold ballpoint pen and a piece of real-paper.

"Dad gave me this whole set for my birthday last year," Camden-Stone said. "A beauty, hey?"

He passed the pen and paper to me. It was the same pen as the one in his office, back in our own time.

"Okay, Joss. Write something from the future. But try not to mess up. That paper costs the earth."

I squatted beside the bedside table, laying the paper carefully on the hard surface.

Camden-Stone slid across the bed, blocking Sunawa-Harrod's view.

"Don't watch, Dan," he said. "It'll wreck the whole thing if we see what she writes."

"This is stupid," Sunawa-Harrod muttered.

I stared hard at the blank piece of paper. What should I write? Something that would show Daniel Sunawa-Harrod that I was really from the future. Really his daughter. Something big. Then I remembered Independence Day and wrote:

Daniel Sunawa-Harrod will receive the Nobel-Takahini Prize for Science on 10/10/50.

I looked at him lounging on the bed. He had dismantled the mouthpiece of his sax and was cleaning the reed. I added:

I know you stole the time-jumping field from Joseph Camden-Stone.

I don't know why I wrote that. I think it was just to let him know that he didn't completely get away with it.

"Are you finished?" Camden-Stone asked.

"Yes."

"Seal it up in this then." He handed me a long ivory-colored envelope.

I folded the paper, slid it inside the envelope and sealed it. Then on the front, I wrote:

To be opened by Daniel Sunawa-Harrod on 10/11/50.

I held it out to Sunawa-Harrod.

"So, will you do it? Will you keep this and open it on that date?" I asked.

He shrugged. "Why not?" He took the envelope, balancing it in his hand.

I touched his shoulder.

"Please, don't forget."

Mav grunted beside me, catching my eye. I nodded.

"We've got to go," I said.

"You should look us up in the future," Sunawa-Harrod said. "We could all get together and have a party." He laughed at his own joke.

Camden-Stone caught my arm.

"Can I have my pen back?"

"Sure. Sorry." I handed it over.

"No problemo. Maybe I'll see you later." He smiled and opened the bedroom door.

That's when I remembered the shadow in the lab.

The Shadow

Mav and I had just reached the camouflaged Jumper when the watch beeped and vibrated against my wrist.

"We've only got five minutes left," I said.

He nodded, pulling the mask off his face. I deactivated the holo unit and the stun stakes. The dark splodge that concealed T3 wavered then disappeared. Mav jumped into action, ripping up the stakes and shoving them into the carrybag. I pulled open the cabin hatch and climbed in.

The T3 countdown clock read three minutes, twenty-four seconds.

Mav passed me the bag. I jammed it under the console, pushing my legs down on either side of it. Mav swung into his seat and slid the hood back off his head. He shook out his ears.

"What are we going to do about that shadow in the lab?" I asked. "What if it's Camden-Stone?" I pulled the hatch closed, securing the cabin seal.

"Refmol is there," Mav sang confidently. "Refmol will protect us."

He was right. The Chanter would help us. Maybe it

could even work out another way to save Mav. Then I remembered Refmol's own desperation and my mouth was flooded with sour fear. This had been Mav's last chance and we had failed.

Mav grabbed my arm.

"Look, only one minute to go. This time I do not shield my eyes."

"Well I'm keeping mine glued shut," I said, swallowing hard. I never wanted to see my own skeleton again. I took Mav's hand in mine.

The clock counted down. I watched the red figures flick past. Ten seconds. I suddenly thought of Sunawa-Harrod's blue-stained finger. Should I have warned him about his future? Should I have warned Camden-Stone? Then I saw the metal skin of T3 start to ripple. I closed my eyes. Concentrated on my breathing. Circular. Deep. There was only my breathing. No sound, no sight. My head crackled with oxygen. Mav shuddered against me. Then he relaxed.

Ten seconds later I opened my eyes.

Too much light. I blinked fast. Then Lisa and Refmol blurred into view, still standing at the console. Lisa stepped forward, smiling. I turned my head towards the door. The figure was too slight for Camden-Stone.

"Behind you," I shouted, but the T3 cabin swallowed the sound.

I hit the harness buckle with my palm and pushed

against the hatch. It popped open. I pulled myself out, stumbling over the cabin seals. Lisa ran forward, in between me and the door.

"You did it," she cried.

A silent laser-blast hit her in the shoulder. She twisted and hit the floor, skidding on her own blood. A long shiny-wet smear.

At the doorway, Tori Suka stood silently. She raised the snub nose of the laser, the red guider-light flowing over my chest. She was looking straight at me through the sight. I could see her frown of concentration, her teeth biting her lower lip.

"No!" Mav shrieked behind me.

Tori Suka's eyes widened. Her mouth opened, as if to say something. Then she collapsed onto her knees, falling forward on top of her gun. A long thin knife stood upright between her shoulder blades.

A man stood in the doorway. A large man in an ugly denim suit. The steroid guy.

Lisa groaned.

"You should get your friend to a doctor," the steroid guy said, gesturing at Lisa. He stepped over Suka's body.

I grabbed onto the side of the T3, holding myself upright.

"Who are you?"

"Just call me George," he said. "Lenny hired me to guard you. Good thing, too."

Refmol ran over to Lisa. "The life liquid leaves her. Quick, Mavkel. Assist."

Mav took hold of my arm.

"Come. Sit down," he sang gently.

He steered me towards Refmol. I leaned against him. I couldn't seem to walk properly. He eased me down on the ground beside Lisa. Refmol was holding her wound together, the blood oozing between his fingers.

"I think I'm going to be sick," I whispered, pressing my hand against my mouth.

"Put your head between your legs," George advised.

I dropped my head between my knees. It helped.

"How did Lenny know Suka was after me?" I asked, lifting my head. George was inspecting Suka's body. I put my head down again.

"Lenny didn't go into specifics. He just told me to keep an eye on you. An extreme eye." He lifted Suka's shoulder and pulled the gun out from under her.

"Joss, we must bring a human doctor for Lisa," Mav sang urgently.

"I'll get someone," I said, pushing myself onto my knees.

That was as far as I got. The strange hiss-pop of another laser shot sounded. George collapsed next to Suka.

I looked up at the doorway. Camden-Stone. His gun was still raised. He poked Suka's body with his foot.

"Stupid bitch," he said. "Couldn't hit a rabbit nailed to the ground."

"You're the one who hired Suka!" I said, all the pieces of the puzzle locking together.

"Of course I did," Camden-Stone said. "You're not getting my Centre, Aaronson." He stepped over the two bodies and pointed his gun at me. "You're not getting it."

"I don't want it," I said.

"It's mine now. I've done the work. I've built it up. It's mine."

"It's yours," I said desperately, but he wasn't listening. He was in some kind of overdrive.

Refmol held up his hand. "Professor Camden-Stone, do not . . ."

Camden-Stone swung the gun around and fired. The shot pushed Refmol sideways into Mav.

"He wants to kill," the Chanter gasped, clawing Mav's shoulder. "I felt it in his mind. We must Rastun. Rastun now!"

Rastun?

The mind weapon!

Mav grabbed my arm, jerking me across his body. He held my head hard against his chest and began to keen. The sound pulsed in time with his heartbeats, shuddering through my head. I tried to pull away, but his hand held me down.

The pulsing became faster and faster. My mind was being ripped apart by sound, by rhythm. I gasped for breath as waves of pain became smooth seamless agony. Far away, I heard Mav's voice. What was he saying? I curled closer, trying to hear.

Refmol's keen merged with Mav's. It merged with mine. I was screaming. Rolling in a fireball. Mav was trying to join. He was saying we can join now. He was strong now.

Then he pulled me up, out of the pain.

We were floating just above it. We were with others. Refmol, Molref, Gohjec, Jecgoh. So many others. Our eyes turned to the one who was hurting us. Camden-Stone. He was with us, too. Floating. We could see all of him. All of his plans. We felt his pain. Deep inside him we saw the purple. Serenity. Peace. So small, but we could reach it. We heard his cry. *Why did Danny do it?* It washed through him, darkening the colors of his mind with black bitterness. We had to cut away the blackness. Leave only the purple. We sliced through the oily darkness. Hacking, cutting, clearing. But when we reached the purple, it was too small, too weak. The purple was dying. Camden-Stone was dying. We cradled the purple as it faded into blue. Cold pale blue that spiraled into nothing.

Joseph Camden-Stone was dead. We keened, mourning the victory of the black bitterness.

Slowly, we disengaged. The others slipped away, exhausted. Only Mav and Joss joined. Exploring. The slow knowing of new joys and old scars. So much to know.

Suddenly the pain reached up and snagged me, dragging me down. I heard Mav calling, but I couldn't stop my fall. I plunged deeper into pulsing molten pain. Then something cold and hard pressed against my neck. A sour taste burst at the back of my throat.

The last thing I heard was a pale green whisper in my mind. *I am with you, Joss.*

There was only pain in my head when I opened my eyes. Mav's mind whisper was gone. I shivered, squinting against the light bouncing off the white ceiling. A heavy lavender smell didn't quite filter out the bite of antiseptic.

"How are you feeling, Joss?" A man's smiling face leaned over me. Biggest set of teeth I'd ever seen. He cupped my cheek in his hand. "We were wondering when you were going to wake up."

I tried to say my head hurt, but it came out as a groan.

"Joss, do you have pain?" It was Mav's voice.

I turned my head towards him. Big mistake. A thousand pinpoints of color exploded in front of my eyes, blotting out the room.

"Take it easy," the man said. "That head of yours needs a bit of TLC. But don't worry, you'll be up and about before you know it."

"Mav?" I whispered.

"I am here. See."

The pinpoints cleared. Mav's face hovered above me, his ears at worry height.

"Are you okay?" I asked, reaching towards him.

"I am well." He took my hand, his thumbs cradling it.

The nurse tapped an entry into the bedside computer.

"The doctor will be here in a minute. Do you want something for the pain?" he asked.

"Yes. Please."

He nodded. "Take care of her for a moment, Mav," he said as he left the room.

"I will take the pain away, Joss," Mav said. He reached his hand over towards my forehead. I flinched.

"You fear my touch?" His ears flicked back, stiff.

"No. It's just that my head hurts so much."

"Yes, that is because your mindway has been opened." He squeezed my hand. "The pain will pass."

"You mean we're joined. Properly?"

"We are joined. Refmol says we will not be joined all the time, but it is still a joining."

"Is it enough for you?" I asked. The pain in my head thudded in my ears as I held my breath.

Mav gently lowered his forehead against mine.

"It is enough," he said softly.

He placed his hands around my head. The thudding eased, leaving a faint green calm. I strained to form *glad* in his mind. Pain crackled through my temple.

"Me, too," he said, pulling away. "However, there is much mind practice for you to do when you are upright again."

He picked up a package from the bedside table and held it out to me. It was wrapped in gold paper with a tangle of silver ribbons hanging off it.

"Look, here is a get-healthy present."

I laughed. "You mean a get-well present. Will you open it for me?"

"Is that allowed?"

"It's okay if you're asked to open it."

He placed the present on the bed, ripping open the paper with a flick of his thumb claw. It was the thought cube. Again.

He had a long way to go.

We both did.

Last Word

We heard today that Lisa is going to get the use of her arm back. It was touch and go there for a while, but the medics say she'll make a full recovery. Though she reckons if she gets one more needle in the bum, she's going to hit someone with her good arm.

Refmol is recovering, too. Luckily Chorians don't have their hearts in the same place as humans do, or Refmol would have been in a lot more trouble. As it was, the Chanter just got the equivalent of an unexpected appendectomy.

Mav filled me in on what happened after the Rastun killed Camden-Stone. When the link disintegrated, Gohjec and Jecgoh raised the alarm. In about a minute, the lab was crawling with security people and medics. That's when I got pumped full of Alpheine. Not that I'm complaining.

I think that the Rastun will haunt me for a long time. We peeled back Joseph Camden-Stone to his core and now the man won't go away. In those few seconds I experienced all of his feelings and memories.

I felt his humiliation when he was six and fell off his bike. I felt the sharp edge of Sunawa-Harrod's betrayal, a pain far greater for Joseph than a burned, disfigured face. I also felt his gloating joy when he remembered that Mav and I jumped back in time on his fiftieth birthday. He used that knowledge to place Suka in the Time Building so she could kill me when we returned. He knew it had to be when we returned, otherwise history might have changed and he might not have been in charge of the Centre. Joseph Camden-Stone was a very smart man, and by the time I crossed his path, burned up by black ambition. He had even slipped out of his birthday reception to watch his victory on the time lab security monitors. So when he saw Suka killed by George, I suppose that blackness just took over.

I also know that before the accident and the betrayal, Joe Camden-Stone met a girl named Joss and liked her. Perhaps that haunts me more than anything else.

Mav says that the Rastun ghost will gradually go away. He's going to teach me how to block it. Mav's been teaching me a lot about our mind-link. Refmol was right: Mav and I don't have a full-blown Chorian joining. We're not in touch all the time. It's more like a static-filled old phone connection that drops out a lot. We have to work hard to contact each other, but I'm kind of glad I've got the option of hanging up.

Talking about contact, Ingrid's been calling me a lot during the last two weeks. She wants to make a documentary about the whole thing. Somehow I can't see Lenny being interviewed about spyders and hitmen. He's already spirited

George out of the hospital before the cops can question him. Must all be part of the henchman health plan.

I saw Sunawa-Harrod's solicitor, Mr. Trant, yesterday. Claimed my inheritance. Once all the legal stuff has been done, I'll be the major stockholder in the Centre for Neo-Historical Studies. The whole idea of it makes me spin. Of course, the Board will appoint a new director to run the place, but I don't think I'll be getting expelled from this school. And I can't wait to see Chaney's face when he finds out I'm Sunawa-Harrod's daughter.

As part of my inheritance Trant gave me a letter. A real letter, sealed in a long ivory-colored envelope. Then he left me alone in his office while I opened it. The letter was dated a few weeks ago and read:

Dear Joss,

The day after I won the Nobel-Takahini, I opened your prediction and discovered that you also knew I had betrayed Joseph. My shame was overwhelming then and it is still as keen today. That is why I never contacted you. How could I look you in the eye?

I was never a family man, and I only donated once to the clinic. A long time ago I pulled some strings and saw the clinic records. They confirmed that you are my only child, and I like to think that you at least inherited your gift for music from me.

I know I have left it a bit late to be fatherly, but I offer you

this advice: don't stick IQ chips in your head, don't get hooked
on Bliss, and don't forget that, in the end, everything you do
has a consequence.
Your father,
Daniel Sunawa-Harrod

I was doing okay until I read that last bit of advice—
there was no way I was going to forget about consequences.
Luckily Trant brought me in a pad of tissues. He's a nice
guy, for a lawyer.

At the moment, I'm sewing a patch for Daniel Sunawa-
Harrod. Mav's drawn a whole load of symbols on it that he
says are Chorian instructions for the dead. It looks more like
someone's dipped an ant in ink and let it loose. When the
patch is finished, we'll take it to that old man at the museum.
I think he'll let me add it to the quilt. I've never sewn anything before, so it's a bit messy. But at least you can read the
lettering.

DANIEL SUNAWA-HARROD,
SULON OF JOSS AARONSON.

Acknowledgments

A lot of wonderful people have helped and supported me in the development of *Singing the Dogstar Blues*. I would like to thank:

Charmaine and Doug Goodman for their never-failing support. Karen McKenzie for her friendship, sharp editing skills and honesty, Ron Gallagher for his curiosity, knowledge of science, and his patience. June Wilson, Justin Healy, and Tor Roxburgh for their friendship and critical input. Bonnie Buxton for her friendship and electronic cheering from Toronto. Judy Duffy and the two RMIT novel classes who listened and commented. Fran Bryson, my agent, and her assistant Lucy Williams for their faith and their energy on my behalf. Anna McFarlane, senior editor at HarperCollins, for her enthusiasm, insight, and gentle editing technique. Laura Harris, commissioning editor at HarperCollins, for liking and accepting the book. Lucy Sussex for her interest in my writing and giving me my break. Gerald Murnane for his excellent teaching and advice. Chris Wilson, harp player and singer extraordinaire, for his input on the music sections. A friendly doctor at an IVF clinic who answered all my questions. Unfortunately, the piece of paper with your name on it got lost. And all my family and friends who asked "How's the book going?" and really wanted to know.

In 2006, Alison Goodman was asked to contribute a story to the anthology *Firebirds Rising*—and she chose to write about Joss and Mav after the end of *Singing the Dogstar Blues*. Here it is, appearing for the first time with the novel that was its inspiration.

Turn the page to read

the ReaL thing

Alison Goodman

the Real thing

The mind experiment had seemed like a good idea an hour ago. Now I wasn't so sure; Mavkel and I barely had the basics of telepathy covered, let alone this kind of thing.

"Are you prepared, Joss-partner?" Mav sang, the tips of his double-jointed ears quivering with excitement. He was Chorian, a mainly telepathic race, but when he did speak he used his two mouths to harmonise the words.

He flicked back his second eyelids. I stared into the dark, pupilless eyes of my time-jumping partner and nodded. Maybe this time the mind connection wouldn't hurt so much.

"Then execute the experiment," he sang.

A fiery spike stabbed through my temple. I grabbed the edge of the table and held my breath, exhaling as the pain eased into the soft warm weight of Mav in my mind. Concentrating on the fragile connection, I slowly lifted the real-bacon sandwich and took a bite.

"Well?" I said through the mouthful.

Salt? Lipids? Smoke? the pale green of his mind-voice said. *Chew more.*

I chewed. His primary mouth grimaced.

"You enjoy this food?" he sang out loud.

I winced as our connection broke and his pale green presence vanished from my mind. It had only been a few months since Mav and I first joined during a *Rastun,* a Chorian mind-weapon, and we weren't too slick in the connecting and disconnecting department. I still couldn't initiate proper contact with him—Mav had to set up the link—but considering everyone kept telling us that humans and Chorians aren't meant to join minds, we were doing okay. It was getting a bit easier each time we tried. According to Mav, my mind-voice was developing into a nice shade of orange, which apparently is about the level of a Chorian toddler.

"A girl needs a bit of real-meat now and again," I said, taking another bite and rolling the rich bacon and mayo juices around my mouth. "So, you could really taste it?"

"Not for long, but taste some, yes," he sang, holding up his two-thumbed hand. I slapped it in victory, my palm stinging as it met his squat, immoveable strength.

"Wait till you try a curry," I said.

"If this can be done with food, then it can be done with other things," he sang excitedly. "I am interested in experiencing your sex."

I stared at him, the sandwich halfway to my mouth. *"What?"*

"Your reproductive act. It involves much sensory input, yes?"

"No way, Mav," I said, shaking my head. "Forget it. It's not going to happen." I dropped the sandwich onto my plate. "You Chorians may like an audience, but I don't. And anyway, a human needs a partner and I don't have one."

I couldn't help sneaking a look at Kyle Sandrall. He'd just bought a couple of coffee cans at one of the machines and was heading towards the large table of cadets at the far end of the busy mess hall. It was the unwritten code of the University of Australia Centre for Neo-Historical Studies that the back table in the mess was reserved for the comp-kids, the genetically engineered students. A few weeks ago, Kyle had asked me to join them, but I'd said no. Not because I didn't want to, but because I knew I wasn't a real comp-kid. My mother had only used one gene donor with minimal engineering. She didn't want to risk too many donors or gene manips in case I developed CGD—Cascading Gene Defect Syndrome, a nasty collapse of pleiotropic genes. So, I wasn't a comp-kid, but I wasn't a real-kid either. And a few months ago I'd discovered I also had a bit of Chorian DNA in my mix, too. I didn't feel like trying to explain all that to Kyle, the poster boy for tailor-made kids. He'd probably only asked me to sit with him because he thought I was a real comp.

I watched him slide the coffees onto the table and sit down, hooking his long legs under the stool. He passed a can to the girl beside him, a blonde with her hair twisted into a flawless pleat and her chest in the tightest red halter top this side of an X-vid. Tarrah something-or-other; she was in sixth year with Kyle. I touched my own dark scraggly ponytail. It needed a cut again. And I could probably do with a few new tops, something a bit more feminine than my usual black T-shirts. I brushed sandwich crumbs off my chest, chancing another look at Kyle.

He was looking at me.

He smiled.

He nodded.

I smiled back . . . then realised my hand was still resting on my boob.

"What is wrong, Joss-partner?" Mav sang. "Why do you redden? Are you ill?"

I snatched my hand away. Terrific. Kyle probably thought I was so hot for him I couldn't control myself in public. Out of the corner of my eye, I saw him stand up.

"I'm okay," I said to Mav. "Want to get out of here?"

"No." Mav flattened the tops of his ears and leaned across the table. "Something is wrong. What is wrong?"

"Nothing," I said, waving him back to his seat.

Kyle was definitely heading towards us. I wiped the corners of my mouth with the back of my hand and pushed my hair out of my eyes.

"Have I got mayo on my face?" I whispered.

"No," Mav whispered back. "Should you?"

Then Kyle was standing beside the table.

"Hey, Joss," he said. "Hey, Mavkel."

Mav bowed, his ears lifting. "Kyle Sandrell, this pair greets you most cordially."

Kyle grinned. "Good to see you, too, Mavkel." He turned to me. "How are you, Joss?"

"Terrific," I said. "Fantastic. Brilliant. You know, really good."

I smiled widely, trying to cover my sudden morph from eighteen-year-old college student into babbling idiot.

"Are you two taking Chenowyth's time dynamics class this semester?" Kyle asked.

I nodded, puzzled. All first years had to take Professor Chenowyth's class—Kyle would know that. He licked his lips. They were great lips, kind of full, but not pouty. I dragged my eyes off them.

"Yeah, it's a tough class," Kyle said. "If you and Mavkel ever need any help, just let me know."

"Thanks," I said.

Mav beamed a double-barrelled smile. "You are very kind, Kyle Sandrell."

There was an awkward silence. Mav looked from me to Kyle, his ears hovering uncertainly.

"Why do you stare at one another?" he sang. "Is this a game?" He started jumping up and down in his chair, attracting stares from nearby tables. "This is a courting ritual, is it not?"

I glared at him. His ears collapsed like windless flags.

"I'm sprung," Kyle said, laughing. He rubbed the back of his head, scruffing up his dark hair. "I really came over to see if you'd like to go out Friday night."

"Friday night?" I echoed. Kyle Sandrell—sixth-year demi-god and all-round nice guy—was asking me out on a date? I suddenly had an image of kissing him, and ducked my head.

"I thought we could grab something to eat," he said. "And

a friend of mine is throwing a party. We could drop in on that, too."

"Sure," I said, trying to sound casual. "Sounds good." Underneath the table, I dug my fingernails into my palms.

"Great." He grinned again. "Can you infra me your screen code?" He held out his wrist, a sleek armscreen wrapped around it.

"Sorry, I don't wear a screen," I said. "My stand against constant surveillance."

He laughed. "Not a prob. You're quartered in P3, aren't you? How about I come round sevenish?"

"Seven's good. You'll have to wait in the security office, though. Just get them to comm me."

Instead of the usual student housing, Mav and I had a suite in P3, the state-of-the-art security building. Mav was the first Chorian to study on Earth and he was getting the red-carpet treatment. As his time-travel study partner, I got to go along for the first-class ride.

"See you then." Kyle gave me one last lingering smile. I watched him walk back to the comp-kid table; his rear view was as fine as his front view. When he sat down next to Tarrah, I saw her say something, an impeccable eyebrow lifted. Was she asking about me? I grinned to myself. Who cared about Tarrah tight-top? Kyle Sandrell had asked me out!

"I have read about this," Mav sang. "This is a date, is it not? A first date. I read that it is very important that you do not 'put out' yet."

"'Put out'? Where did you get that from?"

"It is from a late 1900s text. A magazine for young females.

It says you must wait until you know it is 'the real thing.'"

"Wasn't that an old advertisement for some kind of drink?" I said.

I was sure I'd heard our professor mention it in our Beginnings of Pop Culture class. I was taking it because I wanted to specialise in music history, mainly twentieth-century blues and jazz. I couldn't wait to time-jump back to the mid-1900s and see some of the big gigs of the golden age.

Mav's ears flicked. "No, that is not correct. *Sparkle* says that 'the real thing' is a pairing that is fated."

"*Sparkle?*" I rolled my eyes. "You can't take something called *Sparkle* as an authority on human relationships."

"It is on the recommended reading list," Mav sang, crossing his arms.

I looked over at Kyle. He was stretching, the movement hitching his T-shirt up over a flat stomach and cut abs. I didn't know much about fate, but I wouldn't mind testing out the idea that Kyle was the real thing.

"Still sticking to your own kind, Aaronson?" a slimy voice asked behind me. "Comp freaks?"

I turned around. Chaney Horain-Donleavy was sitting at the table behind me with his usual posse of losers. He jerked his head toward Kyle. "I heard they made that model sterile."

His gang sniggered.

I knew that some of the girls in our course thought Chaney was good-looking. He had a whole Renaissance-archangel thing going on: dark red curly hair, high cheekbones, golden tan. But I knew that inside, he was a total snake. He'd made it clear that if you weren't from one of the big-money hyphen families, you might as well not exist. Unless he felt like tormenting you.

"Don't you ever get tired of being a snorkwit?" I said.

His pale blue eyes were unblinking. "Someone's got to make sure you freaks don't get too up yourselves."

"Up yourselves?" Mav sang uncertainly. "What does this mean?"

"It means, flap-head, that comps are trying to stop us from getting into the time-jumping course," Chaney said. He turned to his friends. "They reckon they're better than us, so they should be the first and only choice."

There was a murmur of disgust.

"What a load of screte," I said. "The Centre has strict comp *and* noncomp quotas. It's law."

"Well, you should know," Chaney said slyly. "Aren't you and your mother major shareholders in the Centre?"

I stared at him. How did he know I'd inherited a controlling interest in the Centre? My donor father had left it to me, and I'd had to choose between sitting on the board and studying. It was a no-brainer; who wanted to worry about budgets when they could travel through time? But I thought the whole situation had been kept hush-hush by the Centre bigwigs.

Chaney glanced back at his friends. "That would explain why she got a place. There's no other reason why she's here."

They all laughed.

"I didn't get in because of that," I said.

"No, of course not," he said mockingly. "Come on, Aaronson. Quit zooming. You may be a comp, but you've been kicked out of nearly every school you've ever been in."

He shook his head. "No, you're here because you've got a rich, famous shareholder mother who donated a little admin building. Just like I'm here because my family name is on the library." So he didn't know the whole story. He picked up a veggie fry from his plate and jabbed it into a puddle of tomato sauce. "In the end, it's always who you know and how much you've got that's more important in this world."

"Only in your twisted mind, Chaney," I said.

He pointed his fry at the comp table. "Their parents scrimped and saved and risked CGD to make their kids prettier and smarter than Joe Average. And what for? Just to give them a shot at getting where we already are—at the top. Our families have done it all without any enhancements. Now, you tell me who's better?" He stuffed the fry in his mouth.

Jorel, Chaney's right-hand lout and jump-partner, leaned forward. "My dad says the comp lobby group is getting really strong. He reckons before you know it, the comps will be trying to take over."

Jorel's dad was in government; obviously not a liberal.

"I've heard there's an extremist comp group on campus," Pino said. As usual, he was trying to outdo Jorel. He nodded towards the comps. "Probably them."

Chaney's gang all turned to look at the table at the far end of the hall.

"You should be more careful," I said. "Someone will have you up on a civ charge."

Chaney snorted. "Not if it's true."

"Yeah, not if it's true," Pino echoed. "What about the graffiti painted on the Time Admin building wall: NOT COMP, NOT

GOOD ENOUGH. Bet that was done by comp extremists."

"Haven't seen it," I said, shrugging, but a little coil of unease tightened in my gut.

"Graffiti?" Mav sang. "Is this an artwork?"

"It's like a protest painted on a wall," I said.

"Maybe we should paint one ourselves," Chaney said. "DELETE THE COMP SCRETE."

His gang laughed, loudly repeating the slogan to one another.

Chaney leaned over to me. "I know you're not a real comp, Joss," he said under the cover of their noise. "One donor, enhancements kept to a minimum. You're almost pure. Why do you want go out with someone like Kyle Sandrell?"

I stiffened. Where was he getting all this info about me?

A sudden sharp pain in my head made me wince, but it was gone in a nanosecond. Mav's mind presence washed over me like warm water.

I am here. His mind voice was dark green, strident.

I shot a greasy look at him. I'd told him over and over again he couldn't just barge into my head whenever he felt like it. Especially since I couldn't barge into his head.

But you are alarmed, his mind presence said. *Of course I am here. Contact seemed easier this time, yes?*

It had been easier, but I was too annoyed to agree.

I turned back to Chaney. "I am comp," I said, keeping my voice low. "I may not have ten donors, but I'm still comp."

Why does Chaney alarm you? Mav rocked up in his chair towards the oblivious Chaney, his ears angled back aggressively.

No! No alarm!

Mav stopped and looked at me, then nodded reluctantly. I felt his mind warmth slip away.

"Are you sure the comps will think you're one of them?" Chaney asked. "For a bunch of freaks, they're getting real picky about who makes the grade." He raised his pale red eyebrows. "You should think carefully about who you want to be associated with, Aaronson."

I gritted my teeth, wanting to slap the smug smile off his real-kid-old-money face. He thought he had it all pinned.

"You're absolutely right," I said, standing up. "Come on, Mav, I don't want to associate with these scretes any more. Let's get out of here."

Mav stood up, his ears straight and tense.

"We do not leave you with any cordiality," he said to Chaney.

I couldn't have said it better myself.

"You've got to stop gate-crashing my head like that," I said, waving my security wristband across the lighted door panel. It flashed to green and the door to our quarters slid open.

Beside me, Mav hummed disconsolately with his ears at half-mast, but I wasn't going to fall for his "poor little alien" act.

"It's kind of like walking in on me when I'm getting dressed, except a lot worse."

"But you were alarmed, Joss-partner. I wished to be of assistance."

"I wasn't alarmed," I said brusquely, stepping into our lounge room. "Chaney doesn't alarm me."

"Chorian pairs are always mind-joined," Mav sang plaintively. "We should always be joined, not this sometimes joined. It is a not a real pairing."

I knew why Mav wanted us to be joined all the time—all Chorians had a constant telepathic link to their birth pair as well as to the rest of their race, and Mav's birth pair, Kelmav, had died in an accident. But something in me balked at trying to maintain a constant link. The last thing I wanted was Mav in my head full-time. I didn't want anyone eavesdropping on that constant murmuring stream of reality, fantasy, dream and emotion that flowed through my head. It was my own private narration of my life. And I had a feeling it was an important part of being human.

I headed for my bedroom, Mav trailing behind me. I had dragged him back to P3 as soon as we'd left the mess hall. He had wanted to stop and look at the graffiti, but I was a woman on a mission: to seek out and discover if I had anything to wear on a date with Kyle Sandrall. Poor Mav didn't have a chance—I practically put him in a headlock and marched him past the Time Admin building.

I threw my bag on the bed and slapped my hand against the v-robe sensor. The two virtual wardrobe doors disappeared with a soft pop. I stared at my sad collection of clothes. Apart from the regulation T-shirts and dress uniform, I had three black T-shirts, two red T-shirts, another pair of black jeans and a black jacket. Great for fast packing, not so great for a first date. I picked up an old black cashmere jumper lying on the wardrobe floor and shook the dust out of it.

"What do you think?" I asked.

Mav took the jumper between his two thumbs and held it up. "It will keep you warm and covered."

"Great. Just what I want on a hot date."

"Then that is settled," Mav sang happily. "I would like to see the graffiti now."

I snatched back the jumper. "No, it's not settled. I can't wear that on Friday. I need something . . . sexy."

Mav's ears flattened at the top. "Sexy? The 2-D images in *Sparkle* indicate that human sexy is achieved with much skin and little cloth."

"That's not really me." I couldn't see myself in one of Tarrah's little red halter tops, or a skintight cling dress. "I need something that is . . . well, at least not totally sexless."

"Lisa," Mav said.

"What?"

"Lisa will help you. I heard Jorel tell Pino that Lisa was sexy."

I frowned, conjuring up a mental picture of our friend Lisa. Long brown hair, savvy grey eyes, nice teeth. Was she sexy? I had never really thought about it. When someone gets shot on your behalf, you never really think of anything but their courage and spirit. A few months ago, she'd helped Mav and me jump back in time to save Mav's life and had got a laser through her shoulder for her trouble. I suppose she always wore makeup, but not much, and her hair was always shiny. Her clothes weren't anything special, although they did kind of skim her body. In all the right places. Damn, Mav was right; Lisa was sexy. And classy.

"Good idea," I told him. "Maybe she'll be able to lend me something."

His ears lifted. "We will visit the graffiti now. If we leave now, we will have six minutes to view it and two minutes to travel to our next class."

Sure enough, by the time we were standing in front of the graffiti on the south wall of the Time Admin building, the clock tower showed we had exactly eight minutes before the start of class. Who needed an armscreen with Mav around?

I stared up at the large slogan. Someone had gone to a lot of trouble; the outline of each letter was sprayed in red and filled in with yellow. The colours of the Genetic Enhancement Lobby Group. The big, beautifully drawn letters boldly declared war: NOT COMP, NOT GOOD ENOUGH. My gut tightened again.

Mav rocked back on his hind claws. "It is very neat," he sang. "And the lettering is aesthetically pleasing. Is this not art?"

"No, it's trouble."

"Why?"

"There's a lot of comps who are wondering why they should apologise for being better."

Mav looked back at the wall. "Comps consider themselves superior to nonenhanced humans?"

"I suppose some do," I said reluctantly.

"Is this not the aim of their genesis. To create superiority?"

"Superior attributes, but not superiority."

"Ah"—Mav nodded—"a semantics problem."

"Sometimes," I said drily, thinking of all the times I had been called a freak or unnatural. "It's just that a lot of humans like to think we're all equal, or that we at least start off equal. Some people think comps have an unfair advantage. Like it's cheating."

"Cheating?" Mav wrinkled his noses. "But if an attribute is created by the fortuitous combination of two unknowns, then it is considered not cheating?"

"Then it's good luck."

Mav's ears flattened. "Luck is acceptable, but design is not?"

"Luck is better because it doesn't need tons of money. Anyone can have luck," I said. "Not everyone can afford to take the chance out of luck."

"I do not understand," Mav sang dolefully.

I turned away from the wall. I wasn't sure I understood either. I just knew that sometimes I felt guilty for being alive.

"Come on," I said, wanting to get away from the graffiti. "We've only got one and half minutes to get to class."

Mav took the bait. "Incorrect, Joss-partner," he shrilled behind me. "We have two minutes, six seconds and four one-hundredths."

"I brought a whole load of stuff," Lisa said, dumping a pile of clothes and shoes on my bed. "Didn't know where you and Kyle were going, so I figured I'd cover all possibilities." She absently adjusted her tank strap over her bandaged shoulder. "You should have commed me sooner. We could have gone shopping."

It was D-Day—Date Day—and Lisa had jumped at the chance to make me over.

I poked at the clothes. "It's not a big deal," I said. Maybe if I said it enough times I'd believe it. "It's only going to be some dinner somewhere and then maybe a party." I pulled a bright blue slip of silky material out of the stack. "What's this? A scarf?"

Lisa snatched it out of my hand. "Very funny. It's a top. Looks great with blue jeans."

"I can still wear jeans?" I'd been imagining microshorts and cling tops.

"Of course. I don't think you should make any drastic changes. Just move away from wearing so much black and smarten things up a bit."

She pulled back her fall of brown hair and deftly twisted it into a loose bun, tying it into itself. Amazing. All I could ever do with mine was whack a band around it and hope it held, or stuff it under a beret.

I pushed the clothes aside and sat on the edge of the bed. "So, you've been studying here for five years. What's the Kyle story."

Lisa got down to business. "For the last year or so he's been a bit of a serial dater," she said. "But before that, he and Tarrah were a couple right through to fourth year." She made a wry face. "The golden comp couple. They were probably whipped up in the same laboratory." She realised what she'd said. "Screte. I'm sorry, Joss, I didn't mean anything by that." She touched my arm in apology. "I think I was channelling my stepfather."

"Not a comp fan, huh?" I said tightly.

"You could say that. Both Mum and Leo are old-line religious. You know, 'Love thy neighbour as long as thy neighbour isn't a comp.' They're always saying that the scientists are playing God and that we shouldn't be messing with the

Lord's creations." She met my eyes. "Look, I'm a big girl now. I don't buy into their beliefs. I say live and let live. Okay?"

I nodded. "Okay." I stood up, wanting to physically shake off the sudden awkwardness between us. "So what went wrong between Kyle and Tarrah."

"Not sure," Lisa said, obviously relieved to be talking about something else. "One rumour was that he found her in a clinch with another guy. Another one said Tarrah started getting a bit too intense about the Comp Lobby and Kyle wasn't so into it."

"They're still friends, though, aren't they? I saw them in the mess together."

"Absolutely. Kyle's a nice guy, he likes to be friends with everybody," Lisa said. She pulled out a top in a soft pink knit. "Try this on. We're about the same size, so it should fit you." She picked up a pair of jeans. "And these, too."

I took the clothes just as Mav loped through the doorway.

"Lisa," he sang. "This pair greets you with great pleasure." He gripped Lisa's hand and bowed, entwining her thumb in the complicated Chorian friendship grip.

Lisa bowed back. "Hi, Mav. You're looking good."

"Yes, I feel much equilibrium. Does your injury heal?" Mav asked, his hand hovering over her shoulder. He began to hum softly.

Before he became a time-jumping student on Earth, Mav had been studying to be a Chanter, the Chorian version of a doctor. He'd once tried to explain to me how he'd been learning to sense injuries and emotional states through sound vibrations, but I'd got lost about five minutes into it.

"It's a lot better," Lisa said. "The doctors say I'll be a hundred per cent in a month or so."

Mav nodded. "They are correct." He dropped his hand and looked at the clothes on the bed. "You bring much cloth for Joss." His ears flattened. "She says I cannot accompany her on her first date to observe human sexual courting behaviour."

"Not on the first date or any date," I said firmly, ignoring Lisa's snort of laughter.

"She feels much apprehension about this first date with Kyle Sandrell," Mav sang. "It is good that you are assisting her to be at least not totally sexless."

I covered my face with my hands. "Think I'll go and drown myself in the bather now."

"While you're in there, try those on," Lisa said, still laughing. She pushed me towards my ensuite. "And don't forget the shoes." She handed me some sandals.

I stepped into the bathroom. "For the record, I am not nervous about this date," I said loftily. I hit the sensor pad, closing the door. My reflection stared at me from the far mirror. "Not one bit," I told it. It nodded.

Eight clothes changes later, we had a winner. I stepped out of the bathroom in a crisp fitted white shirt with thin stripes of blue and silver, a pair of mem-jeans that were already settling themselves around my shape, and silver sandals.

Lisa nodded. "Oh yeah, that's it." She stood up. "Just one thing." She reached over and undid my top two shirt buttons, creating a deep V.

Mav walked around me, considering. "It is pleasing," he

finally announced. "However, it needs a decorative metallic neckpiece."

Lisa and I stared at him.

"You know, he's right," Lisa said. "Have you got a silver necklace?"

I found a twisted silver chain and clasped it around my neck.

"So?" I asked. I changed the v-robe doors into mirror mode and looked at myself.

Lisa and Mav nodded. I smiled at them in the reflection of the mirror.

"You're gorgeous," Lisa said. "I've seen your mother reading the news tons of times, but I've never really noticed how much you look like her. Except she's blonde and you're dark, of course."

"That's what she ordered," I said. "The Eurasian version of herself—wouldn't want another blonde bombshell in the family, would we? And just enough multi-ethnicity to boost her audience numbers."

Even I heard the bitter edge in my voice.

"I'm sure your mother didn't want you just for that," Lisa said softly.

I turned to look at her. "My mother chose to manipulate the genes that create symmetrical facial structure, athletic body type and good teeth. Looks, looks and looks. I think that says it all."

Lisa and Mav looked at me solemnly.

"So all those brains you've got are natural?" Lisa finally said, smiling.

I reluctantly grinned back. "Must be."

Lisa stood up. "Well, it doesn't matter what way you got that face and body. I say, if you've got it, flaunt it." She zeroed in on me. "Come on, we've got to do something with your hair and makeup."

I turned to face the mirror as she smoothed back my fringe. Lisa was wrong. How you got it was important, and my gut told me that flaunting it might soon be very dangerous.

A few minutes before seven, the CommNet jingle sounded from the computer on the bedside table. Lisa was holding a pair of silver hoops against my ears and we both jumped as the screen moved smoothly around to face us.

"Joss, you've got a comm message from Sergeant Vaughn at the P3 Security Office," the computer said.

I met Lisa's eyes. This was it. She snatched away the earrings and stepped back, nodding encouragingly.

I took a deep breath. "Okay, connect."

Vaughn's fashionably altered face appeared on the screen. "Well now, don't we look purty." He leered. "Your little boyfriend is waiting for you."

I gave him a cool death glare, but my heart was already picking up pace.

"Thank you. Tell him I'll be out in five. Disconnect." The screen flicked back to the CommNet logo.

"Okay, he's here," I said, standing up. "Looks like I'm going now." I felt strangely reluctant to leave.

"Are you sure I cannot accompany you?" Mav asked, his ears hiking up hopefully.

"She's sure," Lisa said. She handed me a ridiculously small silver evening bag. "Good luck. And have a great time."

That was the plan.

⊠ ⊠ ⊠

Kyle tapped his spoon against the toffee crust of the crème brûlée that sat between us on the table. "Want to help me break it?" he asked.

I nodded and picked up my spoon.

He sat up straight, holding his hand over his heart. "I dedicate this crème brûlée to all those who believed in it and held the dream in their hearts of a better, happier dessert."

Laughing, we broke through the thin layer, exposing the smooth pale custard underneath.

"I think we've struck gold," he said softly, and I had a feeling he didn't just mean the dessert. "You go first."

I dug out a spoonful of toffee and custard and tasted it.

"Ohmigod," I breathed, letting the honey vanilla melt on my tongue. "That is fantastic."

"Told you," Kyle said, helping himself.

I looked around the crowded café. It had been quiet when we arrived and the headwaiter had seated us in the open double windows that looked out into Mall 11, the boutique area of the Melbourne central mall network. Now the restaurant was buzzing, and the energy in the place was pumping through me.

Kyle and I had talked nonstop about the Centre, discussing our majors (history of architecture for him, music for me), the tough fitness program, the best and worst teachers, and the first terrifying ten seconds of a time-jump. We'd even discussed Mav and the mind link, although I had moved the conversation on fairly quickly—it felt too much like talking behind Mav's back. The arrival of dessert had created a natural break in conversation, but I sensed that we were about to shift into more personal territory. And for once, I didn't mind. I spooned out some more of the crème brûlée, concentrating on scooping up as much toffee as possible.

"That Horain-Donleavy kid from your class cornered me yesterday," Kyle said.

That made me look up—Chaney had never been high on my list of romantic dinner topics.

Kyle shook his head. "One of these days someone's going to buck the civ laws and lay into that kid. And with that mouth on him, he'll deserve it. He wanted to have a 'little chat' about you."

I hurriedly swallowed my mouthful of dessert. "What did he say?"

Kyle shrugged. "That you weren't really comp."

The lingering sweetness in my mouth turned sour. The next time I saw Chaney, he'd better start running.

"I am comp," I said. "I may only have one donor, but I'm enhanced. I'm still comp." It came out more vehemently than I expected.

Kyle held up his hands. "Hey, I'm with you—if someone's enhanced, then they can call themselves comp. I know some comps wouldn't agree with that, but they're a bit hard-line." He picked up his glass and drained it. "You know Tarrah, don't you?"

"I've seen her around, but we haven't met," I said, trying not to sound too happy about it.

"She's well in with the Comp Lobby, and she told me they're trying to get some kind of criteria set for comp status.

A certain number of donors and things like that."

I looked at Kyle's beautiful face, a horrible thought hitting me like a hammer between the eyes. "Would it matter to you if I wasn't a comp?"

It was like everything in the café ground to a halt while I waited for his answer. Was this gorgeous, funny guy the flip side of Chaney? I had very specific ideas about where this evening was heading, and they would all disappear in a flick of a clean sheet if he said yes.

He shook his head. "Of course not."

The magic words. My evening was still intact.

"But I've kind of stopped dating noncomps now," he continued. "Not that there's anything wrong with them—it's just that they don't really understand what it's like. You know what I mean."

"Sure, but . . ." I had been about to say that anyone with an ounce of empathy would be able to work it out, and that went both ways. But earlier, Lisa had delicately suggested I tone down my attitude, especially on the first date. *Leave it to the second date*, she'd said. So, I swallowed the comment, although it kind of stuck in my throat.

Kyle looked at me expectantly. "But what?"

"But do you want coffee?" I said lamely.

"How about we skip coffee and head to the party?" Kyle said. "I promised we'd drop in, but we don't have to stay long."

I caught the lilt in his voice. My thoughts exactly.

We took the Venturi Loop back to campus. I've never been keen on the underground trans system—being sucked through a tube in a metal capsule without windows always creeps me out—but it seemed like a good idea to get to the party as quickly as possible. The sooner we got there, the sooner we could leave.

It was being held in Trinity College, the sixth-year-student quarters. Kyle and I took the most direct route through campus, along the wide tree-lined central boulevard. The huge oaks had formed a canopy over the walkway and the University had installed old-fashioned streetlamps that created pools of buttery light and soft shadows. Although it was officially autumn, the night air was still warm, courtesy of the ever-expanding ozone hole, and a number of other couples were strolling hand in hand. It seemed like a good idea. I glanced across at Kyle. He met my eyes and smiled, both of us moving at the same time. I yelped as my finger mashed against his palm. We jumped apart then started laughing.

"I think we got our timing wrong," he said. "Let's try that again."

Our hands slid together. Something inside me lurched as I felt his long fingers curl around mine.

We walked up the steps to the arched entrance of Trinity College.

"What do you say we only stay for half an hour," I said, tightening my grip.

The door to the party dorm was opened by a sixth-year girl with short black hair intricately twisted back into beaded sections. She kissed Kyle on the cheek then pointed in the direction of the eating area.

"Drinks down there," she yelled over the pounding music.

I followed Kyle through a crowded living room and into the eating area. James, a cheerful fifth-year I'd met through Lisa, was manning the food dispenser.

"Hey Joss, how are you doing? I didn't know you belonged."

Belonged? To what? I opened my mouth to ask, but James had turned to Kyle.

"So what do you want to drink?" he asked.

"Beer?" Kyle said, turning to me for confirmation.

"Sure."

I took the cold glass and studied the group of people. Something was bugging me, but I couldn't work out what.

"Kyle!" a girl's voice yelled. We both turned around. Tarrah was heading towards us in a pale green cling dress, her blonde hair falling in VR star waves. She kissed Kyle on both cheeks, her bright hazel eyes on me.

"So glad you decided to come. And you, too, Joss," she said, smiling widely. "It's always good to have a new member."

Member? And then it clicked. Everyone in the room was a comp. I shot a look at Kyle.

"Member of what?" I asked.

"The Comp Lobby," Tarrah said. "Didn't Kyle tell you this is a meeting?"

"Me and Joss are just here for the beer," Kyle said.

"Come on, Ky, you're going to have to get off your fence one day." Tarrah turned around to face the crowd. "Hey, turn the music off," she called. "It's time to start."

There was immediate silence. I scanned the room; everyone had turned expectantly towards Tarrah.

"I'm not going to rave on for very long," she said. "This is just a prelim to see who is interested in the march on the Director's offices next week."

Four heavyset guys with rugby player necks raised their beers and cheered.

"Let's storm the place," one of them yelled. A few girls near them giggled.

"Thanks for your enthusiasm, Liam," Tarrah said. "But for the moment we're just marching. And that reminds me, although we all appreciate the sentiments of the graffiti on the admin building, it would be better if the artists played it cool for a while. Until the march is over."

"What are you marching against?" I asked.

Tarrah looked back at me and smiled. "Everyone, say hello to Joss. She's in first year, so all you old hands can give her some pointers about surviving the course," she said.

A friendly buzz of *hellos* rippled around the room. I caught a thumbs-up from the black-haired bead girl and a wink from James. I smiled, the warmth of the crowd surprising me.

Tarrah brushed back her hair. "We're marching against the quotas," she said, a strident note entering her voice. "It's just institutionalised prejudice against us. We're supposed to be living in a meritocracy, but potential comp students are being turned away, even though they're outstripping the noncomps in all areas."

"Don't the quotas work both ways?" I asked, curious.

Tarrah nodded. "It used to work both ways. But we're not just oddities any more. At the moment, five per cent of births are comps and that's rising. More and more comps are coming through the school system. Why should they give way to the mediocre?" She turned back to the room of people and raised her voice into a rallying cry. "I say that if you're better, then you should get into the course. And I've seen the statistics—comps are better! Let's face it, that's why our parents took the chance."

The room erupted into a frenzy of whoops and cheers and clapping. Liam and his mates started chanting "Not comp, not good enough!"

"If you want to march, go see Birri over there," Tarrah yelled, pointing to a tall black woman at the back of the room. "Put your name down. Let's show them we mean business."

People started to move towards the sign-up. Beside me, Kyle drained his glass and put it on a nearby table.

"Want to get going?" he asked.

I nodded. "You don't seem very impressed with all this," I said, taking a last swig of beer.

"Are *you* impressed?"

I looked around the room. "I don't know. I suppose I'm impressed by the solidarity."

Kyle raised his eyebrows. "Yeah, Tarrah's good at that."

"Did I hear my name?" Tarrah said, moving away from the four rugby players.

"We're taking off now," Kyle said smoothly.

"Already?" Tarrah looked put out. "I hope you'll come again, Joss," she said. "We comps have to stick together, right?"

"Sure," I said.

She gave me an appraising look. "Think about it, Joss. I know you've had your fair share of screte from noncomps. Do something about it." She quickly kissed Kyle on the cheek. "Don't be like Ky, here. He doesn't like to get involved. Do you, darling?"

"Only with the right person," he said lightly. And although he didn't look at me, I felt a rush of heat through my body.

Tarrah's laugh was brittle. "Always sidestepping the issue. See you tomorrow." Then she was gone, surrounded by her disciples, her voice urging and caressing towards the sign-up table.

Kyle took my hand and we made our way towards the door. I looked back at the milling group waiting to sign their names; arms draped over friends' shoulders, bursts of laughter, loud teasing, and underneath it all a real sense of camaraderie. Of belonging. James was standing at the back of the room and caught my eye. He motioned towards the sign-up table, his eyebrows raised. I shrugged. He nodded and smiled, mouthing "Next time." Perhaps I would, next time. I waved as Kyle gently tugged at my other hand.

Outside, in the warm night air, we paused at the top of the steps.

"Sorry about that," Kyle said. "I didn't know she was going to turn it into a rally."

"It's okay. I can sort of see where she's coming from. And I really liked the vibe."

"Yeah, it's nice to relax with your own kind," he said as we walked side by side down the steps. I felt a fleeting twitch of unease at his phrasing. "That's why I go," he continued. "To hang with other comps. I'm not so keen when Tarrah starts politicising."

"I wouldn't mind hanging with them again," I said.

As if we could read each other's mind, we both turned towards one of the smaller paths that branched off from the main boulevard. A more secluded path. The lamps were farther apart, creating soft-edged spotlights in the darkness. Kyle caught up my hand again and we walked in silence, the energy between us building. Every centimetre of my skin was aware of the warmth of his body, the flat smooth planes of his muscles, the soft curve of his lips. As we moved into the glow of one of the lights, I glanced up at him and saw him staring at me. The flare of his dark pupils pulled me towards him. I stopped and draped my arms over his shoulders. He leaned into me, his body firm against mine. As I rose to meet him, our bodies pressed closer together and I thought I could feel his heartbeat, as quick as mine. The kiss was gentle, a soft taste of each other, but I wanted more. I opened my mouth, feeling him move with me, all my focus on the shivering sensation running though my body.

I feel your desire, Joss-partner! It is beautiful!

I jerked back, the intrusion like the slash of a cold knife.

"What's wrong?" Kyle asked anxiously, his arms still around me.

My mind flamed into burnt orange fury.

No! Get out!

The link snapped, a whisper of lime green remorse colouring my consciousness.

I slammed my wristband across the security panel of our front door. Barely waiting for it to slide open, I stalked into the hexagonal living room. Behind me, Kyle paused in the doorway.

"Mav, get out here," I yelled.

There was no answer. His bedroom door was closed, the lock panel glowing red. I slapped it anyway.

"Mav, don't you try and hide."

"I will come when you no longer shout," he sang.

I glared at the door. That was going to be a long time coming.

"Maybe I should go," Kyle said.

I turned back to him.

"Screte! I'm sorry, Kyle." I ran my hand through my hair, messing up Lisa's careful styling.

"Look, don't worry. You've got stuff to work out here. How about we catch up tomorrow night?" He hesitated. "That is, if you'd like to."

"I'd love to," I said. I walked over to him. "Thanks. And I'm sorry."

We kissed, brief but full of promise. I watched the door close behind him.

Damn it. I marched across to Mav's door again.

"You wrecked my date. You can at least come out and face me," I said, trying to modulate my voice.

The door slid open. Mav stood in front of me, his ears flat against his head.

"This is the correct time to say sorry, yes?" he sang meekly.

"'Sorry' doesn't cut it," I snapped. "I was having a fantastic time until you barged in!"

"I know," Mav sang.

"Do you know how creepy that is?" I said tightly. "To have someone in your mind when you're . . . " I stopped, not really wanting to describe what Kyle and I were doing.

Mav's ears raised placatingly. "On Choria, it is always an honour to be joined at such times."

"I don't give a damn if it's an honour on Choria," I yelled. "I don't want to share my love life with you. Do you understand?"

"Yes," Mav sang contritely. His ears flattened again. "But tell me why you still want Kyle when you do not trust him? I do not understand."

"What?" I stared at him, crossing my arms.

"You do not trust Kyle. I felt it through your desire."

"I don't know what you're talking about. You're just trying to change the subject."

"No, Joss-partner. Deep in you there is not-trust. Why do you fail to acknowledge this instinct?"

"Deep in me is pissed off. With you." I stamped across to my bedroom. "Don't even think about coming near me for a few days. I don't want to see you."

I didn't look back as my bedroom door slid shut. I slapped the lock panel then dived, full-length, onto my bed. I trusted Kyle, just fine. And anyway, what did Mav know about trust? I'd trusted him to stay out of my head for one night, and he couldn't even do that. Maybe this partnership wasn't going to work, after all.

The next day was Saturday, rest day, and Mav took me at my word; whenever I came out of my bedroom, he ducked back into his room. I heard him leave the suite about midday.

As soon as I heard the front door slide shut, I commed Kyle and organised to meet him at the University basketball game at eight. Then I hotfooted it over to Lisa's quarters to borrow more clothes. She lent me a soft, sexy red jumper and red heels, then made me promise I'd go clothes shopping with her later in the week. I didn't mention my fight with Mav—he was wrong, but Lisa had a bad habit of looking at both sides of a situation.

At about a quarter to eight, I left our quarters. Mav was still out. We usually spent Saturday nights together at the Buzz Bar, catching up with our friend Lenny Porchino, the bar owner. Was that where Mav was now? In Lenny's private booth, listening to the house blues band? Sometimes I'd jam with the band on my blues harp and Mav would harmonise my line with intricate humming. We always got encores. It felt strange not being there with him.

I hurried over to the huge, central gym. The basketball game was between the University team and their old adversaries from Monash Uni. It was already crowded when I made it into the stadium. I scanned the seats for Kyle, but couldn't see him. This was one of the times when not wearing an armscreen backfired. Maybe I'd have to get one, now that I *wanted* someone to contact me. I saw Chaney and Jorel in the top row, throwing chips down at four big guys crammed together in the small seats: Liam and his friends from Tarrah's party. They already looked wasted. And now they also looked pissed off—Chaney liked to live dangerously.

I still couldn't see Kyle. Had he decided not to come? I

pushed down a hollow feeling and studied the rows, one by one. Finally I saw him guarding a spare seat in the far corner. A few girls were looking back at him, trying to catch his eye, but he was obviously on the lookout for me—bad luck, girls. I couldn't help grinning as I made my way across the bleachers.

"Hey, just in time," he called when he saw me climbing over legs and bags. He stood up to let me pass. As I brushed past him, I smelled hot man and citrusy cologne. It made me want to drag him out of the stadium.

I'm sure I cheered our team in the right spots and yelled at the refs' decisions, but I can't really remember. All I noticed was the energy between me and Kyle. He held my hand the whole time, softly stroking my palm, sometimes my arm. I pressed my thigh against his, and then my hip, until the whole of our sides were touching, the heat from our bodies only partly due to the crowd around us. By the end of the game, I felt like my whole body was vibrating against his and I knew, from the dark intent of his eyes, that we weren't going to be hanging around for the victory party.

By the time we made it out of the stadium, most of the crowd had cleared.

"It's still early," Kyle said. "Did you want to get a drink or something?"

I stared him in the eyes and shook my head slowly.

"No," I said, and smiled.

He grinned back. "My roomie has gone to stay with a mate," he said. "Want to come back to my place?"

"Why, thank you, Mr Sandrell. Don't mind if I do."

He laughed and squeezed my hand. "Let's cut through the science buildings. It's faster."

We started running, hand in hand, across the stadium quadrangle, leaving behind the last stragglers of the basketball crowd. Kyle led me in between the tall, dark science buildings, through a deserted arched walkway, and down a steep set of steps.

"Wait," I panted, laughing. "I can't run in these silly shoes."

I dragged on his hand. He stopped and we stood for a moment in a dark alleyway. I pulled him closer, angling my face to kiss.

The small space suddenly echoed with a sharp cry and the scraping sound of struggle.

I pulled back. "What's that?"

"Dunno, but it's from over there," Kyle said, turning towards the far end of the alley.

We started towards it, the sounds of heavy breathing and pain-filled gasps more insistent. I rounded the corner into a shadowy courtyard. For a second all I saw was a dark mass on the far edge. Then it became four heavy guys kicking two hunched forms on the concrete. Liam and his mates belting the screte out of two kids. Even before I saw the night-bleached flash of red curly hair, I knew it was Chaney. And Jorel.

Chaney covered his head with his arms as Liam savagely kicked him.

"Don't ever call me a freak again, you little bastard," Liam said.

I started forward, but Kyle's hand dug painfully into my arm, pulling me back.

"Don't," he whispered.

"What do you mean? We've got to stop it!" I jerked my arm away.

"It's not our fight."

"What's that got to do with it?"

Kyle's face was set. "You know Chaney and his friend were asking for it."

I stared at him. "You can't just walk away from people getting hurt."

"It's the only thing those type understand," he said harshly, stepping into the shadows of the alley. "Leave it, Joss. Don't get involved." He went to grab my arm again, but I jumped back.

"No, we have to do something. They're getting creamed."

"Look, I'll call Security," he said.

"They'll be too late."

He took a step back, shaking his head. "I'll call Security."

"Don't knock yourself out," I said as he disappeared down the alley.

I turned towards the fight, suddenly feeling very alone. One of the rugby thugs was down, writhing on the ground. Nearby, Jorel was lying very still on the concrete. Chaney was curled into a ball with the other three thugs on top of him.

"Oi," I yelled, running towards them. "Get off him."

Liam looked up. "Get lost."

He turned back to Chaney. His mistake. I punched him in the side of the head. My mistake. I should have gone for his gools.

"Bloody hell," he roared. And swung. I jumped back. He only grazed my shoulder, but it felt like a sledgehammer.

"Didn't I see you last night?" he demanded.

All three of his mates turned their attention to me. Not so good. On the ground, Chaney groaned, one side of his head covered in blood.

"So?" I said, slipping off my shoes. I couldn't fight in them and they had handy heels. Two of the guys had got up and were circling around me.

"You're comp," Liam said.

"So what?"

"So, these guys are lousy bigots. We're just teaching them a little lesson."

"No, you're not. You're bashing the screte out of them. Leave them alone."

"You're going to stop us, are you?" the thug on my right asked. He swung another kick into Chaney.

"Too right," I said. At least my voice was steady.

I felt the warmth of a body behind me just as Liam rushed me. I should have kept an eye on Left Thug. I zeroed in on Liam's crotch and kicked. Liam buckled as pain burst through my toes. Then I felt Left Thug's arms tighten around my chest.

"Silly bitch," Right Thug yelled.

The rush of adrenaline masked the pain of his first punch to my stomach, but it didn't soften the ground or the kick into my side. I heard Liam moaning near me, and saw Chaney try to get up and pull one of the thugs off me. Mav! I needed Mav! I strained every fibre of my being towards his mind, screaming as the burning pain in my body matched the orange fire in my head. *Hear me! Mav, hear me!* The edges of my sight faded into grey haze as I gasped for breath. Something heavy on my chest. Can't breathe. *Mav!* I pushed against the human weight. Pushed against the confines of my mind. Screaming inside. Outside. Until there was no more breath.

Joss? His mind voice was startled, jubilant, darkening into anxiety. *I come.*

And then I knew why Mav wanted to be joined all the time. Waves of Mav, of everything that was Mav, broke over me, filling me with the certainty that I was not alone, would never be alone. A swirling, dizzying closeness, understanding, acceptance. Joss melding into Mav into Joss, a merging of minds and spirits. A joining of stories, thoughts, emotions, dreams. We flowed together; pasts, presents, futures fused into a rolling, endless stream. We were Pair.

We will be there soon. We will stop the pain. We will be together. We are Pair.

No!

Deep down, part of me struggled for separateness. A bolt hole of isolation. Nothing but the bare essence of Joss. Alone. Human. *One.*

I don't know if it was that, or the punch in the face that suddenly blacked out the world.

I heard humming. Insistent, annoying humming. I licked my lips. Dry. I tried opening my eyes. Bright, painful light. Antiseptic. White walls.

Hospital.

I focused on a hand hovering over my face. Two thumbs.

"Mav?"

The humming stopped.

"Joss-partner. I am here."

Mav's double-barrelled smile appeared in front of me.

"We've got to stop meeting like this," I croaked.

"You are bruised on your face and body and have one rib broken," Mav sang. "All will be well."

"Can't feel anything," I said. Must have been full of Alpheine. "How are Chaney and Jorel?"

"They both live," Mav sang somberly. "Jorel is still unconscious. He is injured inside and is now in the place of special care. Chaney is cut and swollen on his face and also has ribs that are broken. He is much grateful to you."

"What about Liam and his friends?"

"Those who attacked you? They are with your law enforcers. There is loud shouting and anger about comps and noncomps."

I tried to nod, but the effort was too great. The comp trouble had finally come.

"Kyle Sandrall wishes to see you," Mav sang. "He waits outside, asking about your health."

I closed my eyes. How did I feel about that? An image of Kyle disappearing down the alleyway flashed through my mind.

"All right, let him in."

Mav touched the wall panel and the door slid open. He motioned Kyle inside.

"Hi, Joss," Kyle said hesitantly.

He was holding a posy of flowers.

"Hey," I said, trying to summon up a smile. I shifted in the bed as my body remembered his arm across my shoulder, the warmth of his lips against mine.

Kyle looked across at Mav then back at me. "Could we have a moment alone?"

Mav's opaque eyelids flicked shut, shielding his eyes.

"I'd like Mav to stay," I said.

Kyle's face tightened. "Okay." He looked down at the flowers. "I just wanted to say I'm sorry."

"Why'd you take off like that? You left me there."

"I know. I'm sorry. I did call Security, though."

What had Tarrah said about him? Always sidestepping the issue?

Mav crossed his arms. "It was not proper courting behaviour," he sang stiffly.

Kyle nodded. "Joss has got a lot of guts," he said.

"It is not only guts," Mav sang, his ears high. "Joss has much generosity."

Kyle frowned. He didn't understand. He probably never would.

"Well, thanks for coming by," I said, suddenly feeling very tired.

He held out the posy. "Still friends?"

I took the flowers and laid them on the bed beside me. "Sure, Kyle. Maybe I'll see you round."

He smiled—he was still gorgeous, but something was missing. Honour, perhaps, or maybe empathy. Mav had been right about my instincts, after all. Not that I'd ever tell him that—I'd never hear the end of it.

Kyle walked out, the door sliding shut behind him.

Mav flicked back his second eyelids. "There is still much to like in Kyle Sandrell," he sang gently.

I blinked, trying to clear my eyes.

Mav peered at me. "You are weary. Shall I go?"

"No, stay." I swallowed against a dry ache. "Got any water there?"

Mav picked up a glass and held it to my lips. I took a small sip, the coolness slipping down my scratchy throat.

"Thanks."

He put the glass down.

I squinted with effort, trying to focus my mind. *And thanks for help.*

You called me. I came. His mind voice was bright green, pulsating with joy. *You called me!*

"I know. It was amazing," I said, picking up his hand and closing it around my fist. The closest I could come to the Chorian friendship clasp right now. "I feel honoured to know you in that way."

"It is my honour."

"But, Mav, I can't have you in my mind all the time," I said slowly. "I'm sorry, I just can't. Humans are separate. I have to think my own thoughts, narrate my own life."

Mav sighed. "I know, Joss-partner." He sat forward, his thumbs tightening around my hand. "But now you call me. We will make our own joining. And sometimes we will make a paired story. Is this good?"

Yes, it is good.

Turn the page for a taste of
Alison Goodman's award-winning
New York Times bestseller

EON

From the Primer Scrolls of Jion Tzu

NO ONE KNOWS how the first Dragoneyes made their dangerous bargain with the twelve energy dragons of good fortune. The few scrolls and poems that have survived the centuries start the story well after the deal was struck between man and spirit-beast to protect our land. It is rumored, however, that a black folio still exists that tells of the violent beginning and predicts a catastrophic end to the ancient alliance.

The dragons are elemental beings, able to manipulate *Hua*—the natural energy that exists in all things. Each dragon is aligned with one of the heavenly animals in the twelve-year cycle of power that has run in the same sequence since the beginning of time: Rat, Ox, Tiger, Rabbit, Dragon, Snake, Horse, Goat, Monkey, Rooster, Dog, and Pig. Each dragon is also the guardian of one of the twelve celestial directions, and a keeper of one of the Greater Virtues.

Every New Year's Day the cycle turns, the next animal year begins, and its dragon becomes ascendant, his power doubling for that twelve months. The ascending dragon also unites with a new apprentice to be trained in the dragon magic, and as this boy steps up to his new life, the prior apprentice is promoted to Dragoneye and into his full power. He replaces his master, the old Dragoneye, who retires exhausted and fatally debilitated by his twenty-four-year union with the dragon. It is a brutal bargain that gives a Dragoneye enormous power—enough to move monsoons, redirect rivers, and stop earthshakes. In return for such control over nature, the Dragoneye slowly gives up his *Hua* to his dragon.

Only those boys who can see an energy dragon can hope to be a Dragoneye candidate. It is a rare gift to be able to see the dragon of your birth year, and even rarer to be able to see any of the other energy dragons. Every New Year, twelve boys, born twelve years before, face the ascending dragon and pray that their gift is enough for the beast. One of them is chosen and in that moment of union—and only for that moment—all men can see the dragon in all his glory.

Women have no place in the world of the dragon magic. It is said they bring corruption to the art and do not have the physical strength or depth of character needed to commune with an energy dragon. It is also thought that the female eye, too practiced in gazing at itself, cannot see the truth of the energy world.

CHAPTER ONE

I LET THE TIPS of both my swords dig into the sandy arena floor. It was the wrong move, but the dragging pain in my gut was pulling me into a crouch. I watched Swordmaster Ranne's bare feet shuffle forward, rebalancing his weight for a sweep cut. Training with him always made my innards cramp with fear, but this was different. This was the bleeding pain. Had I miscounted the moon days?

"What are you doing, boy?" he said.

I looked up. Ranne was standing poised, both of his swords ready for the elegant cross cut that could have taken my head. His hands tightened around the hilts. I knew he wanted to follow through and rid the school of the cripple. But he didn't dare.

"Are you spent already?" he demanded. "That third form was even worse than usual."

I shook my head, gritting my teeth against another clamping pain.

"It is nothing, Swordmaster." I carefully straightened, keeping my swords down.

Ranne relaxed his stance and stepped back. "You're not ready for the ceremony tomorrow," he said. "You'll never be ready. You can't even finish the approach sequence."

He turned in a circle, glaring at the other candidates kneeling around the edge of the practice sand. "This sequence must be flawless if you are to approach the mirrors. Do you understand?"

"Yes, Swordmaster," eleven voices yelled.

"Please, if you allow, I'll try again," I said. Another cramp twisted through my body but I didn't move.

"No, Eon-*jah*. Get back in the circle."

I saw a riffle of unease run through the other eleven candidates. Ranne had added *jah*, the old ward against evil, to my name. I bowed and crossed my swords in salute, imagining the feel of driving both blades through his chest. Behind Ranne, the huge opaque form of the Tiger Dragon uncoiled and stared at me. He always seemed to rouse with my anger. I concentrated on the Rabbit Dragon, bringing him into shimmering outline, hoping the Keeper of Peace would help calm my rage.

In the candidate circle, Dillon shifted and looked around the arena. Had he sensed the dragons? He was more aware than the others, but even he couldn't see an energy dragon without meditating for hours. I was the only candidate who could see all of the dragons at will, not counting the Mirror Dragon, of course, who had been lost long ago. It took all my focus to see the spirit beasts and left me weary, but it was the only thing that had made the last two years of hard training bearable. It was also the only reason why a cripple like me was allowed to stand as a candidate—full dragon sight was rare, although, as Swordmaster Ranne liked to remind me, no guarantee of success.

"Get back in the circle. Now!" Ranne yelled.

I tensed and stepped back. Too fast. The sand shifted under my bad leg, wrenching it to the right. I hit the ground, hard. One heartbeat of numbed shock, then the pain came. Shoulder, hip, knee. My hip! Had I done more harm to my hip? I reached across my body, digging my fingers through skin and muscle to feel the malformed hip bone. No, there was no pain. It was whole. And the other aches were already fading.

Dillon shuffled forward on his knees, spraying sand into the air, his eyes wide with concern. Little fool—he would only make things worse.

"Eon, are you . . . ?"

"Don't break formation," Ranne snapped. He kicked at me. "Get up, Eon-*jah*. You're an insult to the Dragoneye profession. Get up."

I struggled to my hands and knees, ready to roll if he kicked again. There was no blow. I grabbed my swords and pushed myself upright, another cramp catching me as I straightened. It wouldn't be long now; I had to get back to my master, before the blood showed. Ever since my body had first betrayed us six months ago, my master had kept a supply of soft cloths and sea sponges locked away in his library, away from prying eyes.

The half-hour bell had just rung—if Ranne gave me leave, I could get to the house and back again by the full hour.

"Swordmaster, may I withdraw from practice until the next bell?" I asked. My head was respectfully bowed, but I kept my eyes on Ranne's blunt, stubborn features. He was probably born in an Ox year. Or maybe he was a Goat.

Ranne shrugged. "Return your swords to armory, Eon-*jah*, and don't bother coming back. Another few hours of practice won't improve your chances tomorrow." He turned his back, calling his favorite, Baret, to take my place on the sand. I was dismissed.

Dillon looked over at me, his face worried. We were the weakest candidates. He was of age—twelve, like all the boys in the circle—but as small as an eight-year-old, and I was lame. In the past, we wouldn't even have been considered as Dragoneye candidates. Neither of us was expected to be chosen by the Rat Dragon in the ceremony tomorrow. All the gambling rings had Dillon at a 30:1 chance. I was at 1000:1. The odds might be against us, but even the council did not know how a dragon made its choice. I pretended to yawn at Ranne's back, waiting for Dillon to smile. His mouth twitched up, but the lines of tension did not ease.

Another cramp dragged at my innards. I held my breath through it, then turned and walked carefully toward the small armory building, my bad leg scattering the fine sand. Dillon was right to be worried. Candidates no longer fought for the honor of approaching the mirrors, but we still had to prove our strength and stamina in the ceremonial sword sequences. At least Dillon could complete the approach sequence, even if it was poorly done. I had never once managed the intricate moves of the Mirror Dragon Third.

It was said it took a lot of physical and mental toughness to bargain with the energy dragons and manipulate the earth forces. It was even whispered among the candidates that a Dragoneye slowly gave up his own life force to a dragon in return for the ability to work the energies, and that the pact aged him beyond his years. My master had been the Tiger Dragoneye during the last cycle and, by my reckoning, would only be a few years over forty. Yet he had the looks and bearing of an old man. Perhaps it was true—a Dragoneye did give up his own life force—or perhaps my master had aged under the strain of poverty and ill luck. He was risking everything for the chance of my success.

I looked over my shoulder. Ranne was watching Baret go through the first form. With all of the strong, able-bodied boys vying to serve him, would the Rat Dragon really choose me? He was the Keeper of Ambition, so perhaps he would not be influenced by physical prowess. I turned to the north-northwest and narrowed my mind until I saw the Rat Dragon shimmer on the sand like a heat mirage. As though he was aware of my focus, the dragon arched his neck and shook out his thick mane.

If he did choose me, then I would hold status for twenty-four years; first working as apprentice to the existing Dragoneye and then, when he retired, working the energies myself. I would earn a mountain of riches, even with the 20 percent tithe to my master. No one would dare spit at me or make the ward-evil sign or turn their face away in disgust.

If he did not choose me, I would be lucky if my master kept me as a servant in his house. I would be like Chart, the slops boy, whose body was permanently twisted into a grim parody of itself. Fourteen years ago, Chart was born to Rilla, one of the unmarried maids, and although my master was sickened by the infant's deformity, he allowed it to live within his household. Chart had never been beyond the confines of the servants' quarters, and he lived on a mat near the cooking stoves. If I failed tomorrow, I could only hope my master would show me similar mercy. Before he found me four years ago, I had labored on a salt farm. I would rather share Chart's mat by the stoves than be returned to such misery.

I stopped walking and reached out further with my mind toward the Rat Dragon, trying to touch the energy of the great beast. I felt his power spark through my body. *Talk to me*, I begged. *Talk to me. Choose me tomorrow. Please, choose me tomorrow.*

There was no response.

A dull pain in my temple sharpened into white agony. The effort to hold him in my sight was too great. The dragon slid beyond my mind's eye, dragging my energy with it. I dug a sword into the sand to stop myself from falling and gasped for air. Fool! Would I never learn? A dragon only ever communicated with his Dragoneye and apprentice. I sucked in a deep breath and pulled the sword out of the ground. Why, then, could I see all eleven dragons? As far back as I could remember, I had been able to shift my mind into the energy world and see their huge translucent forms. Why was I given such a gift in such an ill-favored body?

It was a relief to step off the sand onto the paving of the armory courtyard. The sharp cramps in my gut had finally settled into a dragging ache. Hian, the old master armsman, was sitting on a box beside the armory door polishing the furnace black off a small dagger.

"You been thrown out again?" he asked as I passed him.

I stopped. Hian had never spoken to me before.

"Yes, Armsmaster," I said, tucking my chin into a bow to wait out his scorn.

He held the dagger up in front of him and inspected the blade. "Seems to me you were doing all right."

I looked up and met his eyes, the whites yellowed against his forge-reddened skin.

"With that leg, you're never going to get the Mirror Dragon Third sequence right," he said. "Try a Reverse Horse Dragon Second. There's a precedent for it. Ranne should have told you."

I kept my face expressionless but couldn't help the skip of hope that caught in my throat. Was it true? But why was he telling me this? Maybe it was just a joke on the cripple.

He stood up, holding on to the doorjamb to help him straighten. "I don't blame your mistrust, boy. But you ask your master. He's one of the best history keepers around. He'll tell you I'm right."

"Yes, Armsmaster. Thank you."

A loud yell made us both turn toward the candidates on the sand. Baret was on his knees in front of Ranne.

"Swordmaster Louan was considered one of the best approach ceremony instructors. It's a pity he retired," Hian said flatly. "You've got practice swords at home?"

I nodded.

"Then practice the Reverse Second tonight. Before your cleansing ritual starts." He walked stiffly down the two steps, then looked back at me. "And tell your master that old Hian sends his regards."

I watched him walk slowly to the gateway that led down to the forge, the distant clang of hammer on anvil drumming his progress. If he was right and I could replace the Mirror Dragon Third with a Reverse Horse Dragon Second, then I would have no difficulty finishing the approach sequence.

I stepped into the cool, dim armory and waited for my eyes to adjust. I was not as convinced as the armsmaster that the council would allow a change to the ceremony, particularly to the Mirror Dragon sequence. The Dragon Dragon was, after all, the symbol of the Emperor, and the legends said that the Imperial Family was descended from dragons and still had dragon blood in its veins.

Then again, the Mirror Dragon had been gone for over five hundred years. No one really knew why or how he had disappeared. One story said that a long-ago Emperor offended the dragon, and another told of a terrible battle between the spirit beasts that destroyed the Mirror Dragon. My master said that all the stories were just hearthside imaginings, and that the truth, along with all the records, had been lost to time and the fire that took the Mirror Dragon Hall. And he would know; as the armsmaster had said, my master was a great history keeper. If there was an old variation to the approach sequence, then he would find it.

But first I had to tell him, a day before the ceremony, that I could not complete the Mirror Dragon form. I shivered, remembering the welts and bruises of his past displeasure. I knew it was desperation that provoked his hand—in the last ten years, my master had trained six candidates and all of them had failed—but I did not look forward to his anger. I gripped the hilts of the swords more tightly. I had to know if the Reverse Horse Dragon Second was allowed. It was my best chance.

My master was not a fool; he would not beat me too hard before the ceremony. Too much rode upon it. And if his history scrolls agreed with Hian, I'd have at least four hours before the cleansing ritual to practice the new form and its bridges. It was not long, but it should be enough. I raised the swords in the overhead cut that started the Reverse Second and sliced the left sword down shallowly, conscious of the limited space.

"Oi, don't fling those around in here," the duty armsman snapped.

I pulled up, lowering the points of the swords.

"My apologies, Armsman," I said quickly. It was the skinny,

sallow one who liked giving lectures. I held out the two hilts to him, angling the blades down. I saw his hand clench briefly into the ward-evil sign before he took them.

"Any damage?" he asked, holding one out flat to check the steel.

"No, Armsman."

"These are expensive tools, you know, not playthings. You have to treat them with respect. Not hack away with them indoors. If everyone—"

"Thank you, Armsman," I said, backing toward the door before he could go into a full tirade. He was still talking as I cleared the steps.

The easiest way out of the school was back across the arena and through the main gate, but I didn't want to walk over the sand again, or draw the attention of Ranne. Instead, I took the steep path down to the school's southern gate. My left hip ached from the strain of the practice session and the cramping in my gut made me breathless. By the time I reached the south gate and was passed through by the bored guard, I was sweating from the effort of not crying out.

A dozen or so house-shops lined the road behind the school, forming the outer edge of the food market. The smell of roasting pork fat and crispy-skinned duck oiled the air. I leaned against the wall of the school, letting the stone cool my back, and watched a girl in the blue gown of a kitchen maid weave through the tight knots of gossiping marketers and pause at the hatch of the pork seller. She was about sixteen—my true age—

and her dark hair was scraped back into the looped braid of "unmarried girl." I touched the end of my short queue of black hair, the candidate length. If I was chosen tomorrow, I would begin to grow it to my waist until I could bind it into the double-looped queue of the Dragoneye.

The girl, keeping her eyes down, pointed at a cured haunch on display. The young apprentice wrapped the meat in a cloth and placed it on the bench. The girl waited until he had stepped back before laying the coin beside it and picking up the package. No conversation, no eye contact, no touching; it was all very proper. Yet I sensed something between them.

Although part of me knew it was not honorable, I narrowed my eyes and focused on them as I did with the dragons. At first there was nothing. Then I felt a strange shift in my mind's eye, as though I was stepping closer, and a surge of orange energy flared between the girl and boy, swirling around their bodies like a small monsoon. Something soured in my gut and spirit. I dropped my gaze to the ground, feeling like an intruder, and blinked away my mind-sight. When I looked back, the girl was already turning to leave. There was no sign of the energy around them. No sign of the pulsing brightness that had left a searing afterimage in my mind. Why could I suddenly see such intimate human energy? Neither my master nor any of my instructors had ever spoken of it; emotion was not the province of the dragon magic. Another difference to keep hidden from the world. I pushed away from the wall, needing to work the backwash of power and shame out of my muscles.

My master's house was three roads away, all uphill. The pain in my hip had changed from the familiar ache of overuse to a sharper warning. I needed to get to a hot bath if I wanted any chance of practicing the approach sequence. The alley beside the pork seller was a good shortcut. If it was empty. I shaded my eyes and studied the narrow walkway. It seemed safe; no dock boys sharing a quick pipe or waiting for a limping diversion to chase. I took a step out but hesitated as a familiar wave of motion moved through the crowd; people scrambled to the edges of the road and dropped to their knees, their chatter suddenly silenced.

"Make way for the Lady Jila. Make way for the Lady Jila."

The voice was high but masculine. An elaborately carved palanquin was moving down the road carried on the shoulders of eight sweating men, the passenger concealed behind draped purple silks. Twelve guards, dressed in purple tunics and carrying curved swords, formed a protective square around it—the Shadow Men, the soldier eunuchs of the imperial court. They were always quick to beat down those who did not clear the way or bow fast enough. I dropped onto my good knee and dragged my bad leg beneath me. The Lady Jila? She must be one of the emperor's favorites if she was allowed out of the Inner Precinct. I lowered into the "court noble" bow.

Beside me, a stocky man in the leggings and oiled wrap of the seafarer sat back on his heels, watching the approaching procession. If he did not bow down, he would attract the attention of the guards. And they were not careful about whom they struck.

"It is a court lady, sir," I whispered urgently. "You must bow. Like this." I held my body at the proper angle.

He glanced at me. "Do you think she deserves our bows?" he asked.

I frowned. "What do you mean? She's a court lady, it doesn't matter what she deserves. If you don't bow, you will be beaten."

The seafarer laughed. "A very pragmatic approach to life," he said. "I'll take your advice." He lowered his shoulders, still smiling.

I held my breath as the palanquin passed, squinting as the dust raised, then settled. Beyond us, I heard the crack of a sword laid flat against flesh: a merchant, too slow in his movements, knocked to the ground by the lead guard. The palanquin turned the far corner and a collective easing of muscle and breath rippled through the crowd. A few soft remarks grew in volume as people stood, brushing at their clothes. I dropped my hands to the ground and swung my leg out, preparing to stand. Suddenly, I felt a large hand under each armpit, pulling me upward.

"There you go, boy."

"Don't touch me!" I jumped back, my arms across my chest.

"It's all right," he said, holding up his hands. "I just wanted to return the favor. You saved me from a sword across my back."

He smelled of fish oil and old sweat and seaweed. A memory flashed through me: holding up a heavy string of black pearl kelp, and my mother, nodding and smiling and coiling it into the basket strapped across her slight body. Then the image was gone. Too quick to hold, like all the others I had of my family.

"I'm sorry, sir, you took me by surprise," I said, tightening my arms around my chest. "Thank you for the assistance." Bowing politely, I stepped away from him. The shock of his grip was still on my skin.

The alley opposite was no longer empty; a group of dock boys had congregated near the far end, squatting around a game of dice. I'd have to take the long way around. As if in protest, the pain in my hip sharpened.

The seafarer stopped beside me again. "Perhaps you will help me once more," he said. "Can you tell me the way to the Gate of Officials?"

There was no suspicion or puzzlement on his face, just polite inquiry. I looked at the dock boys again, then back at the seafarer. He was not overly tall, but his chest and shoulders were powerful and his face was tanned into stern lines. I glanced to see if he was armed; a knife was slung through his belt. It would do.

"I'm going that way myself, sir," I said, beckoning him across the road toward the alley. It was not strictly in the direction he wanted to go, but it would still be quicker than the main streets.

"I am Tozay, master fisher of Kan Po," he said, pausing at the mouth of the alley. He clasped his hands together and nodded—adult to child.

From my ley line studies, I knew that Kan Po was on the

coast. It had one of the most fortunate harbors in the realm, ' shaped like a money pouch and ringed by seven hills that trapped good luck. It was also the port access to the islands and beyond.

"I am Eon, Dragoneye candidate." I bowed again.

He stared down at me. "Eon? The lame candidate?"

"Yes," I said, keeping my face impassive.

"Well now, isn't that something." He dipped into an "honored acquaintance" bow.

I nodded awkwardly, unprepared for the sudden change in status.

"We've heard all about you from the news-walker," Master Tozay said. "He came through our town a few months back. Told us the council had decided to let you approach the mirrors. Did my son a lot of good to hear that. He's a year younger than you, just turned eleven. By rights, he should be fishing with me, learning his craft, but he lost an arm in a net accident last winter." Master Tozay's broad face tightened with grief.

"That must be hard for him," I said.

I looked down at my twisted leg—at least it was still intact. I didn't remember much about the accident that had crushed my left hip, but I did remember the physician holding a rusted saw over me, deciding where to cut. He was going to take my whole leg off, but my master stopped him and called for the bonesetter. Sometimes I could still smell the old blood and decaying flesh on the jagged teeth of the saw blade.

We started walking again. I sneaked another look at the end

of the alley—the dock boys had already shifted into a watchful line. Beside me, Master Tozay stiffened as he noted the lounging gang.

"It is hard on him. On the family, too," he said, brushing his fingers across the hilt of his knife. "Wait, I have a stone in my shoe," he said loudly and stopped.

I turned and watched as he bent and dug a finger down the side of his worn boot.

"You're a shrewd one, aren't you," he said, his voice low. "Well, then, if you want a bodyguard, you'd better move to my other side." The look in his eyes made the soft words a command, but he didn't seem angry. I nodded and shifted to his left.

"I just hope you're not taking me too far out of my way," he said as he straightened, keeping his eyes on the boys.

"It *is* a shortcut," I said.

He glanced across at me. "More for you than for me, hey?"

"For both of us. But perhaps a little bit more for me."

He grunted in amusement and placed his hand on my shoulder. "Keep close."

We walked toward the group, Master Tozay shortening his stride to match my slower pace. The largest boy, thickset, with the darker skin and bull-necked strength of the island people, casually kicked a cobblestone into our path. It skipped and bounced, narrowly missing my foot. His three friends laughed. They were city boys, thin and sharp, with the aimless bravado that was always in need of a leader. The island boy picked up a large stone, rubbing his thumb across its surface.

"Afternoon, boys," Master Tozay said.

The islander spat out a wad of tannin leaf, the fibrous mess landing in front of us. His movement made a pendant swing out on a thin leather cord from his clothing; a pale shell carving in the shape of bamboo branches enclosed in a circle. Master Tozay saw it too and stopped, checking me with a hand on my arm. He pushed me behind him, then turned and faced the islander. The other boys nudged each other closer, keen for a show.

"You're from the south, aren't you?" Master Tozay said. "From the far islands?"

The boy's shoulders stiffened. "I'm from Trang Dein," he said, lifting his chin.

I leaned to my right to get a better look at him. A year ago, the emperor had ordered raids on the Trang Dein people as punishment for their bold independence. It was whispered in the city taverns that all the male Trang prisoners had been viciously gelded, like animals, and forced to serve on the imperial ships. This boy was only about fifteen but big enough to pass as a man. Was he one of the Trang cattle-men? My eyes dropped, but he wore the loose tunic and trousers of the dock laborer. I couldn't tell by just looking.

Or could I? A cattle-man's energy would be different from a whole man's energy, wouldn't it? Maybe my new mind-sight would work on him as it had with the kitchen girl and apprentice. The memory of watching their bright monsoon union made my skin prickle with shame, but I still narrowed my mind into the energy world. There was the same strange sensation of stepping forward, and then light, so bright that tears came to my eyes. I couldn't separate anyone's energy; it was a roiling blurred mass of red and yellow and blue. Then, like a flickering cloud shadow, another presence. And pain, deep and low in the belly. Ten times worse than the monthly pain, as though barbs were being dragged through my innards. Only a power born of evil spirits could have such agony ride with it. My mind-sight buckled. I drew in a shuddering breath as the alley twisted back into view. The pain vanished.

Never again would I intrude upon such savage energies.

Beside me, I heard Master Tozay say, "I fish the Kan Po coast. Hired a few of your people as hands on my boats. That was before the raid, of course. They were all good workers."

The island boy nodded warily.

"The islands are quiet now," Tozay said softly. "Not so many soldiers in Ryoka. Some of the missing are making their way home."

The boy let the stone drop to the ground, his hand groping for the shell carving. Holding it like a talisman, he glanced back at his friends, then faced Master Tozay and hunched his shoulders as though to separate himself from his companions.

"Are you hiring now?" he asked, stumbling over the words.

"I may have a place," Master Tozay said. "If you're looking for honest work, then meet me at the Gray Marlin dock tomorrow. I'll wait until the noon bell."

Master Tozay turned, herding me with his body. As we walked out of the alley and into the busy Sweet Sellers Road, I looked back at the island boy. He was staring at us, oblivious to his friends, his hand clenched around the pendant.

"What is that thing he wears around his neck?" I asked Master Tozay as we crossed the road. "A good luck symbol?" But I knew the pendant had to be more than that.

Master Tozay snorted. "No, I wouldn't say it was good luck." He looked closely at me. "You have a politician's face, Eon. I'd wager you know a lot more than you show the world. So what have you noted about the change in our land?"

More beggars, more raids, more arrests, more hard words against the imperial court. I had also overheard my master in low conversation with others of his rank: *The emperor is ill, the heir too callow, the court split in its loyalties.*

"What I have noted is that it is safer to have a politician's face and a mute's tongue," I said wryly.

Master Tozay laughed. "Prudently said." He looked around, then pulled me over to the narrow space between two shops. "That boy's pendant is an islander totem, to bring longevity and courage," he said, bending close to my ear, his voice low. "It's also a symbol of resistance."

"To the emperor?" I whispered, knowing the danger of such words.

"No, child. To the real power in the Empire of the Celestial Dragons. High Lord Sethon."

The emperor's brother. The son of a concubine. According to the old ways, when the emperor came to his throne, he should have ordered his brother Sethon killed, along with all the other male children born to his father's concubines. But our emperor was an enlightened man, an educated man. He let his eight younger brothers live. He made them his generals, and Sethon, the eldest of the eight, he made his commander in chief. Our emperor was also a trusting man.

"But High Lord Sethon commands the armies. What can islanders do against such might?" I asked.

Master Tozay shrugged. "Not much. But there are others, more powerful, who remain loyal to the emperor and his son." He paused as an old woman stopped at the shop-hatch next to us to poke through a display of yeast cakes. "Come, this is not the talk for such an open place," he said softly. "Or indeed for any place." He straightened. "I fancy a sweet bun. How about you?"

I longed to ask him who opposed High Lord Sethon, but the subject was clearly at an end. And I had not had a sweet bun in a very long time—there was no money for such excesses in my master's household.

"I should not dawdle. . . ." I said.

"Come, it will not take long. We'll get them as we walk. Can you recommend a seller?"

I nodded. One bun would not take long. I spotted a break in the slow-moving crowd and led Master Tozay through it to the corner of the White Cloud Market. It was busier than usual, the afternoon sun driving people under the shade of the broad white silk sails that had been stretched between carved poles. We passed Ari the Foreigner serving some merchants in his coffee stall, the heavy perfume of the strange black drink thick in the air. Ari had once given me a bowl of his coffee, and I had liked the rich bitterness and the slight buzzing it left in my head. I touched Master Tozay's arm and pointed at the pastry stall to our left, its counter blocked by customers.

"The red bean ones are said to be good here," I said, standing on my toes to see the trays of buns arranged in neat lines.

The nutty smell of bean paste and sweet dough radiated in a wave of heat. A sharp roil of hunger joined the ache in my gut. Master Tozay nodded and, bowing politely, managed to neatly insert himself ahead of a woman hesitating over her choice. As I watched his broad back and sunburned neck, I felt another flicker of memory; of being carried on a big man's back and the salty warmth of sun-leathered skin against my cheek. But, once again, I couldn't make the image stay. Was it a memory of my father? I no longer had any clear idea of what he looked like. A moment later Master Tozay turned, holding a bun in each hand, wrapped in a twist of red paper.

"Here you go," he said. "Be careful. The seller said they're just out of the steamer."

"Thank you, sir." The heat from the bun stung my palm through the thin wrapping. I slid the paper down, fashioning a handle. It would be best to wait until it had cooled, but the smell was too tantalizing; I bit into it, juggling the steaming pastry around with my tongue.

"Tasty," Master Tozay said, fanning his mouth with his hand.

I nodded, unable to speak as the hot, dense filling made my jaw seize and ache with its sudden sweetness.

He motioned forward with his bun. "Is this the way to the Gate?"

I swallowed and sucked in a breath of cooling air. "Yes, you follow the white sails until they end," I said, pointing at the silk roof, "and then turn right. Just keep walking and you'll come to the Gate of Officials."

Master Tozay smiled. "Good boy. Now, if ever you make the journey down the coast to Kan Po, you must look for me. You can be always sure of a welcome." He hesitated, then put his hand on my shoulder. "If that dragon has any sense tomorrow, he'll choose you," he said, giving me a gentle shake.

I smiled. "Thank you, sir. And travel well."

He nodded and raised his pastry in salute, then joined the flow of people in the center of the walkway. As his solid form merged into the shapes and colors of the crowd, I felt as though he was taking my mother and father with him. Two half memories that were already fading, leaving only an imprint of a smile like mine and the smell of sun-warmed skin.